# THE CAUSE & THE CURE

Mark Devlin

The Cause & The Cure
Mark Devlin

Paperback Edition First Published in Great Britain in 2019
eBook Edition First Published in Great Britain in 2019

ISBN: 978-1-913438-09-8

aSys Publishing
http://www.asys-publishing.co.uk

# FOREWORD FROM THE AUTHOR

Although this book represents my first forays into the world of fiction, there is nevertheless much truth encoded within the narrative. As such, it can be read and comprehended in layers.

I hope that in the surface narrative I have created a story that will be engaging and thrilling to any reader – and particularly those with any personal knowledge of Oxford, and memories of what life was like in the UK in the early 1990s. The story draws heavily on my own recall of these times, and experiences of working in a radio newsroom.

Beyond this, however, the book contains many spiritual and occulted truths – some of it spoken by the various characters, some of it embedded into aspects of the plot, and some of it drawing on the documented history of Oxford. There are also symbolic metaphors and allegories, meaning those readers with a propensity towards such things will be able to decipher the clues, messages and teachings contained. The city of Oxford serves as a microcosm for the entire world in this regard, and there is much to be gleaned about how Organised Society works from that which occurs within the city ring road. Multiple readings of the book will likely bring forth different aspects of what has been encoded each time round.

Parts of the story will doubtless be considered shocking and 'controversial' by some, but so be it. The story appears exactly the way I intended, and each reader must make of it what they will.

Further coding occurs with the names of the characters, all of which reveal something of their true nature and/or motives. (Tip – a small few are anagrams!) The only non-coded exceptions are the DJs at Lux FM, and Colin Cole, Richard Owen and Mateo in the newsroom. All other names represent a treasure trove of clues to be deciphered. (I have also permitted myself a couple of un-named Alfred Hitchcock-style cameos along the way!)

All of the places mentioned are real locations, with the exception only of the abattoir on the Watlington Road, Herzlos's laboratory and the underground tunnel from Carfax Tower, (although rumours do persist of one connecting the Mitre and Chequers Inns under the High Street!) The picture section in the centre contains many photographs of places documented. Any readers wishing to fully absorb themselves in the TCATC experience may choose to tour some of these sites. They would make for a fascinating day out!

Similarly, many of the news stories mentioned, such as the first Gulf 'War" (invasion,) the Poll Tax riots, the demise of Margaret Thatcher, and the burgeoning rave scene, are accurate renditions of real events.

Overall, although I certainly enjoyed the creative process of assembling a novel, it was always my intention for this book to be a device for conveying inspiring and potentially liberating truths, as my previous non-fiction tomes were. The methods by which humanity gets this information aren't important. That they grasp and apply these in their lives, for the sake of true freedom for all – is.

If *The Cause* & *The Cure* can achieve that, I'll know it was worth the effort.

**Mark Devlin**

# *Acknowledgements*

*Huge thanks goes out to Nick Smith for the excellent cover design, John 'Razor Eye' Hamer and Erick van Dijk for the proofreading, and Nicola Mackin of aSys Publishing for the production assistance.*

# Also by the author

## MUSICAL TRUTH, VOLUMES 1 AND 2

To most people, the music industry represents a source of harmless fun and entertainment. Beneath the glossy veneer, however, lies the devastating truth of who really controls these institutions, and the deeply malevolent agendas for which they're being used.

Mark Devlin is a long-standing DJ and music journalist. The two volumes of *Musical Truth* are the culmination of his several years' of research into the true nature of the industry and its objectives – from dark occult rituals, to mind-controlled artists, and all points in between. The book shows how these agendas fit into the much wider picture of what's really going on in the world, and - crucially – how the power lies with us to bring it all to an end.

Both volumes are available at Amazon and Barnes & Noble. Signed copies may also be obtained direct from the Author, however.

Please e-mail *markdevlinuk@gmail.com* to arrange.

## THE SOUND OF FREEDOM

TSOF is a free showcase of conscious music, old and new, compiled by Mark Devlin. It stands as the inspiring antithesis to the corporate agenda, offering meaningful music by switched-on, awakened artists.

The full archive so far is available at:

*https://www.spreaker.com/show/the-sound-of-freedom*

TSOF can also be found on Mixcloud and iTunes.

# GOOD VIBRATIONS

A free, ongoing series of conversation-based podcasts, covering a huge array of topics within the truth/ conspiracy/ consciousness/ spirituality fields.

The entire archive so far is available at:

*https://www.spreaker.com/show good-vibrations-podcast*

# THE CAUSE & THE CURE
# DISCUSSION GROUPS

The Author welcomes all feedback and communication, (as long as it's civil,) to the following e-mail address, and guarantees a personal reply to all messages received

*markdevlinuk@gmail.com*

In particular, he is interested in receiving feedback from readers as to the coded aspects of the book, and what allegories, metaphors and symbolism they feel they have deduced.

To this end, a couple of on-line discussion groups have been set up to explore the above ideas and encourage conversation among readers.

The Facebook group is here:

*https://www.facebook.com/groups/585956482202931/*

Alternatively, (and for any non-Facebook users,) a Reddit discussion group has been set up here:

*https://www.reddit.com/user/djmarkdevlin/comments/dc9j4b/
the_cause_and_the_cure_by_mark_devlin_discussion/*

See you in the chat.

# THE CAUSE & THE CURE SOUNDTRACK

This may well be the first novel to come with its own movie-style soundtrack!

Compiled by Mark Devlin, this two-hour sonic journey brings the TCATC story to life with a selection of the music that was around during the book's timeframe, interspersed with news footage, radio station recordings and other relevant snippets from the times.

The soundtrack audio can be streamed or downloaded for free from the following link:

*https://www.spreaker.com/user/markdevlin the-cause-the-cure -soundtrack*

Mark Devlin's main website:

*www.markdevlin.co.uk*

Please subscribe to The Author's YouTube channel, containing a huge archive of live talks, Q&A sessions, interviews and podcasts:

*www.youtube.com/markdevlintv*

# THE CAUSE AND THE CURE

## By Mark Devlin

*"We must outgrow the cause. There can be no problem overcome unless the cause of it is outgrown. It is not outgrown by ages of suffering, but by proper intelligent education."*

*Manly P. Hall*

*"If we find ourselves with a desire that nothing in this world can satisfy, the most probable explanation is that we were made for another world."*

*C.S. Lewis.*

# CHAPTER 1

## Thursday 22nd March 1990

*"I saw a rabbit with its eyes full of tears,*
*The lab that owned her had been doing it for years.*
*Why don't we make them pay for every last eye,*
*That couldn't cry its own tears."*

*Paul McCartney: 'Looking For Changes'.*

It had been marketed so seductively. "Get an alert sent directly to a phone number of your choice whenever anything disturbs the network of laser sensors," read the pamphlet. "This is new state-of-the-art technology involving devices communicating with each-other electronically, and will be a staple part of the way our entire society will be run in the future."

Professor Gottfried Herzlos had snorted derisively at the exaggeration of the last part as it was regurgitated by the salesman in red braces who would probably have told him that the earth was flat if it meant a quick sale. As he'd barked some sardonic response, he could barely conceal his contempt for these talentless yuppy dropouts, earning at 21 what he'd had to work three decades and achieve two degrees and a doctorate to attain. But still, getting a heads-up on any potential disturbance at his laboratory and being able to get on-site ahead of even the police, had seemed a very attractive idea when he had signed the contract three months prior.

It seemed less attractive now, at 2.57am, as he tore his Range Rover along Banbury Road, ignoring every red light with a sleepless, but keen eye in the rear-view mirror for any blue ones. The word 'savage' spray-painted in red across the rear windscreen didn't make navigational tasks any easier. Neither did the snapped passenger side wing-mirror bashing into the door as it hung on its last two wires. Herzlos lurched sharply to the left into South Parks, left through another red light into Hinschelwood Road, and swung the machine sharply left again into the University's Bio-Chemical Research Division, roaring up to the car park wall and stopping only within inches of the blue railing.

Flying out of the jeep, and leaving the headlights blazing, he darted around the side of the railings, and through the back courtyard to the staff entrance. A department like this really should be using biometrics to open doors by now, he briefly reflected, as he scrabbled in his pockets for the thick bunch of keys. Retinal scans would be far more convenient. The alarm unit on the side of the building was flashing its white lights wildly, but silently.

Herzlos was a walking stereotype. With wiry, greying hair growing wildly on both sides of his head, he epitomised the quintessential 'nutty professor' look. It had taken him precisely six and a half minutes to get from the warmth of his bed in Davenant Road to this point. It was only now, having been operating on a combination of R-Complex-brained instinct and hazy sleep deprivation, that it occurred to Herzlos that he had not given thought to defending himself against any threat to his safety that may lurk within the quiet darkness of the laboratory rooms. But he reassured himself that the sensors had most probably been triggered by a spider walking across its path, as the smarmy youth had warned him could occasionally happen. Indeed, he couldn't recall a time during his tenure when the rooms had ever been dusted for cobwebs.

As he reached the top of the first set of stairs, he fumbled again in the dark for the big bunch of keys, cursed as he dropped them, then felt for the one that unlocked his laboratory. His heart pumping wildly and his eyes wide in the semi-darkness, he cautiously opened the door, cursing again as the un-oiled hinges let out their characteristic squeak.

As he gazed in, the familiar sight of his lab gazed back at him, slightly illuminated in orange by the streetlamp filtering in through the curtain-less windows, along with the white light of the still-flashing alarm unit on the side. There was the soft sound of scurrying as he moved gingerly into the room. Herzlos was unalarmed. It was a sound he was used to. Two or three of the rabbits in the cage to the left had moved to the edge of their enforced prison, noses twitching at the wire grille, as the rest of their number slept on. The rats with the shaven backs were grabbing their only relief from their daily torment through sleep. It was a similar situation in the gerbil cage as the awakened ones started turning in circles, anticipating another incursion to their number.

Herzlos switched off from the expected sounds, trying to fine-tune his senses to any out-of-place ones. He heard nothing. He shot a gaze at the red blinking light of the sensor in the corner of the lab. Had it really been a spider that had set it off? It must have been. What a ballache to have to go through all this for the sake of a bloody spider. That cleaning firm was going to get it in the neck. Still, he reflected, he couldn't be too careful. This contract was far too important, and those bloody activists had already shown their steely commitment to their cause.

He moved his eyes, still squinting in the partial light, around the room. Was anything missing? First things first. The microscopes were still where they should be. Test tubes, flasks, evaporating dish, measuring scales and bunsen burner were all in their place on the wooden bench. Creeping over to his desk he tested the drawers, which were locked as they should be. So was the steel filing cabinet.

Collecting his thoughts, he began to move back towards the door, preparing himself for re-setting the alarm and returning home to the sanctuary of his bed. As he turned on his heels he sensed a slight swish of air, and in a split fraction of a second his brain was already racing through the possibilities.

There was a sharp crack of a blunt object hitting flesh and bone, and Gottfried Herzlos' world went black.

* * *

Twenty-five minutes had passed by the laboratory's wall clock before Gottfried Herzlos began making a low snuffling sound. His slumped head started to twitch and dim light seeped in through his fluttering eyelids, bringing him his first forays back into consciousness. Within seconds, the terrible truth of his predicament had become clear.

He was bound by rope to a plastic chair in the centre of the room, his arms tied behind him, his legs shackled to those of the chair. The back of his head throbbed in intense pain. The dark shadow of his assailant loomed over him, dressed in black, a ski mask concealing his features. Through his watery bloodshot eyes, and illuminated by the beam from his assailant's flashlight, Herzlos could just make out a small selection of items laid out on the plastic table in front of him; a fully-loaded syringe, a plastic bottle of soap solution, another of bleach, a cigarette lighter, a packet of 20 Dunhill cigarettes.

The assailant spoke for the first time.

"It's nothing you haven't brought upon yourself. It was always your choice. I'm just the delivery agent for the retribution."

It took a few seconds for the words to sink in. Herzlos' first instinct was characteristic apoplexy, but before this could display itself by way of a verbal outburst, he was able to temper his reaction.

Even in this extreme state of trauma, Herzlos' scientist mind got analytical. Was there an accent there? How about the intonation? These things might be important later. What the assailant knew but Herzlos didn't is that there wasn't to be much of a later. Not in this life, anyway.

Herzlos decided quickly on a diplomatic response.

"What do you want? Please. I have money. We can make a deal. Please just let me go. I've done nothing to you."

"Not to me. But the harm you have put into the world goes way beyond the two of us."

The assailant had said all he was going to. Now it was time for action. In one swift move his black-gloved hand grabbed a section of Herzlos' sweat-soaked hair and yanked his head sharply back. The other hand now contained the soap solution which he moved closer to Herzlos' face, seemingly oblivious to the now desperate cries of protestation.

Outside of the thick brick walls of the laboratory, the dimly amber-lit streets of Oxford slumbered on for the remaining hours of the night.

# CHAPTER 2

## Thursday 22nd March 1990

*"Nineteen ninety, Chubb Rock jumps up on the scene, with a lean and a pocket full of green."*

*Chubb Rock: 'Treat 'Em Right.'*

The vocals thundered out through the speakers.

"Nine, nine, nine, nine, nine, nine, nine, nine, nine, nine..."

The vibrations caused a drinking glass to start trembling, water spilling over the top and cascading down the side.

"Five, five, five, five, five, five, five, five, five..."

"Shit. Hold on," said the dreadlocked 25-year-old host, grabbing the glass and mopping up the water with a tea-towel before it seeped into the bass bins.

"Eight, eight, eight, eight, eight, eight, eight, eight, eight..."

The host stood back proudly, glancing over at his eighteen-year-old companion for a reaction, as the audio switched to a bass-heavy bomb sound, giving way to the next vocal samples.

"The number one rap show inna de UK. De Capital Rap Show with Westwood. Listen dis! (listen dis, listen dis.)"

The heavily reverberated sound effect was joined by a swooping sample. The eighteen-year-old was grinning a bad-toothed smile, the peak of his baseball cap tipping up and down as he nodded his approval.

"Wicked system, bruv!"

His host looked back towards the hi-fi system, satisfied.

"You're listening to the number one radio programme in our timeslot. And that's no lie! (and that's no lie, and that's no lie.) ..."

The sounds overlapped, melding into a glorious sonic melange augmented by the radio station's on-air processor, and captured so faithfully on the chrome cassette tape. The show's idents gave way to the opening beats of *911 Is A Joke*, announcing the imminent arrival of Public Enemy's *In Fear Of A Black Planet* album.

"Right, so that's this Saturday's show," confirmed the host, terminating their shared soundbath by pressing the stop button, rewinding the cassette, ejecting it and placing it carefully in its case. He handed it to his keen young guest.

"How the fuck do you get the signal so clear all the way from London?" asked the youth.

"State-of-the-art aeriel, my brother," replied the host, beckoning with his eyes towards the hulking antenna solidly affixed to the brickwork outside his living room window. "It's got a range of up to 70 miles, and the pull is strong enough to handle the drop in signal strength that you normally get after the cut-through on the M40."

"Yeah, I always lose the London stations in the car coming through there," confirmed the youth. "Fucking pain in the ass."

"And this is the Friday late-night show." The host offered another gold TDK tape, the wording on the label written in black felt-tip in a stylish graffiti-style script: 'Westwood: Capital Rap Show, Friday 9/3/90.'

"He played plenty of PE on that one, plus some joints from the new Tribe Called Quest and 3rd Bass albums. Now, what else you interested in? I got Jeff Young, Radio 1 from Friday night, Pete Tong on Capital, Saturday, or Rodigan's Reggae from Saturday night."

"Nah, 'low Pete Tong and Jeff Young, but I'll have the Rodigan," the youth replied, his heavy Oxfordshire lilt revealing the locality of his upbringing.

"Safe," replied the host. He put the three cassettes into a pile and handed them to his customer who, in turn, handed him three crumpled five-pound notes.

"Wait 'til Kiss FM goes legal in September," said the host. "I'll have a whole world of stuff every week then."

"Innit?," his guest replied. They touched fists. The youth reached for the ready-rolled spliff he had placed behind his ear, and he exited the living room. As the host pocketed the fifteen pounds, he detected the arrival of someone at the front door as the youth was leaving. "D in?" asked the voice. "Yeah, he's there," replied the youth.

His cousin stepped into the room, beaming a full smile.

"Yes, V!" the host grinned back, reaching out to offer an embrace.

"So wha? You a still hustlin' good wid de radio cassettes?" asked his new arrival.

"Fe' real! It mek a nice likkle sideline, and it all legal too!" came the reply. The host's accent had now switched from Estuary English to exaggerated Caribbean, heavy on the patois.

"Tea?" he asked.

"Please."

Drew Hunter walked through the open door to his kitchen and headed for the kettle. In the living room, his 23-year-old cousin, Verity, took off her jacket and got comfortable on his sofa. She thumbed through the pile of tapes on the coffee table next to her, quietly admiring the cottage industry her cousin had created. From the kitchen came the sound of a match being struck, and a few seconds later, the pungent aroma of a freshly-lit joint.

"So what brings you here?" Drew shouted from the kitchen. "Shouldn't you be at work, Thursday morning?"

"Just on the way in." All hints of a Caribbean dialect had now gone, as both reverted back to their English-born accents. An outsider would have detected a hint of the same Oxfordshire twang that the visiting youth had displayed, though the pair could never recognise it in themselves. Verity reflected for a few seconds on how curious it was that the two of them instinctively went through this ritual whenever they saw each other – adopting the patois for the initial greetings, then going back to 'normal' talk. Even more curious that they lapsed into Jamaican patois in spite of their Bajan heritage. She realised she did it with many of her other black friends, too. It defied any kind of logic, but she didn't plan on changing any time soon.

Drew lit an incense stick to help neutralise the scent from his spliff. He placed it in his favourite holder, a gift from Barbados, fashioned in the form of a demonic face, and designed for the smoke to waft through the entity's nostrils.

"Mum's doing one of her famous lunches on Sunday. Wants to know if you can make it?"

"Sure. As long as she's still a beast with the rice an' peas, count me in."

Drew emerged from the kitchen with two steaming mugs, placing one down on the coffee table besides Verity. He took the other over to the armchair opposite.

"So, how come you're starting so late?"

"Shift patterns. It never was a 9 to 5. I've had to work all week to get Sunday off."

"How's it all going there? Still enjoying it?"

"Mixed," replied Verity, cautiously sipping from her hot mug. "Jess is still giving me some skivvy tasks. I only really get let loose on the small local stories. Acting like she still needs me to prove myself. I don't know how long it's going to take."

'But you're still the last one in, right?"

"Apart from the work experience kids, yeah."

"Most jobs like that involve biding your time 'til the right break comes along," came Drew's reflection. "There'll come a time when you're right where you need to be, right when you need to be there. Things happen only when they're ready, never a moment before. The Universe sees to it that way."

"Seen," said Verity, absorbing Drew's words as she continued to sip her tea.

Fifteen minutes later, Verity said her goodbyes, descended the two flights of communal stairs, and headed out of the blue-and-white painted building. She climbed back into her white 1978 mini, registration plate BBP 216S, counting her blessings that it had remained unvandalised on this occasion. She drove out of North Way, and immediately right on to Bayswater Road, out of the Barton estate, straight over the Headington Roundabout, and on down the Eastern Bypass. After a brief stop at the Slade traffic lights, the mini veered left on to the Horspath Industrial Estate. A first left on to Pony Road, and she was at work. The unremarkable building, a former furniture warehouse now decked out in imposing red and blue-painted decor, loomed large as she took the remaining parking space at the side.

Not that she needed it, but a reminder of the nature of her workplace was on offer immediately as she walked through the main door and nodded a greeting to Geraldine the receptionist. "On 99.9FM, and 91.1 in Banbury," came the vocals from the reception speakers, "THIS is Lux FM." There was a dramatic stab of strings, before the syndicated Independent Radio News bulletin beamed by satellite from London kicked in. "The eleven o'clock news, I'm Howard Hughes."

Verity nodded another greeting through the reinforced glass window to Pete Hollis, the on-air presenter, who was taking the opportunity of the news break to tidy up the pile of blue cartridges that had built up on the desk in front of him. She walked out of reception, around the side of the studios, and upstairs to the newsroom.

"Morning," she called to anyone who was in earshot. Mateo, the sports editor, mumbled an unenthusiastic response as he sat reading the racing pages in *The Sun*, his feet up on his desk as ever, and a Benson & Hedges blazing idly in the ashtray next to his phone. Jess Hewitt, their boss, sat opposite, seemingly unperturbed by his stance. Verity wondered how his self-employed status allowed him to get away with so much that her fellow staffers couldn't. Jess hadn't looked up from her typewriter, but grunted a nonchalant greeting.

The other two reporters, Richard Owen and Colin Cole, didn't reply and looked bored, sitting below the grey fug created by their listlessly-held cigarettes.

"Nuttin' a gwan?" asked Verity, mischievously.

"Mmmmm?" asked Cole confusedly.

"Slow news day?" she clarified.

"Yeah, you could say that. Looks like we'll be leading with a cat stuck up a tree in Kennington and a Jam Festival in Berinsfield at this rate."

"News is what you make it," piped up Jess Hewitt, still without looking up, and reinforcing one of her favourite 'truisms.'

"Well, you can't force murders and rapes, though sometimes I wish you could," replied Cole detachedly.

Verity put her blue sequinned jacket on the back of her seat opposite Cole's, at phone extension 216, and got herself comfortable ready for the long hours ahead. Mateo's phone rang and he removed his feet from the desk to take down the latest racing results. At the large table on the other side of the office, James Cody was shuffling through some new seven-inch singles as he prepared to take over from Pete Hollis later. Through the glass window in the news prep room was someone Verity didn't recognise. Looking barely old enough for work, a pale skinny teenager was working his way through a pile of blue carts, scrubbing them clean of their audio ready for re-use by shoving them into the magnetic erasing device whose powerful field had incapacitated many a staff member's wristwatch.

Another phone rang. Owen's this time.

"Newsroom?...Yes..." A long pause. Verity glanced up from her papers to see Owen's bored expression change to one of great interest. His eyes widened as he began scribbling on his notepad.

"Right...Shit!...Yes...Oh my god!...OK. I'm on it right away."

Replacing the receiver, he leapt up from his desk. "There's been a murder. A professor at the University found tied up in his office this morning."

'What?' asked Jess, a puzzled look on her face. "Who?"

He looked down at his scribbled note. "A Gottfried Herzlos."

"Jesus!" said Jess, in apparent recognition of the name.

"Sounds grisly. The police are there now. Col, come on, Let's get down there."

Owen and Cole hurriedly put on their jackets and each rushed to grab a Marantz tape recorder and plug-in microphone from the side shelf.

Verity glanced over at a still shocked Jess Hewitt.

"Looks like we got our lead then!"

# CHAPTER 3

## Thursday 22nd March 1990

*"The mayor hides the crime rate,*
*Council woman hesitates,*
*Public gets irate, but forgets the vote date,*
*Weatherman complaining. Predicted sun, it's raining."*

*Rodriguez: 'This Is Not A Song, It's An Outburst: Or, The*
*Establishment Blues.'*

As the Lux FM news car, hardly subtle with its garish red and blue livery and broadcast antenna protruding from the roof, turned the same corner into South Parks Road that Gottfried Herzlos had a few hours earlier, there was no doubt that Owen and Cole were approaching a crime scene.

The blue lights of several police vehicles blazed on both sides of the road. Confused onlookers were gathered behind a line of blue tape as a couple of Constables stood on duty on the other side. As the radio car slinked slowly towards the Bio-Chemical Research Division, an officer predictably started strutting towards them, signalling for

Cole to wind down the window. "Press?" he asked. Cole fought hard to resist the reply he wanted to give, ("no, we're joyriders who thought it'd be a right laugh to nick a radio car,") opting for a more career-appropriate one.

"Yeah, senior reporter for Lux FM," he replied, handing the officer his press badge.

"OK, park up next to the police van just there," came the instruction. The Constable's superior attitude didn't justify any further pleasantries in Cole's mind. Having parked as instructed, the two reporters walked as far as they were able towards the police cordon.

Inside, at the site of Herzlos' ultimate fate, the animals, all now awake and hungry, scurried about in their cages. The chair to which he had been tied was still in the centre of the laboratory. Jolyon Morton, the police pathologist, was kneeled down attending to traces of blood on the floor. Lying underneath the patches was a black zigzag line which had been bafflingly painted on to the grey granite floor. While two officers remained, the three others began the walk down from the lab to the blue tape line outside. Their emergence was noted by Cole, who recognised the pair. He worked hard to keep the primal thoughts at bay as he eyed up the figure of Woman Detective Constable May Pearce, reasoning that these were hardly the circumstances in which to get aroused. Beside her were her boss, Detective Inspector Neil Lowe, and his own superior, Detective Chief Superintendent C.C Nomas. So all the big dogs had come out for this one.

Cole seized his chance as Lowe and Nomas reached a pause in their conversation. "Inspector, Chief Superintendent," he said, extending his hand. Nomas reluctantly took it first, giving a limp response. (Yeah, it's a bit different to the handshake you'll be giving down the Lodge tomorrow night, Cole thought to himself.) Lowe's grip was firmer and, by the feel of his hand afterwards, greasier. "You didn't waste any bloody time then" he said, in a voice that, to Cole's mind, would have sounded more fitting coming from the mouth of a dairy farmer than a senior policeman.

"A good reporter always keeps his nose to the ground," Cole smiled, cringing inside at his recital of another of Jess's maxims.

"Helps when TVP Kidlington phone you with a tip-off though, doesn't it?" said Lowe.

"What can you tell us, Inspector?" asked Cole, ignoring Lowe's swipe and noting through the corner of his eye that Owen had wasted no time in talking to W.D.C. Pearce.

"There'll be a full press conference at St. Aldates at 2pm tomorrow," said Lowe. "You'll get everything there."

Nomas, seemingly with more important things to attend to, shuffled off. Once he was out of earshot, Cole tried again. "Come on, Neil. If you can give me something now, I can phone it in ready for the midday locals."

"I've not done Lux enough favours already then, no?" Lowe replied.

"Jess specifically told me to ask for you, and said she'd be extremely grateful," Cole lied, thinking on the spot.

Cole studied Lowe's face for signs of any reaction. Looking around to make sure Nomas had left, Lowe ushered Cole to one side.

"Victim was a 55-year-old Professor of Biology, Gottfried Herzlos. Discovered dead at 08.21 this morning by the Department's cleaner. He'd been bound to a chair. Ultimate cause of death was cardiac arrest brought on by shock. Soap and acid had been poured into his eyes, and there were cigarette burns on his face and arms. The pathologist has indicated the presence of drain cleaner in his stomach. Estimates the time of death as between 0300 and 0500."

Knowing Lowe would not go on the record himself before the press conference, Cole didn't bother reaching for his microphone, but instead scribbled everything he'd been told on to his pad.

"Thanks, Inspector. I know she'll be grateful," said Cole, glancing at his watch to see how long he had left before the midday news, and starting to turn on his heel. Unimpressed to note that Owen was still talking to May Pearce, he hollered at him to head back to the radio car.

"See you at the press conference," said Lowe.

Cole smiled wordlessly, the closeness to the midday news still extinguishing any other concerns from his mind. He and Owen hurried to phone in their report. The radio car dash display indicated that it was 11:48.

W.D.C. May Pearce had now joined her superior.

"Surprised to see Chief Superintendent Nomas turn out for this one, sir. I got the impression he knew the victim?"

Lowe regarded her curiously. "Everyone knows everyone at a certain level in this town, Constable," he replied, his fumbling hand producing a rustling sound from his jacket pocket.

"Must have been an absolute psycho. It's horrific." W.D.C. Pearce shook her head, affected by the graphic nature of the events in which she'd unwittingly become embroiled.

"Spare a thought for the friggin' cleaner! There's one who'll be down the Job Centre as soon as she can face leaving the house again."

"Who the hell would do such a thing?"

Lowe's hand emerged from his jacket pocket clutching a bag of pork scratchings. He ripped it open and popped three in his mouth as he spoke. It was so close to lunchtime and yet not close enough.

"I think you'll find that's where our jobs come in, Constable."

Lowe began to walk back towards his car. "Either way, the world keeps turning for the rest of us."

# CHAPTER 4

## Thursday 22nd March 1990

*"1990's time for the guru,*
*1990's time for the guru."*

*Guru Josh: '1990 To Infinity.'*

Verity knew that it was just shy of 8pm as she turned the key to the front door of her rented terraced house on Abingdon Road. The trees lining the parkland on the opposite side of the road swayed wildly in the evening breeze as the closing theme to *Coronation Street* wafted out of the slightly-opened window to the student house next door, along with the potent scent of cheap skunk. As she shut the rest of the world out for another day with a slam of the door, some different sounds drifted out of the living room to the right.

"It's All Possibility waiting to play out, according to the Will and the Intent of we conscious co-creators of our own realities," proclaimed the emphatic voice. Verity rolled her eyes at the all-too-familiar tones as she kicked off her shoes and hung up her jacket on the wall peg.

The voice continued, burning with passion.

"Anything COULD happen. So we COULD have a world steeped in justice, holistic intelligence, connectedness to source, harmonious with nature, and with abundance for all. That's an option available to us any time enough of us want it, and therefore bring it into being.

"Everything has to exist in mind before it can become reality. The house that you live in only exists because a property developer decided to build it and an architect used his imagination to design it. That's why the first Hermetic principle detailed in *The Kybalion* is The Principle of Mentalism: 'the Universe is mental,' or, 'all is mind.'

"Another option – because it's All Possibility, remember – is a world of human slavery, suffering and hardship. Of artificiality, immorality and manufactured scarceness, where human potential is stifled, and where most people live synthetic lives completely separated from higher consciousness. Sound familiar at all? It should. But we're ONLY living in those conditions within the infinite number of POSSIBLE playouts, because, collectively, we've chosen it. And we've chosen it through our lack of spiritual CARE.

"How degraded and utterly destroyed does a species have to be to CHOOSE that second option when the first one is available to them any time they want it … but they don't even realise that it is!"

Verity headed for the kitchen kettle, permitting another couple of minutes of the diatribe to continue.

"NOWHERE NEAR enough people are responding to Truth and exercising Care, and the way Natural Law works is to dish out consequences in a direct response to the Free Will decisions that we make. Unfortunately, that happens on a collective and societal basis as well as an individual one, which means that the small number of us who DO care and take personal responsibility, are going to be dragged down and made to suffer by the larger number in society who won't.

"That's why those of us who have come to these comprehensions have the right – and I would go further and say the duty – to teach these principles to those who are doing great harm to the whole of humanity by their ignorance of these dynamics.

"That's why I'm PISSED OFF that I'm having to do this with my life. And I have a right to be pissed off! I do it out of an obligation to Truth, to Creation, because I recognise that, in taking on these comprehensions myself, I also took on a moral obligation to teach them to others. But are there other things I'd much prefer to be doing with my time? You bet your fucking life there are!"

"How's the job search been going?" Verity teased as she entered the room, a mug of tea in hand.

Oh, hey," replied Keith Malcolm, reaching for the stop button on the cassette player, and exhibiting the kind of embarrassment that might have occurred in another household had a man been caught by his girlfriend watching porn, rather than listening to a cassette of streetwise spirituality from a renowned local speaker in the field. As Verity stretched herself out on the sofa and closed her eyes, Keith leaned forward for a quick kiss on the lips.

"The tape arrived today. It's powerful stuff. Not sure your mum would be in agreement with what he's saying, though."

Pausing for a few seconds to let the veracity of the words contained on the tape sink in, he remembered himself.

"Decent day?"

"Horrible," she replied. "Dark."

"Yeah, I heard about that Professor. Have you been on that?"

"Not in the fine detail of what happened. Thankfully. Just the donkey work, as usual. I had to get his biography together for *The Lux Report*."

Keith put the case to the cassette he had been listening to on top of another, which contained a 1985-recorded tape of the pioneering American conspiracy researcher Mae Brussell. These rested on the three books that sat on the handmade wooden table next to the sofa – G. Edward Griffin's *World Without Cancer*, James H. Billington's *Fire In The Minds Of Men*, and Jim Marrs' *Crossfire: The Plot That Killed Kennedy*. He headed to the kitchen to reboil the kettle as Verity shouted after him.

"He'd been targeted multiple times by animal rights activists. They're becoming the obvious candidates for what happened."

"Yeah, well, turns out there might be a bit more to all of that," Keith shouted back.

Though they remained closed, Verity screwed up her eyes in apparent confusion.

"What do you mean?"

As the kettle began to boil, Keith re-entered the room. "Well, it seems he had a few extra-curricular activities going on. Outside of his University position, he'd been working on some private research contracts. For Clive Tuns."

Verity opened her eyes. "Clive Tuns? The pharmaceutical giant?"

'Yeah. Seems he'd been carrying out research for them on a personal basis, but using the University's funds and resources on the sly."

Verity paused for a few seconds. "Where the hell did you hear that? Who's the bloodclaat journalist here, you or me?"

"That's the word according to Phil."

"I thought it might be. What does he think he knows?"

"Just saying what I heard. It does add a slightly different perspective to things."

"What, so somebody at the Uni found out he was doing work on the side and decided to take him out to teach him a lesson? Seems a little 'extreme,' don't you think?"

Sensing a lightening of the tone might be appropriate, Keith perched on the edge of the sofa and stroked Verity's shimmering and newly (expensively) straightened hair. "Hungry?"

"What you got in mind? Pot Noodle?" she asked, her eyes now closed again. "Oh, that reminds me. Mum's doing family lunch at hers on Sunday."

"Ah," said Keith awkwardly.

"What?" came the inevitable reply.

"Well, it's just that…Max Zeall's doing an all-day seminar at the Pegasus on Sunday. Phil's going. I really wanted to join him. It'll be the first chance I've had to hear him in person since getting into his stuff." He beckoned at the cassette.

Verity's eyes were open again, now burning with vexation. She pushed his hand away from her hair. "Fine! Got your priorities straight then!"

"V! Don't be like that," Keith protested meekly.

"No, no, it's fine. I'll just take Colin fucking Cole from work along with me. After all, why would I want my boyfriend to be at a *family* gathering?!

Keith got up to go and make the tea, sensing a withdrawal from the scenario was called for. Must be the time of the month, he reasoned. He knew his place.

# CHAPTER 5

## Sunday 25th March 1990

*"The ground beneath my feet,*
*I know was made for me,*
*There is no any one place where I belong.*
*My spirit's meant to be free,*
*And soon now everyone will see,*
*Life was made for us to be what we wanna be."*

*Gil Scott-Heron: 'It's Your World.'*

"Who here can tell me what a right is?"

The voice was clear, eloquent and authoritative, and rang out through the PA system of the Pegasus Theatre in Magdalen Road. The assembled crowd of 50 or so remained silent, their collective gaze fixed on the tall, bearded figure speaking from the lectern.

"I repeat, who here can tell me what a right is?"

The silence was broken by a male voice from the front row. "It's an action that is legitimate for humans to undertake."

"Legitimate according to ...?" quizzed the speaker.

"According to the government of that land," ventured the respondent.

"WRONG!" Max Zeall's voice rasped through the speakers and was joined by a heavy thud as he crashed his fist down on the wooden lectern, and a high-pitched smash as the glass of water dropped from the lectern and shattered on the stage. "There is ZERO legitimacy to Government! Zero! Government is SLAVERY!"

The respondent, realising his grave tactical error, stayed silent. There was a reason why the speaker had warned, at the start of the lecture, that attendees would find his style markedly different from that of other lecturers, and that many would likely get offended at some of what he had to say, because it would fly in the face of so much of what they had been entrained, through a lifetime of societal conditioning, to accept as 'truth.'

"See, this is the problem, and this is why human slavery continues to thrive upon this earth," continued Zeall, much to the satisfaction of Keith and his old college buddy Phil Meritus in the third row, who had been so looking forward to hearing their mentor embark on one of his characteristic diatribes. It seems it didn't take much to get him going. "Because the dark-occult priest class which *really* runs everything in this world, has managed to instil a belief in the vast majority of people that 'rights' come from this magical entity called 'government.'

"TRUE Rights come from the creative force behind the Universe itself, and they make an absolute mockery of the notion that mankind gets to make up what's 'right' and 'wrong' according to time, location, circumstance or personal whims and preferences. Eternal, unwavering Truth doesn't change according to whether any one individual likes it or not, what year it is, or what imaginary "country" someone might happen to be in at any given time.

"Prior to 1967, you could have got jail time for being openly homosexual in England. Now you're more likely to get put away if you oppose it. Certain taxes are applied in wartime that aren't applied during so-called times of 'peace.' You can smoke cannabis 'legally' in certain geographical 'states,' but the minute you set foot over some imaginary line that somebody whose name you'll never know has plotted on a piece of paper you can be arrested and thrown in a cage. Some governor or minister who nobody has ever met, enacts some so-called 'law' according to their own personal preference, and everyone else just falls into line because they're told it's 'illegal' not to."

A vein stood out on Zeall's forehead and his face became redder as he continued his impassioned delivery.

"It's a sick joke. Really. You can't designate a right that doesn't exist for somebody else to set into place on your behalf, and the right DOESN'T exist for one person to dictate what everybody else must or must not do, according to whether they've decided that they like it or not! You hear how ridiculous it sounds? Something is either Right or Wrong Action, and will always be so, everywhere.

"So the correct answer to my question can be expressed in the apophatic – describing what something is by eliminating from the equation that which it is *not*. Okay? So a right is any behaviour which does *not* cause harm or loss to another living, sentient being. That's it. That's Right Action in Creation, That's Natural Law in effect, and it's been set into place by the creative force behind everything in this Universe. If you want to call that force 'God,' that's fine. Call it whatever you will. It doesn't make a difference."

The student who had called out was beginning to realise this now.

"If an action *does* put harm into physical manifestation, it's Wrong Action, we have no *right* to be doing it. And we will be held accountable, through the moral code of the Universe, for that chosen action.

"Because everything is a choice. Free Will is our greatest gift. So, sure, you *can* choose to undertake Wrong Action – because you'd be nothing more than an automaton if you didn't possess the capacity to make that choice. But you *can't* choose to escape the karmic *consequences* of making that choice. They will *always* be there."

(Though Keith had tried his best to stay focused on the words, he found the jibber-jabber of his over-burdened mind occasionally over-writing his concentration. At Zeall's mention of the words "always be there" he had recalled the creepy bathroom scene from *The Shining*, where the spirit of the murderer, Grady, had exclaimed to Jack Nicholson's character, "I'm sorry to differ with you, sir, but *you* are the caretaker. You've always been the caretaker. I should know, Sir. I've *always* been here.' Snapping back into conscious thought, he shook the diversion from his mind and refocused on the lecture.)

"And we reap these consequences on both an individual basis, for the personal decisions we make, and on a collective basis, as a result of the actions an entire society undertakes. And that's why we live in a world of immorality, injustice, chaos, violence and slavery, folks. Because people can't grasp basic morality and basic Truth, and don't know how to determine Right from Wrong Action.

"It's simple enough for a child of five to understand, and if this information were taught in primary school from that age, we'd see a dramatically different dynamic in society as a result. So it speaks volumes that it's not. But, despite it being simple enough for a five-year-old to comprehend, apparently a society of grown adults can't – or won't – grasp these most basic of teachings."

Zeall paused for dramatic effect as the assembled throng continued to hang on his every word.

"Told you he'd be on fire," whispered Phil. Keith didn't answer, eager not to miss the next words. His gaze remained fixed on the speaker as he mused on why it was that all gurus, sages and seers seemed to be bearded, as if they somehow channelled their wisdom from the ether through their facial hair. Keith had been studying Zeall's mannerisms closely. A steely passion burned in his intense eyes as he spoke, his head nodded back and forth gently, and he unconsciously gesticulated with both hands when he spoke multi-syllabled words.

"Government is slavery. I realise how provocative that statement will sound to many people, but it doesn't stop it from being true. To determine whether or not Government is a moral institution, we only need to examine how taxes are collected. Do people pay taxes voluntarily, or does Government extract them through coercion and force? The government does not politely ask that you pay your taxes. It threatens you – just like a mafia. If you don't pay them, the government will kidnap you and throw you in a cage. Let's call it as it really is.

"The only difference between the government and a mafia is the *belief* that political authority can be wielded virtuously, and that Government has a moral Right to threaten and coerce its citizens into paying taxes. Threats of violence are *never* okay, and Government is a fundamentally violent institution that will *never* bring about true freedom, peace, and prosperity."

Five hours later, the lecture had concluded to a standing ovation for the speaker, who, rather than disappear backstage, walked down the steps into the throng, and was immediately besieged by attendees wishing to shake his hand and engage him in conversation.

Keith and Phil swigged the last of the beer from their plastic cups and put on their jackets. "Whoah! Brotherman sure dropped some truth bombs today!" exclaimed Phil.

"It's cool that he gets involved with the audience like that," Keith replied.

"What kind of arrogant asshole would he be not to?" challenged Phil. "It'd kinda go against everything he preaches about elitism."

"Max Zeall's got to be a made-up name, right?"

'I don't think it is. The Universe has a funny sense of irony. You often find people whose real names tell you something about their character. Hey, you want to grab a word? I can introduce you."

Keith glanced at his watch. 5:08pm. "I'd better not, you know. V's had some family gathering today and I'm already on her shit list for being here instead. I'd better get over there and pick up the pieces."

Phil began singing the chorus to Godley & Creme's *Under Your Thumb*. Keith uttered an affectionate "fuck you" and headed towards the theatre's front door.

Outside, he climbed into his pale blue Austin Maestro. The radio blasted into life as he turned the ignition. He pushed the button to the separate graphic equaliser, still not entirely sure what it did. '1990's time for the Guru' went the song's hook, right on cue, as 99.9 Lux FM played Guru Josh's new *1990 To Infinity*. Careering off, Keith negotiated the annoying speed humps of Magdalen Road as quickly as he could without damaging the car's suspension. Just as he was free of them near the Mecca Bingo Hall, a red Nissan Micra driven by an elderly Asian pulled out from a parking space.

"This year would be nice!" yelled Keith, as the Micra moved agonisingly slowly towards the junction with

Cowley Road. Mercifully, the driver turned left, as Keith headed right.

Within minutes, he pulled up outside the semi-detached house in Littlemore, (or "Likklemore" as her mother liked to call it,) that was Verity's mum's home. Knowing the front door would be unlocked, he walked straight through and hollered to announce his arrival. He found himself among the dying embers of a social event that had peaked some hours before. Verity's mum walked through from the living room, pausing directly underneath the hand-painted portrait of a black Jesus, yellowing around the edges from age. "Wh'appen, Keith" she remarked, giving him a loose hug. "Hi, Joy," he replied. So sorry I couldn't make it earlier. Did you have a good day?"

Drew answered the question for him as he followed through from the living room, his hands laden with plates. "Ya man, de rice an' peas was wicked as always, star!"

"Hey, Drew," Keith replied. "Where's the Goddess at?"

Verity was next to appear from the lounge, right on cue. "Sorry to be so late," said Keith. "The event went over a bit."

"That's OK," replied Verity. "You're right on time to do the washing up."

# CHAPTER 6

## Wednesday 4th April 1990

*"Did you read the trespass notices? Did you keep off the grass?*
*Did you shuffle up the pavements just to let your betters pass?*
*Did you learn to keep your mouth shut? Were you seen but*
*never heard?*
*Did you learn to be obedient and jump to at a word?"*

*Ewan MacColl & Peggy Seeger: 'The Ballad of Accounting.'*

The driver of the shiny black Mercedes S-Class swung the machine with arrogant aplomb sharply to the left out of Worcester Street, the Ashmolean Museum to his left, and the martyrs' memorial off to his right. 434 years earlier, the Anglican bishops Thomas Cranmer, Hugh Latimer and Nicholas Ridley had paid the ultimate price for disobeying the dictates of Queen Mary 1, being burnt at the stake just a stone's throw away into Broad Street. A group of students on one side of the road, and a family of Chinese tourists on the other, stood aghast as the car steamed straight through the red traffic light.

One of the students mouthed an obscenity that was unrecognisable to the driver as he glanced into his

41

rear-view mirror. Hubris seeped from his every pore as his eugenics-inclined mind considered the utter insignificance of these people in the grand scheme of things. They occupied no more of his thoughts than the few seconds it took him to proceed along St. Giles, hooting and cursing at two cyclists as he prepared to swing in to the left.

He manoeuvred the Mercedes into a vacant parking spot between a Vauxhall Astra GTE and a Ford Fiesta. His erratic braking attracted the attention of the young traffic warden on duty, who glanced up from the windscreen of the Austin Allegro on which he'd just slapped a parking ticket. As the driver hurriedly pulled himself out of the Mercedes and strode away from the ticket machine, he directed a scowl towards the warden. "Don't even think about it," he warned, flashing up some kind of badge that the warden couldn't quite identify.

Detective Chief Superintendent C. C. Nomas of Thames Valley Police Oxford C.I.D. pushed on the oak door of the ancient Eagle and Child tavern and headed immediately to the intimate snug area on the left. Seated alone at the wooden table inside, nursing a pint of lager and with a Benson & Hedges blazing in the ashtray in front of him, was Detective Inspector Neil Lowe, just as Nomas had known he would be. Lowe could always be found in his favourite spot. Always to the left.

As Lowe became alerted to Nomas' sudden presence, instinct kicked in and he prepared to stand up. "Sit down, Neil," said Nomas immediately, having anticipated the usual playout of this ritual.

"I was just about to head off," said Lowe, the rapid darting around of the pupils in his beady eyes betraying the lie, the full pint glass and one quarter-burnt cigarette reinforcing it.

"Neil, consider it a business meeting," replied Nomas, ordering himself two double brandies from the barmaid who had noted his arrival and come into the snug to ask what she could get him.

Lowe's eyes continued to study Nomas' silently, as the D.I. pondered whether he was being surveilled. Nomas' words set his mind at rest.

"A few developments on the Herzlos case." The yellow manila file blew the ash of Lowe's neglected cigarette as it was tossed down on the table.

"I was wondering how that was going," offered Lowe.

"The alarm was triggered at 2.57am. Herzlos had a remote electronic link set up to a pager which he kept at home. It was set to ring whenever the sensors were disturbed at his lab."

"Isn't it normal for University department alarms to be connected to us, rather than to private individuals?"

"It is indeed, Neil. This is what first roused my curiosity. Herzlos had personally hired a state-of-the-art security company to secure this system and had seemingly paid for it out of his own pocket, whereas ordinarily, Uni funds would be allocated towards security systems. This all suggested to me that our Mr. Herzlos was acting more towards his own agenda than that of the Uni department with which he was employed."

Lowe started leafing through the manila folder, pausing for a swig of his beer and a pull on the cigarette which he had just remembered. Decades earlier, to the rear of the tavern, the celebrated writers C. S. Lewis, J. R. R. Tolkien, Charles Williams and Hugo Dyson had held their regular lunchtime gatherings as The Inklings to discuss literature, theology and philosophy, and Lewis had first unveiled the manuscripts to his *The Lion, The Witch And The Wardrobe* to his peers. Now, 40 years later, Neil Lowe was scrutinising a different kind of document, the details less poetic and far more sordid. Lowe's brow furrowed as he continued piecing together the scenario in his mind.

"Anyway, from quizzing his staff and from some interesting documentation found when we cracked open the safe in his lab, it turns out that Herzlos had a few extra-curricular activities on the go."

"Do we know who he was undertaking this work on behalf of?"

Nomas eyed him silently.

"Neil, take out your ID badge for me, please," said Nomas, his heavy ring clinking against the glass as he took a swig of the brandy which had now arrived.

Lowe obeyed.

"What's the full wording where you see your name?"

Lowe's eyes stayed focused on his superior's as he responded, 'Detective Inspector Neil Lowe."

"Bingo!" remarked Nomas sharply. "That means it's time for you to do some detective-inspecting. It's time for you to justify your position to the poll tax-payers of Oxford."

Nomas swigged back the second of the brandies and stood up to leave. He pushed the two glasses towards Lowe.

"Put those on your expense account. I'm playing golf at Frilford this afternoon. Come and see me first thing in the morning and let me know what you've found."

Nomas strode out of the darkened tavern into the bright sunlight of Wednesday lunchtime. The red border of the parking ticket carefully placed on the windscreen of his Mercedes immediately caught his eye. He ripped it off and paced purposely towards the young traffic warden who was about to apply another such ticket to the screen of the white van parked in the motorcycle bay.

From becoming aware of Nomas' imposing figure approaching, he barely had time to react before a strong arm had him pinned up against the trunk of one of St. Giles' elms. The warden caught the full brunt of Nomas' brandy-infused breath as he sneered at him. "I guess you didn't read the badge that I showed to you earlier. I'll let this one pass, but don't ever try it again, sonny, or you'll be trading this career for a promising new one over there." Nomas nodded towards the underground toilets toward the end of St. Giles, opposite the side entrance to the Ashmolean.

"Good luck trying to make this stick," he said, as he stuffed the screwed-up ticket into the warden's top pocket, before striding back to the Mercedes, climbing in and tearing off.

A couple of minutes later, Detective Inspector Neil Lowe emerged out of the Eagle and Child doorway. Finishing his cigarette and tossing the dog-end to the ground, he walked over to his own car, the paid parking ticket dutifully displayed. He turned the key to the lock, started the ignition, and headed out of St. Giles back into the city centre.

# CHAPTER 7

## Monday 16th April 1990

*"So if you want the Truth, go to God! Go to your gurus. Go to yourselves! Because that's the only place you're ever gonna find any real truth. But, man, you're never gonna get any truth from us. We'll tell you anything you wanna hear."*

*Peter Finch diatribe from the movie 'Network' (1976)*

It was an entirely normal scene as Verity arrived at Lux FM for the start of another week. As she greeted Geraldine the receptionist, the record being played by James Cody through the reinforced glass window to the studio was highly relevant. The line "at five I must have left, there's no exception to the rule, a matter of routine, I've done it ever since I finished school" drifted out of the reception speakers. Verity nodded a greeting to James, who had a stack of blue carts lined up ready to play the ads and the 11 o'clock news jingle.

Giving the lyrical observations some thought, Verity opted to take the stairs to the left of reception, up past the toilets and in past the kitchen, the managing director's office and the boardroom, rather than her usual route to the front of the studios. "Live a little, V," she mumbled smilingly to herself, reflecting on how much it sounded like something Keith would say.

Her alternative route to the newsroom, past Sales and Commercial Production, took her past the desk where the presenters prepared the content for their upcoming shows. Dave Vickers was in early ahead of his *Red Lux* evening show. He glanced up at her as she brushed past. "Hey, Verity," he called. "Here, come and take a listen to this."

"Hi Dave. What's up?" she asked, a tinge of caution in her tone as she'd detected Dave's eyes going up and down her legs on more than one occasion. Dave beckoned her to sit down opposite. Verity glanced over towards News where no-one had yet noted her arrival, so figured half a minute would do no harm. "See what you think of this," he enthused, popping a white-labelled tape into the portable radio-cassette player and pressing down on the Play button. After the few seconds of lead-in had passed the tape heads, the track began. Following some epic, ballad-tempo instrumentation, the soulful vocals began to soar: "Treated me kind, sweet destiny, carried me through desperation, to the one that was waiting for me."

"Who's that, Whitney Houston?" Verity asked.

Dave smiled. Everyone says that. Listen ..." Dave poked his finger down on the fast-forward button, advancing the tape by a couple of minutes. The singer was now in full operatic flow, showcasing a stunning vocal range as she blasted out the song's impassioned chorus. Verity raised her eyebrows, impressed. Dave tossed over the case to the cassette. "Maria Carey, who dat?" she remarked, regarding a slim, shapely figure with frizzy blonde hair in a black dress, clutching a vintage microphone.

"Not Maria – it's *Mariah*, as in Mount Moriah," Dave corrected her. "It just arrived on promo. Released next month. It's awesome. She's only 20. Just got signed to Columbia. And she's white...I think? Trust me – she's going to be massive!"

"You could be right," replied Verity, peering towards News again. This time, Jess Hewitt was glancing over her glasses in her direction. Verity stood up to leave, noticing Dave's fleeting glance towards her cleavage, concealed yet pronounced under her black sweater. "Laters, Dave," she said, beginning to walk across the grey-tiled carpet towards News. After a few paces she quickly turned around, catching Dave removing his gaze from her backside and towards his playlist printout on the desk. She tried to work out whether she was annoyed or flattered. Acknowledging the faint smile that had formed on her lips, she realised it was more of the latter.

The young tech-op guy was visible through the open door to the music library, going through a pile of 7-inch vinyl singles in white cardboard sleeves. The reporter in her reminded Verity that she really should find out his name one of these days and establish exactly what his role was in the station. Afternoon presenter Gary Grant emerged from the music library and walked over to the presenters' desk. "Here he is," said Dave. "Gary 'Chit Chat' Grant, the only presenter who can talk all the way up to the vocal on *Song For Guy*." Grant clipped him around the back of the head with a 12-inch copy of Snap!'s *The Power*.

The usual grey fog hung in the air over the news area, as the reporters all puffed on cigarettes between looking at papers and bashing the keys of their electric typewriters. "Morning all," offered Verity cheerfully. The expected non-committal grunts came from Colin Cole and Richard Owen. A more enthusiastic "hi, hun," came from Amy Noble, Verity's only female ally in the newsroom jungle, who, she noted, was looking more like Suzanne Vega every day. The two touched fists in their usual work-place horseplay, before Amy turned her attention back to the home-made avocado and chickpea salad she'd been consuming.

Over at the sports desk, his legs up on his typewriter as usual, Mateo feasted on yet another packet of Lemon Scampi fries liberated from the downstairs storage area, the remnants of the previous Christmas's Lux Box charity appeal. While the tinned goods had proven very popular, it seemed Oxford's homeless community had little use for the many boxes of Lemon Scampi fries that had been donated by a local pub. These had formed the main basis of Mateo's lunch for the previous four months.

"Oh, look, it's Lady V!" enthused Mateo as he noted Verity's arrival. A familiar routine was about to break out. "Oh, look George, it's Verity, here to do some *proper* reporting." Mateo effected a perfect voice rendition of Zippy from the children's' television show *Rainbow*, before launching into an impersonation of the show's George character that might have made an onlooker assume he was the original voice artist. "Yes, I know, Zippy. I can see. Hello, Verity. You're looking very pretty today."

'Hi Mateo," she replied, smiling. No matter how predictable the routine, it was still amusing and reassuring. "Nutritious lunch again, I see?" "Oh yes," he replied, still in George mode as he tossed the finished bag of Lemon Scampi fries into his red wastepaper basket, where it joined a melee of dot matrix printer paper, cigarette ash, apple cores, and other Lemon Scampi bags. The concept of recy-cling has yet to hit Lux FM, Verity mused.

"Well, the lung cancer will probably get you before the malnutrition," she ventured to add, happy that she knew him well enough that he would treat the comment as affec-tionate banter, rather than taking offence. "You'll have to apply for an outside reporting job when smoke-free offices come in," she added, mischievously.

"Bollocks," came the reply. "You'll be waiting a long time for that! Never happen."

"We'll see," she retorted good-naturedly as she made a headway towards Jess Hewitt's desk, reasoning it was about time she made an official start to her shift.

"Grab a seat, Verity," said Jess, looking up again over her reading glasses. and taking a pause from bashing at her typewriter keys.

Verity duly pulled over a red foam office chair and took a perch, anticipating some sort of imminent reprimand.

Her worries proved unfounded.

"Are you ready for your first stint presenting *The Lux Report* this evening?" Jess asked, handing Verity a folder-full of printout papers and typed news-scripts.

"What . . . seriously?" Verity's hesitance and shock was in no way contrived. *The Lux Report* was the pinnacle of the station's news reporting – a live one-hour show from 6pm which brought together the day's local, national and international news in a fast-paced magazine format. A Lux journalist was considered to have earned their stripes when they were given the programme's anchor slot.

"Do you think I'm ready?" Verity continued.

"I wouldn't offer it to you if I didn't think you were. I've picked up that you don't think I've been giving you enough responsibility, and that you feel ready to climb the ladder a few rungs. So I want to put you on the TLR rota. You can do tonight and tomorrow and we'll see how it goes. Dave V will tech-op you."

Verity's immediate reaction of panic became overwritten with relief that her boss did have some faith in her abilities after all, and the pride of knowing that this was going to be a major milestone in her developing career.

"Well, … thank you, Jess," Verity replied appropriately. "I'll give it my very best shot."

"I know you're nervous," Jess managed a half-smile, "but once you get the first ten minutes out of the way it'll be plain sailing. Have a word with Rich to get some tips, and make sure you go through it all with Dave in advance."

Verity's afternoon passed interminably slow, the butterflies in her stomach working overtime. Eager to break her news to Keith so his words of encouragement could stabilise her anxieties somewhat, she glanced at the office clock. 2.16pm. Each hour, she'd gone to the printer that was hot-wired to Independent Radio News HQ in London, ripping off the latest printout to see what the stories of the day were:

*'Saddam Hussein threatens to "destroy half of Israel with chemical weapons" if it opposes his intentions to annexe Kuwait. Bush administration says it cannot rule out the possibility of military intervention'.*

*'Pressure increases on Mrs. Thatcher over Poll Tax reforms.'*

*'Appeal launched over John Poindexter role in Iran-Contra affair.'*

"Here's the local leads," said Jess, ripping a sheet of A4 out of her typewriter. Verity glanced at the headlines:

*'Number of children reported missing in Oxford area increases by 25 per cent.'*

*'Rover Group launches a new version of its Metro supermini, which has been the Cowley plant's best-selling BL/ Austin Rover car since its 1980 launch.'*

At 5.45pm, Verity walked ominously down the stairs to the studios brandishing a black cartridge holder stuffed with scripts. Dave Vickers followed, clutching a pile of blue carts, a fresh reel of Zonal tape in its white and mauve-patterned cardboard box, a smaller reel of yellow leader tape, a razor blade, and a tiny reel of splicing tape.

As Dave entered Studio A, waiting for James Cody to play his last record and fire the carefully-backtimed sequence of ads, Verity composed herself on the other side of the glass, breathing steadily in nervous contemplation. The moment came around all too soon, and she found herself voicing the words she had anticipated so often over the past several months:

"It's six o' clock, I'm Verity Hunter, and this is *The Lux Report*."

Jess had been right. By the time she had nervously but dutifully read the first few stories and signalled through the glass for Dave to fire the corresponding audio, Verity found herself able to relax somewhat, reflecting that Dave, juggling reports, ads, jingles, and the mic feed from her studio, probably had a more demanding task than she did. Within the show's first few minutes he had called over the intercom, advising Verity to project her voice further upon observing that the mic levels were peaking at around 2-3 rather than the required 5-6 on the meter. Listeners to the station wouldn't have noticed much of an audio deficit, however, with Lux's processing amplifier automatically boosting the volume to a standardised level.

Her emerging sense of ease was suddenly interrupted, however, by Studio B's door being wrenched open and Jess reaching in with an additional sheet of A4. "New local lead," she barked. "Do this next. Push the Rover story further on." She was gone as abruptly as she'd arrived. Verity quickly perused the typed headline:

*'University Professor's murder likely the work of animal rights extremists.'*

As seven o'clock finally arrived, and the IRN news melded into Madonna's *Vogue*, Dave Vickers's new Power Play, Verity collated her papers and emerged from Studio B to a chorus of cheers from her colleagues. Even Mal

Knight, the station's Managing Director was there. "You finally popped your TLR cherry!" he exclaimed. "Right, put your scripts down, you have an urgent engagement at the Chequers." As the tech-op youth that Verity had christened 'The Boy With No Name' collected the pile of carts ready to archive the audio on to a reel of tape, and the scripts to put away in the filing cabinet, the small group filed out of reception into three of the Lux-branded cars out front, and headed to the company's pub of choice in nearby Horspath village.

As the collective filed noisily into the pub's main bar, and Jess secured the usual table by the window, Knight made a headway to order the drinks. "Say hello to the host of this evening's *Lux Report*, George," he bellowed joyfully to the landlord, beckoning in Verity's direction. A haze of cigarette smoke was already marking out the radio station's table as Mal Knight placed down the tray of drinks, causing lager to slop over the sides of the pint glasses in the process.

"I'd better just have a lemonade please, Mal," remarked Verity. "I've got to drive home."

"Haven't we all?" he retorted boisterously. "You can let go of those sensibilities, Verity. You're well and truly on the winning team now!"

As the table erupted into loud conversation, Jess reached into her handbag and pulled out a red cassette in a clear case – a C60 with 30 minutes of audio on each side.

"I had Dave run off a tape of your first show for you. You'll want to keep that."

"I sure will," said Verity, putting it away in her own bag, then seizing the opportunity for a quiet word away from the others.

"That Herzlos story. The police putting it down to animal rights activists."

"Anti-vivisectionists. Apparently he'd been targeted by them before. Police think it's some hardcore unhinged activists who objected to his use of lab rats."

"I'd heard there was some kind of link in his work with Clive Tuns?" Verity ventured, reciting what Keith had mentioned to her.

Jess's demeanour immediately switched from convivial to defensive.

"Where did you hear that?"

"I...don't remember. I just picked it up somewhere the other day," said Verity, shocked at the attack.

"You don't remember? Not much of a reporter if you can't remember your source, are you?" Jess prolonged her scowl, eventually adding. "Just read the scripts you're given, Verity, and forget all about any involvement from Clive Tuns. Clear?"

Nothing was clear. But it would become so in time.

# CHAPTER 8

## Friday 20th April 1990

*"It's 1990,*
*How we've made it this far is beyond me.*
*Another decade, another error made in history,*
*Will repeat itself and this species,*
*Called mankind will be zapped out totally."*

*MC Wildski: 'Wonderful World.'*

As Verity turned the key to the Abingdon Road door, she realised her Friday night sanctuary would not get to be enjoyed just yet, as she heard Keith's vocal tones joined by another male voice. She groaned to herself as she kicked off her shoes, hung up her jacket and bag, and got the inevitable over with. "Hi Keith. Hi Phil," she offered routinely, putting her head around the doorway to where her boyfriend was sat opposite the stocky frame of his best mate, the pair deep in intense conversation. "Hey, Goddess," Keith replied, convincingly.

Phil put his nose to the air and began sniffing. A smile came to his lips. "Is that weed? Have you been bunning, Verity?"

"No, but Drew has. I stopped off at his first. It's 4/20, isn't it?"

"Like he needs that as an excuse," contributed Keith.

"Ah, the date of sacrifice by fire, and of celebration by habitual weed-smokers everywhere," added Phil.

"Tea?" Verity asked, excusing herself in favour of the kitchen.

"Please," replied Keith.

"Hey, guess what?" he called after her. "Phil was just telling me that Max Zeall's been kicked out of the Pegasus Theatre. They've pulled the next two lectures he was due to do there."

"I can't imagine why," Verity called back from the kitchen, filling the kettle.

"The man speaks too much truth. They can't handle it," Phil interjected, ignoring the gentle sarcasm. "His last talk went in big-time on the true nature of Satanism. Seems it was a little too close to the mark for the theatre manager.

"Why? Does he like dressing in robes in a forest at three in the morning and sacrificing chickens around a fire?" remarked Verity wryly.

Phil was triggered. "See, that's exactly the kind of perception most people have of Satanism due to how they've been programmed by society to think of it. Either that, or they take the so-called 'Christian' interpretation of this singular entity called 'the Devil' complete with horns and a trident and blame every evil in the world on 'him'."

An image of her mother in church on a Sunday morning came into Verity's mind.

"Although dark occult rituals do take place in the name of Satanism, that's only a small part of the picture," Phil clarified. "For the most part it's a mindset that's all about selfishness – me, me me. And, if we're honest with ourselves, most people upon this earth are stuck in that mindset. Their only concerns, from the minute they wake up in the morning to the minute they go to bed at night, are about what suits them, right now, in the circumstances in which they find themselves. I learned that much from my dad."

Keith and Verity sat in silence, letting the words register.

"Not a thought for other people, or for the impact their own selfish behaviours may have on the rest of society or Creation. *That's* real Satanism. And so you can say that the vast, overwhelming majority of people are Satanists. And they would be *horrified* to hear that. But they can get as horrified as they like. That doesn't stop it from being true."

Verity gave some acknowledgement to the conflict of thoughts that she was experiencing. Although she found Phil's intensity to be off-putting, and she resented the amount of her man's time that he was now taking up, the sentiments of his words clearly resonated.

He continued with what could well have been a Max Zeall lecture in itself.

"Word," said Keith, nodding in agreement as the words sank in. Verity leaned against the door frame, paying similar attention.

Presently, it became clear that Phil had said his piece, and equally clear that the words had been heartfelt and delivered with sincerity, rather than regurgitated from any kind of script. (Like a *Lux Report* one, Verity considered dryly.)

An awkward silence filled the room. Keith's eyes met Verity's and he took his cue.

"Right, mate, I'll have to be cracking on, and it's time to give the Goddess here some Friday night space."

"Sure," said Phil. The sofa seemed to heave with relief as he lifted his burly anatomy off it and reached for his backpack.

"See ya, Phil," said Verity. Then, as an afterthought: "Hey, Phil, where did you hear about that connection between that Herzlos guy and Clive Tuns?"

Phil paused for a moment before responding.

"Somebody I met at the last Pegasus lecture reckons they spoke to an insider who works at Tuns. Told him about Herzlos being paid backhanders to do research under the radar into the effects of a new cancer drug they're preparing. Using the University's lab facilities to do it on the sly."

"Gotta love whistleblowers," offered Keith. He knew as soon as the words left his lips that he was about to be contradicted.

"It might be useful information, but there's no dignity in having anything to do with a pharmaceutical corporation. Or any corporation. It's no accident that the word is derived from 'corpse,' as it's a dead entity. Having anything to do with an organisation like that – especially making your livelihood from it – is immoral. This person knows about Herzlos doing deals under the table, and how evil vivisection is, yet, as far as I'm aware, hasn't yet walked from his job and found himself a method of making Right Livelihood."

More silence. Even Phil was astute enough to know that the conversation had reached its natural end, and it was time to leave the others to muse on his words in their own time and space.

"Gotta run, guys. I need to get a weights session in at the gym before it closes. Hey, Keith ... "

Keith knew what was coming.

"This is my will, and I apply it," said Phil, reciting what had become something of a double-header catchphrase between the two as they had developed their studies of spiritual truth together.

"As it is willed, so shall it be," Keith replied faithfully.

Take care," said Phil with a smile, letting himself out.

Now able to fully enter domestic relaxation mode, and with her man to herself for the evening, Verity stretched out on the sofa and re-assumed foot massage position. But not before Keith had finished making the tea.

It had been quite the week. Anxiety, then pride over being asked to front *The Lux Report* on Monday had turned to disappointment and resentment when Jess had pulled her off of Tuesday's show, insisting unconvincingly that Richard Owen needed to present it in order to make up some lacking contractual hours. Jess's altered demeanour when she had mentioned Clive Tuns in the pub had played on Verity's mind, all the way until earlier on Friday.

Confusion and doubt were the dominant emotions when Jess had called her over to her desk again, asking her to go with Owen to represent the station at the Rotary Club annual charity dinner. Jess herself always attended, she explained, yet this year, due to how the dates had fallen, was unable to, leaving Verity wondering if this was some tedious task that she'd just wanted to get out of, or whether it was a gesture to atone for her unfair treatment of Verity earlier in the week. Either way, Jess must have thought her adding, "don't worry, they'll have vegetarian meals" would make all the difference.

"You'll be right in the belly of the beast there, V," Keith opined when she had revealed her mission. "The Rotary Club thing will be a respectable public front. You'll be in the midst of a load of Freemasons, for sure. All the big movers and shakers."

"It's not a Freemasons ball, Keith," Verity retorted.

"Not officially. They'll conduct their important activities in private. They wouldn't publicly advertise it to anyone outside of the order. I've been researching how these secret-society fraternities work. It's all done in degrees. The real knowledge and power is compartmentalised, so that only those deemed worthy of it have access to it as they advance through the degrees. The lower levels are the public face of the organisation. Most at that level believe they're genuinely doing good works and serving the community and all that. You'll only ever advance beyond those levels if the higher-ups identify traits in you that can be put to use where the real power lies. At those levels, everything's done by oaths of allegiance and high-level secrecy.

"They put on events like this one to give the impression it's just a harmless old boys' network – a bunch of old Etonians and Oxbridge graduates getting together to hobnob over champagne and canapés. But I'm telling you, you'll see some real high-fliers there. And what they get up to on a Tuesday night down the Lodge will be rather different to what's on display here. A nod's as good as a wink to a blind bat, as they say."

Verity glanced at her watch. 21:06. "This is hardly Friday night-appropriate material, Keith," she said, closing her eyes and prodding him with her foot to begin his massage duties. "Somewhere I read that life isn't *always* supposed to be serious. Somewhere I read that it *is* actually OK to have some fun from time to time. Remember fun?"

"I remember fun," smiled Keith, anticipating the blessing of a Friday evening indoors with his girl.

# CHAPTER 9

## Monday 30th April 1990

*"Mirrors on the ceiling, the pink champagne on ice.*
*And she said, 'we are all just prisoners here, of our own device,'*
*And in the master's chambers, they gathered for the feast.*
*They stab it with their steely knives but they just can't*
*kill the beast."*

*The Eagles: 'Hotel California.'*

Though she knew Lux FM would have no problem affording it, something still felt wrong to Verity about the executive car from Findlay Chauffeur Service that had been booked to take her from Abingdon Road to the Randolph Hotel. Keith could very well have given her a lift, and had offered, but Jess had insisted on the private car. As she alighted the Mercedes S-Class, she instinctively reached for her purse to pay the driver, before remembering that it was all covered on account.

The Randolph's facade was lined with men and women who, like Verity herself, were dressed all in black as per the event's stipulations. Most had similarly arrived by executive car, the door being opened obligingly by one of the hotel's concierges. She joined the queue walking up the steps to the main entrance, presenting her invitation card for the careful inspection of the doorman, before being ushered on to the black-and-white chequerboard flooring of the lobby. Waitresses attended the guests, trays of champagne glasses and canapés in hand. Verity followed the actions of the other guests and took a glass on cue.

"Verity!" Richard Owen appeared, providing a welcome diversion from the social awkwardness. Dressed in a dinner jacket hired from Ballroom Emporium on The Plain, he paced towards her through the throng of identically-dressed male attendees.

"Rich," said Verity. "Help. Tell me what to do."

"Treat it as a piss-up, with time off in lieu to boot," he smiled, raising what was his third glass of champagne. "But keep an ear open for any stories. If there's a roof collapse in this place tonight, it'll wipe out the great and good of Oxford Establishment all in one go."

"Well, Jess would be safe, at least," replied Verity.

"Yeah, I don't know why she wouldn't come. Still, you get an evening out into the bargain."

"Not my type of crowd," said Verity, reflecting on how much more at home she'd feel if she were cutting shapes to some New Jack Swing at Boodles, Downtown Manhattans or Minchery Farm Country Club "But it's an eye-opener either way," she added, as the crowd slowly filtered into the Randolph's sprawling restaurant ahead of the banquet meal and the formal presentations.

A stocky man in his thirties with a jovial air lurched towards the pair. "Richard, you grizzled old hack!" he bellowed loudly, giving Owen a pat on the back that, had he worn false teeth, may well have caused them to fly out. "Martin, you deceitful old adulterer!" Owen teased back.

As Verity mused on this strange ritual of mutual ribbing, Owen made an introduction. "Mart, this is Verity, my colleague in the newsroom. Verity – Martin McLeish, my old college pal from Bailliol, by way of Inverness-shire." McLeish gripped her hand so firmly it almost brought her to tears. "Delighted, Verity," he said. "Now, you let me know if this old pervert starts bothering you, and I'll tell you all about his bizarre fetishes."

"You're from Scotland?" said Verity, working on her social small-talk. 'You don't have an accent."

"That's a public school upbringing for you, darling," said McLeish, in a dialect reminiscent of John Cleese's Basil Fawlty, and putting Verity in mind of the way most of her colleagues in Lux News spoke. Having not gone beyond A' Levels at Oxpens College herself, this was still a culture that was very alien to her. "Ten years at Eton and Oxford could make Paul Gascoigne come out sounding like Prince Charles," added McLeish.

As he guffawed his way to the next grouping, Verity and Owen occupied a corner of the room which gave them a vantage point for some good people-watching. Their eyes scoured the room for familiar faces, and between them, they recognised a few; the Lord Mayor of Oxford, the headmaster of the Dragon School, dons from Bailliol, Worcester and Christchurch colleges, Jeremy Bardwell of Bardwell Books, the editorial director of the *Oxford Mail* Group. The latter two were also on the board of Lux FM. Present also were a couple of their radio rivals, Bill Heine and Bill Rennells of BBC Radio Oxford.

"Isn't he the guy that has the shark in the roof of his house in Headington?" asked Verity, nudging Owen and nodding towards Heine.

"That's him. Also runs the Penultimate Picture Palace in Jeune Street."

"There's Rose Cross," added Owen, indicating towards a woman, senior in years, with wild, white hair. Despite her ballgown, she still carried the air of a lady who might live in Bohemian surroundings in the company of multiple cats. Verity recognised the name. Rose Cross was a veteran broadcaster, lecturer and writer on feminism and women's rights issues and, by all accounts, a mentor figure to their boss, Jess Hewitt. An Oxford graduate herself, she was held in high regard in Oxford literary and academic circles. She was also a shareholder in Lux FM.

Another face familiar to Verity was that of Detective Chief Superintendent Nomas of Oxford C.I.D. who was deep in conversation. The other man, white-haired and bespectacled, was dressed identically to all the other males, but, her trained reporter's eye noted, sporting a particularly distinctive gold ring, adorned with a heavy black stone and some kind of engraved sigil. "Nomas," Verity whispered to Owen, nodding towards the police chief. "Yeah, and getting cosy with Solomon Schwartz."

Verity paused, mid-champagne-sip, at the name. "*That's* Sol Schwartz, Chief Executive of Clive Tuns?"

"The very same," replied Owen. "Doesn't look like that suggestion of him being mixed up in that Herzlos business has done too much harm to his standing in the community, does it?"

Keith's words about secret societies, and how this event would see her right in the belly of the beast, came back to her. "Back in a sec," she said to Owen, as she began nudging her way through the crowd to get closer to the two men.

She reached a position where she could get a clearer look at Sol Schwartz's ring. From what she could detect without making herself too obvious, the motif engraved into the black granite depicted some kind of slithering snake, with a five-pointed star above its head, the apex of the star pointing downwards. The conversation between the pair was drawing to a close, and as Nomas extended his right hand towards Schwartz's, she registered that he was wearing an identical ring. And the handshake that ensued was no ordinary one.

A thought occurred to Verity. She nudged her way back over to where Rose Cross was regaling two elderly men with some anecdote or other. As the old lady paused to bring her glass to her lips, the same engraved ring was visible on her right ring finger.

A few paces from where Verity stood, her back against the wall, an untouched champagne glass in hand, was another newcomer to such events. Just two years Verity's senior, the tall brunette felt equally out-of-place in such social gatherings – particularly as she kept becoming aware of lecherous gazes from several of the male guests, most of them over the age of 60.

No budget had been provided for either a private car or for ballroom dress hire, so she had arrived in the black clubbing dress and high heels that she'd worn out to Parkers wine bar on St. Clements with her friends at the weekend, and hoped for the best. Alarmed to see on arrival that all the other ladies' gowns flowed to their ankles, whereas hers ended above the knee, she'd rushed out to the Asian convenience store in George Street for a pair of tights to tone down the effect. These she had hastily pulled on in the Randolph toilets, managing to ladder them with a jagged toenail in the process. An additional purchase was a nerve-steadying 20 Silk Cut. Though she had pretty much given up smoking some months before, three of these had already been consumed in these moments of weakness.

She, also, had been keenly eying the attendees in the room, making all kinds of mental notes for later follow-up.

W.D.C. May Pearce's attendance was at the behest of her superior, D.I. Neil Lowe, who stood beside her, having traded in his glass of champagne for a bottle of Hobgoblin ale. He himself was a reluctant guest, but the annual Ball had become requirement of his position. He felt only slight guilt at having coerced his Detective Constable into joining him to forcibly hobnob, but had sold it to her on the basis of his making some useful contacts that would stand her in good stead as her career progressed.

Having finished his conversation, Nomas walked back towards Lowe and beckoned him away from May. Looking in all directions to make sure they wouldn't be overheard, he whispered softly.

"Forget all about that lead regarding Herzlos possibly being involved in extra-curricular activities at his lab. We're back to looking at animal rights extremists. Haul in anyone we've previously had dealings with on such matters and question them. Put your whole team on it. Doesn't matter how long it takes."

From her vantage point, May observed the pair's conversation. Though she couldn't hear their words, she got the impression that Lowe was objecting to whatever Nomas had just said to him, but that the latter was pulling rank. They both assumed a social air and walked back to join her.

May was finding amusement from the fact that she and her superiors were standing in one of the iconic settings for Oxford's most famous literary cop, Colin Dexter's *Inspector Morse*. The appropriately-named Morse Bar was straight ahead of them. Ennui and awkwardness had seen her searching for some kind of conversation-starter for several minutes. As Nomas and Lowe walked back to join her, she dropped her intended ice-breaker.

"So, I gather this place is named after Sir Randolph Churchill, the father of Winston? You know, I heard something a while back about Randolph Churchill being linked to the Jack the Ripper murders. According to some, he may have been the actual killer, it was all connected to the Royal Family, and was all covered up in line with some Freemasonic plot. Is there any truth to that?"

Although the general hubbub and chit-chat continued through the rest of the room, in the small section occupied by the three police officers, an excruciatingly awkward silence ensued. Nomas appeared apoplectic. Lowe stared down at his shoes. "Shit. Nice one, May," the W.D.C. thought to herself.

It was Nomas who broke the silence. "Detective Inspector Lowe," he growled. "Kindly keep your dogs on a leash, where they belong," before striding away indignantly. After four steps he paused, turned around and barked, "and by the way, the hotel was actually named after Doctor Francis Randolph!" Nomas turned on his heel and continued his retreat.

"Oh, nice one. Bloody great. You've proper fucked him off now," said an embarrassed Lowe.

"I'm sorry. I just ... "

"You just put your bloody great foot in it, Detective Constable, that's what you did. You don't talk about Freemasonic plots in the company of a man like that. And furthermore, you don't besmirch the name of one of the greatest statesmen this country has ever seen with a stupid bloody conspiracy theory! You think someone like Randolph Churchill could become a Lord if he was involved in something like that, and that the Royal family wouldn't know about it? Get real!"

Lowe began pacing towards the bar. "I need another ale ... Jack the friggin' Ripper. Bloody hell!" And he was gone.

May pictured herself on the checkouts of Sainsbury's Heyford Hill by the end of the week as she pondered whether one badly-judged comment could have ended her career that evening. Heading out into the warm evening air of Worcester Street, she reached for the Silk Cut.

# CHAPTER 10

## Tuesday 1st May 1990

*"And here's a classic from those heady days of 1969 for you. Thunderclap Newman and 'Something In The Air.'"*

*Dean Daniels on Lux Gold, 2.10am.*

A little over two hours later, W.D.C. May Pearce was back in a taxi, headed towards home in Cowley. Experience had taught her that, to have left her departure much later may have made crossing Magdalen Bridge at the end of the High Street and onward to Cowley Road impossible. The gaggle of drunken students in college blazers that suddenly jumped into the road, one of them thinking it pant-wettingly hilarious that he'd placed a traffic cone on his friend's head, served as confirmation that tonight was a special study in Establishment ritual, in this city most steeped in fiercely guarded traditions.

The city centre revelry was a prelude to what would be happening a few hours later at dawn, when the May Morning celebrations that had persisted for the past 500 years or so got faithfully re-enacted once again. These were centred around Magdalen Bridge, which would be closed to traffic from 2am, necessitating a lengthy diversion for anyone looking to get to the East side of the city. "May Morning," May whispered to herself, smiling at the linguistic irony.

In Oxpens Road, as the taxi driver gave a sharp hoot of his horn and wound down his window to shout an obscenity at the youths, one of them hurled the bottle of rum he'd been brandishing at the car. It sprayed the driver with its contents through the still-open window, before ricocheting off the roof and smashing loudly on the other side of the road. The taxi driver screeched to a halt. Both he and his passenger, cop mode kicking in, quickly realised that giving chase would be futile as the youths, now minus the traffic cone, were already running off. "Send the bill to my dad," taunted the bottle-thrower, as his friends guffawed and chortled.

* * *

As the sun came up on the dawn of 1st May, events at Magdalen Bridge played out the same as they had for the past several decades. Few in attendance bore any knowledge of the significance of the rituals, their performance being justified simply by 'tradition,' or it all being 'the done thing' in Oxford. As the church bells struck 6am, the choir from Magdalen College began singing the seven-minute *Hymnus Eucharistus* from the Great Tower. Once completed, a bell-ringing ceremony took place over the following 20 minutes, and after this, the troupe of Morris Men from Oxford and many of the surrounding villages began a procession of ceremonial music and dancing, coercing the bulk of the crowd from Magdalen Bridge along the High Street and into Radcliffe Square where, in the early morning shadow of the Capitol Building-like Camera, the revelry continued.

The city was witnessing the faithful re-enactment of pagan ceremony from centuries past, the activities steeped in symbolism to generate the same states of consciousness in the crowd, here in the last decade of the 20th century, as had been the case for countless generations before. Those proceeding directly from singing Christian hymns to embracing Pagan dancing apparently saw no contradiction in doing so.

This same Spring fertility ritual, given various names including Walpurgisnacht and Beltane, was being simultaneously celebrated in towns and cities throughout Europe and beyond. Many schools had kept alive the ancient tradition of May dancing, with children skipping around the maypole and holding ribbons which emanated from its tip. So shrouded in the mists of time were its origins that few parents held any awareness of the maypole and ribbons being symbolic representations of an erect phallus and the ejaculation of semen, representing the male principle of regeneration at this most significant of times for agriculture and the life-giving properties of the sun in this part of the world.

While the overwhelming majority in attendance were simple-mindedly swept up in the convivial spirit of the celebrations, a small proportion were in full knowledge of why these traditions were still kept alive and had been implanted into the cultural fabric of this city. Some of this chosen few observed quietly from the sidelines, noting the behaviours of many as the combination of the music, the ritual, the archetypal motifs, and the uniquely-generated vibrational frequency, affected them in ways which fell way below the threshold of their conscious minds.

Since 2am, this area of town had been the domain only of pedestrians, with all vehicles diverted until around nine. Emerging out of Cowley Road and walking quickly across The Plain roundabout, was a 17-year-old girl. Her appearance represented a modern-day rendering of tribal attire. Underneath the loosely-fitting denim dungarees, she wore a baggy white T-shirt. Its main logo was obscured by the front of the denim, but had it been visible, an onlooker would have seen a large yellow circle with a smiley face in the centre, and a splattering of red on the upper left edge. Parts of the yellow were starting to peel away. This was a well-worn garment, having been in almost weekly use since the 'Second Summer of Love' events of 1988. On her back, she carried a black rucksack. On her feet she wore black Doc Marten boots. Her yellow-blonde hair evoked an unkempt bramble bush, splaying out wildly in all directions.

Though she was now alone, this had only been the case for the time it had taken her to walk the entire length of Cowley Road from where it emptied out on to the Ring Road near the giant British Leyland works. Her brain and body fuelled up on a cocktail of narcotic stimulants, she had achieved this in a little over fifteen minutes, a fraction of what it would have taken most able-bodied individuals walking at an energetic pace, even taking into account a stop to make a call from the red phone box near the City Arms pub. A supply of coins for the call would not be a problem.

Her friends called her Molly, and a group of them had dropped her near the Cowley works, at her request, as the carload returned from a May Day festival of an alternative kind, in a field somewhere off the A329 towards Wallingford. Though the cosmetic details differed, the many parallels between this group's chosen way of seeing in 1st May, and that of the crowds in the High Street, were all too evident; music, ceremony, signs, symbols and sigils directed straight at the subconscious, and an almost religious state of rapture from the energetic state generated by the proceedings.

It was full daylight, somewhere between 6 and 7am, and unusually warm for the time of day, as Molly crossed The Plain on to Magdalen Bridge. She might have been some kind of celebrity given the amount of students who seemed to recognise her. Several, in turn, approached, and brief conversations were had, always ending in money being taken out of the the students' pockets and being exchanged for small see-through bags which Molly extracted from her backpack. Some contained blue and yellow tablets, a few engraved with the redundant 'L' logo of British Leyland to mark them out as being Oxford-produced. Others contained white powder.

Though superficial efforts were made to be discreet, these transactions still took place within sight of the many uniformed police officers dotted around the bridge area. Their presence didn't seem to faze the enterprising young vendor, though they apparently did one prospective customer. Had an onlooker been present in Oxpens Road some hours earlier when May Pearce's taxi got christened by the rum bottle, they might have recognised the student who was now negotiating with Molly as the one who had thrown it.

Apparently becoming agitated, the student grabbed Molly's arm and led her back on to The Plain and towards the doorway of Club Latino, some distance away from the nearest police officer. Finding a concealed alleyway to the right of the row of buildings, the pair's transaction was completed there, and the student took the opportunity to sample some of the wares that his Hong Kong-based business magnate father's trust fund money had just procured. Molly's regular product was not for him. He had insisted upon the 'Special Blend.'

Getting recognised and accosted twice again en route, Molly made her way through the crowds to a sight which would have alarmed anyone new to the city's traditions, but which was occurring without the batting of an eyelid in actuality. Several students were climbing on to the balusters of ancient Magdalen Bridge, now green with the moss and mildew of ages, and balancing themselves precariously with arms aloft, before leaping off and plunging down into the murky waters of the River Cherwell below. This particular narrow stretch was far from what anyone might have legitimately called deep. At this time, following some weeks without rain, the depth was barely over five feet under the bridge. This fact was not deterring the students gleefully jumping in wearing full college ball attire, however, all drunk either from a night of alcohol consumption, or simply intoxicated by the vibrant energy of the ritual.

As Molly completed a couple more transactions with her characteristic lack of real discretion, the crowd became alerted to a piercing wailing sound and a sense of commotion. The youth with whom Molly had just completed her alleyway transaction was running maniacally through the crowd, pushing to the floor anyone who stood in his path. He had shed the college blazer and frilly white shirt and was now bare-chested. His behaviour had raised the attention of two of the uniformed police officers who were now hurrying across the road, but they were far too slow to prevent him from frantically climbing on the stone rim of Magdalen Bridge and leaping straight off the other side, his piercing screams snuffed out as his body disappeared beneath the brown water.

Several of the alarmed crowd, and the police officers, peered over the bridge in shock. Many seconds had passed, and there had been no movement from the area of water into which he had plunged. As one of the police officers reached for his radio, the other was too slow to stop one of the other students climbing on to the balusters. "I'll get him," he said, as he disappeared over the other side.

Survival and self-preservation instincts kicking in, Molly quietly manoeuvred her way through the hustle and bustle on the Bridge and began striding purposefully up the High Street towards the city centre, and the next available phone box. "Time you weren't here, Moll," she whispered quietly to herself.

As the uniformed coppers continued to peer over the side, looking for signs of life from the troubled jumper, their radios crackled back into life. This communication was nothing to do with their present situation, however. Details of a far more serious event were coming over the radio waves.

# CHAPTER 11

## Tuesday 1st May 1990

*"The lives were taken,*
*For feasts at the table,*
*A life of misery,*
*Ending with a shock.*
*Brutal murder, (brutal murder.)*
*All hands to the slaughter.*
*Mass torture,*
*All hands to the knife."*

*Howard Jones: 'Assault And Battery.'*

The unusually lively activity that had kept Cowley Road buzzing all night wasn't about to abate as, a short while after 7am, a procession of three squad cars raced from Cowley Police Station, sirens and blue lights blazing as they weaved in and out of the ragtag assortment of bicycles, white work vans, taxis, red buses, and vehicles on detour from the High Street.

\*\*\*

The smell of fried bacon filled the downstairs level of one of the unremarkable semi-detached houses that lined the Cherwell Drive end of Marsh Lane, as it did every morning around this time. "Neil – it's ready!" Di Lowe hollered in the direction of the stairs.

"Do well!" said her husband, his slippers slapping and stomach rumbling as he descended enthusiastically, fixing his tie on the way. "Bugger off!" he shouted at his ginger cat Buzz, named after his favourite NASA astronaut, who had almost caused him to lose his balance as he'd run to the side of him. He was cranky, having been deprived of three hours of his normal sleep quota from only having got in from the Randolph event a little before 2am.

The house phone began ringing before he'd reached the bottom step. "Bloody hell! Who's that at this time?" moaned Neil Lowe, anticipating the answer, and vexed at the thought of his breakfast having to wait.

"Well, you won't know unless you answer it, will you?" teased his wife.

He snatched up the receiver. "Neil Lowe?...Yes... What?...Oh, shit...Which one?...Jesus!...What time?...Identity known?...Who's been called?...OK... OK...Yes, I'll be there."

He jabbed the receiver back down.

"Bloody hell. I've got to go. Do us a favour, love – put that bacon in a bap and I'll take it to go."

Within ten minutes, assisted by a blaze of blue lights, D.I. Neil Lowe had swung his police-issue Audi across Headington, through Cowley, out the other side of the Rover works on to the Garsington Road, and past Greater Leys on the Watlington Road. He lurched off right after some distance, shortly after Blackberry Lane, on to an unmarked dusty track, the bath of blue light marking out his destination for him.

He was on farmland. Bushes flanked the perimeter of the concrete courtyard, with wide-open fields to the other side of the stone wall. On this side, though, beyond the two dirty, imposing double-decker trailer trucks, was an ominous looking warehouse-style building. *Al Shaitan Halal Meats. Oxford 231666*, declared the discreet wooden sign above the corrugated iron doorframe, with writing in Arabic underneath.

Lowe flashed up his detective's badge as he exited his haphazardly-parked Audi. Two uniformed Constables who had already recognised him began walking his way. One wore a traumatised expression, the other looked distinctly pale and unwell. There were traces of vomit on the front of his uniform.

"Hope you haven't had your breakfast yet, sir. It's not pretty," said Constable Rissey, gulping as he spoke the words, and appearing, like his colleague Constable Alves, ready to vomit himself. Lowe dabbed at the bacon grease on his tie.

"So I hear," Lowe replied.

"I'm told the pathologist is on his way," added Rissey.

"Right," said Lowe solemnly. "Let's have a look."

The Constables lifted the police ribbon as Lowe climbed underneath. The officers all recognised him, but he flashed up his ID as a matter of course regardless. It seemed no-one in attendance had the right words, as Lowe was led into the dark, cold, foreboding confines of the Halal slaughter-house. The smell of death lingered in the air. The whole place felt wrong. Lowe's immediate instinct was to get away from what felt like the closest thing to Hell in this part of the world. Professional duty forced him on.

Most of the unit's central floorspace housed a twisted arrangement of conveyor belts. Over each was railing descending from the ceiling, with sharp pointed hooks positioned every few inches. Suspended elsewhere from the steel ceiling beams were leather hoists, each strong enough to take the full weight of a cow, arranged around another railing system, all connected to a control box with protruding levers on the left side of the building.

Underneath the belts ran sluices and drains, all of them thickly stained with dark, dried blood. The same stains, almost black, covered the rest of the concrete floor. Towards the other side of the room were several circular vats. On a row of hooks on the wall hung a selection of waterproof coats, each caked with dried blood. Underneath them were pairs of similarly stained wellington boots. On a bench next to the coats was a kettle and a radio-cassette player, an arrangement of *Now, That's What I Call Music* tapes piled up next to it.

"Where?" asked a visibly perturbed Lowe, swallowing loudly.

"In here, sir," said Constable Rissey, leading Lowe through a heavy metal door into the adjoining room. Lowe gulped a sharp intake of breath and his heart rate increased as he registered what loomed before him.

Hanging upside-down off another ceiling-connected steel railing, on hooks, hung the corpses of the several hundred pigs, sheep and chickens that had been routinely slaughtered here the previous day. Beneath them was a trough positioned to catch the rivers of blood that poured from their wide-open throats, flowing at the end into a subterranean drain system. This sight alone was enough to have traumatised the officers in attendance to the point that they would recall this vision of mass pain, suffering, terror and death momentarily through the rest of their lives, regardless of what else they all now had to see.

At the very end of the overhead belt – upside-down – hung the obese, naked body of Sharun Iiblis, chief slaughterman at Al Shaitan Meats. The steel beam descending from the ceiling was buckling under the weight of the hoist belt into which he'd been placed, and looked ready to snap and drop the body into the blood trough at any moment. Iiblis's wrists and ankles were shackled with electrical wire, and his feet had been tied to the steel beam by a mechanical chain. His thick beard was saturated in his own dark blood, as his throat gaped wide open above it. Daubed in blood on the white tiled wall beside him was the phrase *Per furtim prosperabitur.*

Constable Rissey started convulsing and promptly vomited into the trough full of Iiblis' blood.

"Jesus, things ain't what they used to be," commented Lowe as he walked out of the building into the warm Spring morning air. "In my day they'd have just thrown a brick through a butcher's shop window to make a statement. When did that all change?"

# CHAPTER 12

## Tuesday 1st May 1990

*"There's a killer on the road,*
*His brain is squirmin' like a toad,*
*Take a long holiday, let your children play,*
*If you give this man a ride sweet family will die,*
*Killer on the road."*

*The Doors: 'Riders on the Storm.'*

The cafe on Barns Road displayed its usual demographic of clientele for 4pm on a weekday – secondary school pupils smoking outside or grabbing a Coke or a Milkshake inside, students poring over papers with a coffee, and builders, plumbers and labourers enjoying a full-fat fry-up as they clocked off for the day.

A stone's throw away from the cafe was the site of the former estate established by the order of the Knights Templar in 1139, kick-starting this mystical group's presence in the city for the next hundred years. Memoirs of their patronage of the city still remained in place names such as Templars Square Shopping Centre, and Temple Cowley Swimming Baths and Library.

Oblivious to any of this was Detective Inspector Neil Lowe, seated at the table to the left of the cafe counter, where he could always be found. Sitting opposite him was Jolyon Morton, chief forensic pathologist for Thames Valley Police. The cafe owner put down a steaming tea, housed in Lowe's own personalised mug, bearing the face of John Thaw's Jack Regan character from *The Sweeney*, that he kept behind the counter. She handed a bottle of still mineral water to his companion.

"Right, let's have the full story," said Lowe.

"Hardly an orthodox setting for such matters, Neil," remarked Morton, glancing around the cafe. Realising he wouldn't be getting a response, he began relating his findings.

"The victim was 36-year-old Sharun Iiblis, of Saudi Arabian descent, son of second-generation immigrants, and a lifelong resident of Cowley. Unmarried with no dependents. He had been a co-director and chief slaughterman at Al Shaitan Meats for the past eight years. I put the time of death at between approximately 5 and 6am. Cause of death was massive loss of blood through his throat having been cut with one of the razor-sharp knives used routinely in the abattoir."

"Could it have been the work of one man, or would it have required more?"

"It is feasible that whoever did it could have acted alone. He'd have needed to be strong and in good physical shape."

"We've spoken to his co-director. Iiblis finished his shift around 6pm yesterday, saying he was going straight home. He was due back at 6.30 this morning but seems to have got lured back to the warehouse by something – or someone – in the middle of the night."

Morton's eyebrows raised slightly at the words as he fixed his gaze on Lowe.

"Yeah, I know what you're thinking. A parallel to the Herzlos case, right?"

"Bit of a bloody coincidence otherwise."

The intensity of the two men's conversation was broken as the bespectacled, mousy-haired cafe proprietor banged a plate of bacon, sausage and fried eggs down in front of Lowe.

"Do well, Olive. Thanks," said Lowe. He turned back to a bemused Morton.

"You sure you're not hungry?"

\* \* \*

Four hours later, Lowe had called a meeting in the incident room at St. Aldates. Present were Detective Sergeant Sam Haine, W.D.C. May Pearce, Rissey, Alves and three other detective Constables. All sat perched on the edges of the room's desks, none choosing to take a seat. Plumes of steam danced up from the plastic coffee cups next to each officer, melding with the curls of grey smoke from the several slowly-burning cigarettes. A photograph of Sharun Iiblis in his death state was pinned next to a smiling glossy public relations picture of Gottfried Herzlos on the wooden-framed cork notice board on the main wall. The whiteboard mounted next to it was full of scribbled notes and arrows in black and red marker pen, in different sets of handwriting.

"Right, let's get started," said Lowe, the pronunciation of his first and last words acting as further confirmation of his lifelong localness. "Here's what we know."

Lowe moved in front of the boards. Just as he opened his mouth to speak again there was a sudden creak of the incident room door. All looked around to see Detective Chief Superintendent Nomas enter. Nomas glanced at Lowe, touching his nose with his index finger, and quietly moved to one of the desks at the back of the room, perching himself on the corner like the others.

"Here's what we know," Lowe began again, regarding Nomas nervously as he spoke. "At approximately 0600, the body of Sharun Iiblis, proprietor of Al Shaitan Halal Meat, was discovered at the company's warehouse by one of the staff. According to this person, it was regular practice for him to arrive first at around 0630, start to cut down the carcasses that had been hanging overnight, and to prepare for the arrival of new animals for slaughter later in the morning."

May Pearce shuffled uncomfortably on her desk edge and put her hand to her forehead as she stared down into her coffee cup. The other officers remained transfixed on Lowe's words.

"The pathologist's report indicates that Iiblis was first hit over the head with a blunt instrument. The dimensions of the impact indicate that this could have been a cricket bat.

"Once subdued, the victim was stripped naked. His clothes were found stuffed into a drain in the courtyard. The victim's wrists and ankles were shackled with electrical wire taken from a storage area in the warehouse. The assailant was able to place him in a hoist belt and suspend him, upside-down, over one of the blood drainage troughs. According to the pathologist, at this point his throat was cut from side to side with one of the ritual slaughter knives used in the facility. It's possible the assailant waited for him to regain consciousness before doing this.

"The knife was discovered in the drain along with the clothes. No fingerprints, indicating the assailant probably wore gloves. No security system or CCTV in operation at the abattoir. No witnesses."

May's gaze was still in her coffee. The others' were still fixed on Lowe. At the back of the room Nomas wore a poker face. As Lowe paused, the faint rumble of buses in the road outside the incident room window, a gulp from one of the Constables, and a hiss of breath from another were the only sounds.

"The co-worker says he arrived to find the front door bolted from the inside, which he thought unusual. He let himself in with his key through the staff door at the back and discovered the victim. He immediately called 999 and first-response cars were dispatched at around 0635. A BT check on the facility's phone records reveal that the office phone was used to dial Iiblis' home number at around 0300. It would appear that he was somehow lured to the facility, where the assailant was lying in wait. Obviously we don't know what was said, but Iiblis clearly wasn't sufficiently concerned to alert the police, opting to turn up at the facility alone.

"I'll open it to any questions now," Lowe continued, peering over towards Nomas for approval. Nomas nodded.

Rissey was quick to pitch in first. "Sir, it seems there are distinct parallels to the Herzlos case here, with both victims having been lured out to their workplaces in the middle of the night. Are we working on the assumption that this is the same attacker?"

"It's too early to say with any certainty, Constable, but the evidence is certainly pointing to that probability."

"Some kind of animal rights nut?"

Not wanting to be upstaged by his colleague, Alves was quick with his follow-up.

"Sir, is it feasible this murder could have been committed by one man?"

"There's no forensic evidence to suggest that more than one individual was involved," replied Lowe. "Certainly the assailant would have had to be physically fit and strong."

"Also very resourceful, sir," said a female voice out of nowhere. All in the room turned in the direction of

W.D.C. May Pearce, who had now forced the graphic images from her mind and regained her professional composure. "If we really are dealing with the same attacker as in the Herzlos case, he seems to have known a lot about each of them. He knew that the security system at the laboratory was linked to Herzlos' home in Davenant Road. He had access to Iiblis' home number. He presumably knew how long it would take each of them to arrive after being alerted. He must have planned each of these killings for some time and done some serious homework in advance."

"You make some good points, Constable," said Lowe, regarding her through squinted eyes, concealing his vexation that he hadn't raised these points himself in Nomas' presence.

Detective Sergeant Sam Haine was next to speak. "Guv, the assailant must have been in a right state after this slaughterhouse killing. He must have been saturated in the victim's blood. He would certainly have stood out to anyone seeing him fleeing the scene, right?"

"That's right. Sadly, nobody seems to have seen him."

"If the attacker was resourceful enough to have planned through this whole thing as meticulously as he seems to, he may have had a plan for disposing of his own bloody clothes," May added.

"There's nothing but open fields to the rear of the warehouse," said Lowe. "We've got officers scouring the area for anything incriminating. Also, the pathologist suggested he may have used a cricket bat to hit Iiblis over the head – and also Herzlos, if it's the same man. If no bat was found at the scene, this would suggest that he brought his own and took it away with him each time. So we're looking for sightings of a very bloody man carrying a cricket bat. You'd know him if you'd seen him."

Constable Rissey was back with a question. "Guv, what's the story on the phrase in Latin that was painted in the victim's blood on to the wall next to him?"

Lowe paused and glanced over towards Nomas before answering. He would have denied the writing's existence, which was quickly scrubbed away, had he not known that Rissey had seen it with his own eyes.

"We're not treating that as any kind of lead. Seemingly just the ramblings of a crazed madman. All the more reason to apprehend him quickly."

Again, a glance towards Nomas, who nodded discreetly.

"Right, Constable Rissey," Lowe continued. "As you mentioned the attacker possibly being some kind of animal rights nut, I'd like you and Constable Alves to go through all recent arrest records for any kind of animal rights activists throughout the Thames Valley. See what you find. Constable Pearce, I'd like you to pay a visit to all other businesses along that stretch of the Watlington Road. Find out who arrived early for work this morning – between 5 and 7am. Ask everyone if they noticed anything suspicious. Sergeant Haine, get a couple of your men to identify all bus and taxi drivers who were on duty in the Watlington Road area at that time this morning. It was right close to the Oxford Bus Company HQ there, after all. Same questions."

At the back of the room, Nomas rose from his desk-edge and walked wordlessly over to and through the incident room door.

"Gentlemen," said Lowe, dropping his voice so as to enhance the gravity, "err, and W.D.C. Pearce," he added as an afterthought. "It looks as if we're all charged with the responsibility of responding to Oxford's first serial killer."

# CHAPTER 13

## Wednesday 2nd May 1990

*"Somewhere there's hunger, somewhere there's a war,*
*But I can do nothing so I'll just ignore,*
*The cruelty around me, pretending I'm blind.*
*In case I start thinking and wake up my mind.*
*And the days break,*
*And the nights fall and drift into time … "*

*The Uglys: 'Wake Up My Mind.'*

Amy Noble hit the play and record buttons on the mounted Revox tape machine, and the two horizontal spools, protruding like a pair of Mickey Mouse ears, sprang to life and began rotating, as the voice from her Marantz portable cassette recorder, connected to the back of the tape machine by a small jack lead, got imprinted on to the coated quarter-inch tape. She rolled her eyes as the fifteen seconds of the Imam of Sharun Iiblis' East Oxford mosque, praising the late slaughterman as a "model Muslim," blared out of the speakers, before hitting the stop button on both the Revox and the Marantz.

Reaching out to grab a blue tape cartridge from the stack marked '30 seconds,' she slammed it into the Sonifex cart machine, rewound the tape spool to the start of the audio, and with practiced precision, hit the red record button at the same instant as the play button on the tape. With the 15 seconds of audio now transferred on to the cart, ready for broadcast, she pulled a white label off the reel on the work surface to the right and filled in the necessary details. Cut: (she smiled wryly at the irony) 66. Date: 02/05/90. Title: Iiblis Iman. Length: 15" Outro: "example to us all."

"What are Radox leading with?" asked Jess from behind her characteristically-cluttered desk.

"Not sure," said Senior Reporter Tom Atton, twiddling the black dial on top of the newsroom's radio cassette player to retune to 95.2FM, BBC Radio Oxford. "Met Police being called on to justify their violence towards Poll tax rioters, I think." He pressed play and record on the machine to capture the station's next news bulletin on cassette.

Amy Noble stood at the newsroom printer that was remotely linked to Independent Radio News headquarters in London, the source that provided news feeds to the network of commercial radio stations around the UK, awaiting the printout of headlines for the next hour as she prepared to deliver the 11am news bulletin.

"As we wait," she sneered. "Who writes this crap, anyway?"

"Who cares?" remarked Colin Cole. "Our job's just to read it."

Tom Atton began whistling the tune to *Always Look On The Bright Side of Life* from *Monty Python's 'Life of Brian.'*

"Cause life's a piece of shit," he sang.

"When you look at it," contributed Cole.

"How long does this bloody thing take?" growled Amy, now feral as she bore her prominent teeth, the pent-up stress of the day beginning to release itself. "I've been waiting here since about 1971."

"Ladies and gentlemen, Amy Noble – making exaggeration an artform," said Tom Atton, ripping a sheet of A4 out of his typewriter.

"Fuck off, Tom," countered Amy, any hint of good-natured workplace banter now absent.

Tom Atton turned to Colin Cole on his right. "Time of the month?" he mumbled, none too subtly.

"Okay!" barked Jess out of nowhere, startling the others. "What's on your mind, Amy?"

"No problem here, Jess. Just getting the job done," replied Amy, avoiding eye contact.

"Bollocks. You're turning the newsroom into a bloody war zone. What's eating you up? Let's get it dealt with."

"Okay then. I'm just getting pissed off with all these glowing tributes to this slaughterman who, let's face it, was a mass-murderer himself. All this talk of him being a fine upstanding pillar of the community, deeply religious, all this bollocks. He committed murder for a living! Why does nobody talk about that? Why is that considered just fine and oh-so-respectable, for fuck's sake?"

"Amy!" bellowed an indignant Jess.

"You asked!" came the sharp response.

Tom Atton chimed in. "Mass-murderer? Stop being so bloody dramatic, woman. He killed cows, chicken and sheep. So what? It hardly makes him the Yorkshire Ripper."

"'*So what?*' Are you actually serious? So you think because they're 'just' cows, chicken and sheep they deserve to be enslaved and brutally tortured? You don't think cows, chicken and sheep would quite like to just be left alone to live, the same way humans do? You don't think cows,

90

chicken and sheep feel fear and pain, just like humans do? That it's in their instincts to want to stay alive and protect their young, just like humans do? The fact that they try and run away whenever they're approached is a little bit of a clue, Tom. What happens in any slaughterhouse is bad enough, but the Halal method is even more brutal. It's like it's specifically devised to unleash the maximum amount of suffering on the animal before it dies."

"It's a ceremonial practice in line with the religion, Amy," contributed an unamused Jess. "Muslims believe it makes the offering pure."

"I'm very familiar with those old chestnuts, Jess. That's just PR and spin to try and justify the brutality. Dress it up as 'religion' and shut down any argument. There's an 'approved' narrative for everything in 'polite' society." Amy curled her fingers into air-quotes with each sarcastically-emphasised word.

"We should know all about that in our profession, right? After all, we can't have anyone getting 'offended,' can we?"

"It's a more humane method of slaughter, you idiot. The animal loses consciousness quicker." Tom Atton was all out of professional protocol.

"Wow. I can't believe you've actually been drinking the Halal Koolade, Tom. That's a classic piece of meat industry propaganda. 'Humane' slaughter. That's a good one. Hey, how about we invent a new method of 'humane' rape? The rapist places a pillow under the victim's head to make her nice and comfortable while he goes about his business. If we establish it for long enough so it becomes a 'tradition' we can make that a religious ceremonial practice too."

"Whatever. Nothing's going to make me give up my bacon buttie on a Saturday morning. Just too damned tasty!" said Tom, licking his lips exaggeratedly, and giving Colin Cole a high-five.

"Amy, if you can't observe others' rights to their religious beliefs, maybe you picked the wrong career," bellowed Jess.

"Jess, this has nothing to do with anyone's religion. Don't put words into my mouth. I'm happy for anyone to believe and practice whatever they want to practice – so long as it doesn't cause harm to others. My objection here is specifically to the practice of Halal slaughter. I would have the same objection to this practice whatever the religion. Matter of fact, the Kosher method within Judaism is pretty much the same from what I hear, so I have a problem with that too."

The field of intensified energy which had set in over the newsroom had not gone un-noticed by others in the large, open-plan environment. Two of the sales staff, and Dave Vickers and Pete Hollis over at the presenters' desk, had paused their activities to eavesdrop. When the burly figure of Mal Knight appeared from his office, Jess knew things had gone far enough, and found herself regretting the day when Amy's assertiveness and sense of conviction had convinced her to offer her a reporter's post, fresh out of university. Why did she ever imagine these would be useful attributes for the job?

"Right, Amy. Come with me."

"Oh, am I getting a disciplinary?" replied Amy angrily, her cheeks flushed a deep red. If an aura-measuring device had been available, her energetic state would have sent it off the scale. "Have I spoken too much truth? Can't have that in a newsroom, can we?"

As Amy complied and followed Jess to the boardroom for a dressing down at best, her P45 at worst, Tom Atton impersonated the bleat of a sheep, before emitting a sharp expulsion of breath through his teeth. "That girl never did know when to keep it zipped. That bleeding liberal heart will be the death of her."

"Still, it's a sad day when you can't express a personal opinion, right?" offered his more reasonably-inclined colleague. "No matter how unpopular it might be."

"You give up your right to opinion when you choose to enter certain professions, Colin. Journalism would be one."

Their conversation was interrupted by Jess, who was now standing where Mal Knight had been a few moments before. "Tom," she barked. "Get Verity on the phone. Tell her she's presenting *The Lux Report* tonight," before returning to the boardroom, where all of the red window blinds were pulled completely down.

# CHAPTER 14

## Saturday 12th May 1990

*"Sounds of laughter, shades of life,*
*Are ringing through my opened ears,*
*Inciting and inviting me,*
*Limitless undying love,*
*Which shines around me like a million suns.*
*It calls me on and on across the Universe."*

*The Beatles: 'Across the Universe.'*

The scenes around the Blackbird Leys estate may have surprised an outsider whose only perception of life in Oxford had been shaped by scenes from TV's *Inspector Morse*, and who might have imagined the whole city to consist of elegant architecture populated by academic types.

A group of black youths were sat on the bench in the play area next to the school passing around a spliff; in front of the row of shops, a bedraggled tramp, whose actual age was a couple of decades less than was suggested by his grizzled appearance, swigged something from a bottle concealed in a brown paper bag; two young single mothers with prams, both smoking cigarettes, stopped to chat to each other at the bus stop.

To the rear of the Community Centre, the social hub of the neighbourhood, Keith Malcolm parked his silver-blue Austin Maestro amidst the small group of other vehicles, and he and Phil Meritus exited the car in eager anticipation of what the day ahead held. They, along with no more than 15 others, were there to attend an all-day seminar by Max Zeall, now taking place in this alternative venue.

"It speaks volumes that he got kicked out of the Pegasus."

"Yeah, but in many ways this is better. The truth tends to go down more effectively in communities that have experienced hardship. People in the city have cosy, comfortable lives and aren't looking to pay attention to anything that might rock their world."

"True, true."

The pair walked around to the front of the building, bypassing the double doors of the main entrance and instead heading for the door to the right of them, which led to an annexe section. They each paid their £2 entrance fee, and seeing just eight people already in the room, occupied two of the orange plastic chairs in the second row.

"Verity working today?"

"Nah. Shopping."

"Lucky escape for you then."

"Tell me about it."

Less than 20 minutes later, after a few individual conversations with the attendees, Max Zeall had taken to the lectern, and began addressing the crowd. The Shure SM58 microphone he spoke through was wired to the venue's PA system, and also to a cassette deck, tended by an engineer, who was charged with recording the day's proceedings on to a series of C90 tapes.

Within a few minutes, aided by images beamed from a carousel projector on to a portable roll-down screen, Zeall was in full-on performance mode.

"And so we have The Non Aggression Principle, an expression of the Sacred Feminine energy inherent in Creation. It's right-brained thought, it's Care and it can be summed up in the apophatic phrase, "do *not* treat others in a way you would *not* wish to be treated yourself. Or, to put it even more simply, Do No Harm.

"If a behaviour causes harm, or loss, to another sentient being and impinges on their rights, that's Wrong Action, and you have no *right* to be doing it. And this includes the animal kingdom, folks. Sorry if that's inconvenient for you, but you have no right to take the life of another living, sentient being unless it's in self-defence.

"That means that the slaughter of animals in order to eat their bodies – which belong to *them*, and *not* to you – is Wrong Action when alternative food sources are abundantly available. And don't even bother with all the apparent 'justifications' that always come up in this type of discussion – 'it's 'normal', it's 'natural', it's 'necessary,' it's the only way for us to get our protein, it's OK to kill an animal so long as it was lovingly reared, grass-fed and 'humanely slaughtered.' I've heard every single one of them a million times, and I can take them all apart."

There was some uncomfortable shuffling of bottoms on seats as Zeall blasted out his vitriol, and a sense that some in the crowd felt instinctively compelled to jump in and challenge him on his points. Yet all observed etiquette – or sought to avoid potential humiliation – by remaining silent.

Keith found himself reflecting on how much Verity, as a six-year vegetarian, would appreciate this section of the presentation, and was grateful to note that it was being recorded for future distribution on cassette. Recollections of what Verity had told him about the horrific abattoir murder also came to mind. He glanced over at Phil to find him engrossed in the speaker's words.

"If an action does not cause harm to another living, sentient being, well then, it's a right.

"I would say that the number one right that we possess as free, sovereign beings in Creation, is the right to be left alone, free of coercion, intimidation or violence, so long as we're causing no harm. I mean, these sick psychopaths who want to control everyone are a rarity. Regular people have no interest in dominating and controlling others. Isn't that what the vast majority of souls on this earth want more than anything else? Just to be left alone?

"If someone then tries to impinge on your right to be left alone by instigating one of these things against you, that's where you reserve the *right* – and I would even go as far as to say, duty – to enact the Self Defence Principle. This one is an expression of the Sacred Masculine in Nature. It's left-brained thought and it's Action.

"These are the two principles of higher consciousness or enlightenment, and together can be expressed in more catchy street language as, "Do No Harm, But Take No Shit."

Keith instinctively glanced at the slogan printed in white lettering on Zeall's black T-shirt which spelled out that very phrase.

"If somebody tries to instigate violence or coercion against your will, then you take on the moral right to do whatever becomes necessary to make them stop, up to and including the use of deadly force. And that's not you applying violence. That's you defending yourself *against* the violence that's been laid upon you – something that other person had no right to do.

"And it doesn't make a blind bit of difference if it's a cop or a military person who *believes* that they have the right to do what they're doing, or who may have been ordered by somebody else to do it. If it's wrong, it's wrong, and that person forfeits the right to their *own* personal safety the minute they try and bring that violation into somebody else's life without justification!"

"Here is wisdom," whispered Phil, turning towards Keith.

"There's Right Action in the world, and there's Wrong Action, And the list of wrongs really isn't that big. It's not that difficult to remember. They all involve loss. Murder or assault is the loss of your life or your personal wellbeing. Coercion is the loss of your right to be left alone, so long as you're doing no harm and there's no injured party. Theft is the loss of property or belongings of which you are the custodian and have personal need during your time on this earth. Rape is the loss of your right to decide who you have sexual relations with. Wilfully lying is the loss of someone's right to the truth.

"You can ignore the tenets of Natural Law, if you choose to take that most difficult path rather than the other ones which were available to you. But you can't escape the *consequences* of ignoring the tenets of Natural Law. Ever. They will *always* be there."

"And I *do* have a right to get angry about the fact that the vast majority of the human population are in ignorance of these truths. The problem is that other people choosing not to embrace truth and freedom and apply these principles in their lives, affects me and everybody else who *doesn't* wish to live under tyranny and human slavery! These states only persist because of the apathy, passivity and ignorance in the vast majority of the population."

Zeall's voice got louder and more emphatic with each sentence. A look of concern came to his engineer's face as he noted the recording levels on the cassette deck shoot further into the red.

"So those of us who *have* figured these things out are having our *right* in Creation to be left alone taken away by others. We therefore have a *right* – duty – to try and wake these people up, so that the collective state of human consciousness – and freedom – can be improved.

"And THAT'S," (Zeall slammed his fist down on to his lectern, sending another glass of water shattering to the ground, "why those of us engaged in this work do what we do the way we do it."

\* \* \*

A few miles up the Eastern Bypass, Verity's white mini was turning off the Green Road roundabout back on to Barton, pulling up outside the familiar white and blue-painted building. Glancing around beforehand, she placed the Dorothy Perkins bag containing the new tops she had just bought into the boot. She looked at her watch. 2.16pm. She paused before slamming down the boot lid, looked around again, and had second thoughts. Locking the car, she carried the bag with her as she ascended the two flights of stairs and took a left turn towards her cousin's flat.

The pungent aroma of marijuana hit her a few steps before she reached Drew's front door. It was nothing unusual in this building. Verity groaned at how her clothes and hair would stink of the stuff after just a few minutes inside, and she screwed up her Dorothy Perkins bag tightly to at least try and protect her new purchases. Before she rang the bell, the door opened, and a grinning Drew, his bloodshot eyes squeezed into a squint, appeared. "Yes, Miss

V, my Nubian Queen. Wh'appen?" The linguistic ritual was back in session.

Verity and Drew touched fists. "How did you know I was out here?"

"Rasta man know every ting. Me never tell you dat?"

"Me tink you may have mentioned it once or twice," Verity remarked, following him into the flat, and finding the living room engulfed in a haze of grey vapour. She took her usual spot on the sofa, the table next to her full of the latest batch of radio shows recorded to cassette, ready for customers.

Her cousin sauntered over to the pair of Technics SL-1200 turntables and Made 2 Fade DJ mixer on the sideboard, where a new reggae release was playing. Verity recognised the voice of Shabba Ranks toasting over a female singer's vocals. The melody appeared to have been lifted from Terry Jacks' *Seasons In The Sun*, which she knew only too well from its regular rotation on *Lux Gold*. Drew hit the stop button on the turntable and the music ground to a halt.

"Bout time dat dyam Babylon radio station of yours put on a proper Reggae show!" Drew remarked as he sucked his teeth.

"With you as the DJ, right?" replied Verity.

"Nah, me haffi be de *selektah*!"

"I'd settle for some Soul and New Jack Swing. Fat chance of that too. Little time left after all the Phil Collins, Simply Red and Sting."

Drew reached for the spliff, now more ash than anything else, which was burning in the ashtray next to the turntable

"You waan toke?" he teased.

"'Low dat! Yuk mek mi hair an' clothes all frowzy up wid dat bloodclaat ting!" Verity played along.

"De marijuana is a gift from Creation! Dem likkle fools on the estate might smoke it for shits an' giggles, wid all dem deadly tobacco, but dis is plant medicine. Dis is a connection back to Almighty Jah. Dis is de greatest insight into spiritual truth!"

"Oh? I thought that was Lux FM News?" came Verity's riposte. The pair shared a chuckle. As per the usual routine, the patois now dropped and they reverted back to their natural-born dialects.

"Seriously, though. You know me, V. I've never read a book from front to back in my whole life, and I never watch TV. That's all mind-control and propaganda anyway. But I know a lot of things about a lot of things. I get that from talking to the elders around the estates. But I get most of my insights through the 'erb. It opens up a portal into all-knowing awareness. The natural world provides a plant medicine for all ills. For every cause there's a cure."

Verity regarded Drew with an amused look but didn't feel the need to speak. She couldn't deny that she had learned so much from her older cousin, and that she had indeed never known him to read a book. However else conversations with Drew panned out, they were never boring, and there was never any telling what he was going to say next.

"Been shopping?" He directed his gaze towards the Dorothy Perkins bag. Verity was disappointed that the conversation had descended from the profound to the trivial.

"You know us women. Can't keep away from the Westgate on a Saturday."

"Take out the receipt."

Verity looked puzzled for a second but reached into the bag as Drew had asked.

'How much you spend?"

"£21.60," Verity replied, reading the receipt.

"When's your birt'day again?"

"21st June."

"That's right. 21/6. There's a message for you."

"On a Dorothy Perkins receipt?"

"It's not just that. You never noticed the registration plate on your car encodes your birthday? Your phone extension number at work is 216, right? You live at 216b Abingdon Road?"

Verity paused to contemplate the apparent "coincidences."

"Don't try and tell me these are all coincidences," Drew quickly protested.

"What does it mean then?"

"These are all messages from the Universe, V, letting you know that you're on the right path and you're headed to where you need to be. You just need to keep reading the signs and stay on the path. Your name and your birthdate are no random accident, and Creation can give little reminders of this from time to time. 216 is a beautiful number, and part of a very significant cosmic sequence in Nature."

Verity needn't have worried about Drew getting trivial. She gestured with her eyes, giving a look that only black women could give, coercing him wordlessly to elaborate.

"The sequence starts with 27. You double it each time and the numbers always add up or reduce back to nine. It's the only numerical sequence in Creation that works in this way. So you get 54, then 108, then 216, 432, 864.

"432 Hertz is the harmonic frequency. We should be listening to all of our music pitched to A=432hz," (he gestured with his spliff hand towards his turntables,) "instead of the devilish 440 that we now have. There are 86,400 seconds in a day—43,200 for day, and 43,200 for night. You know, Yogic schools teach that all living beings inhale and exhale 21,600 times a day. The Kali Yuga lasts 432,000 years.

"So you see how blessed you are to have a birthdate as part of this sequence, and also at the sun's ultimate zenith on the Summer Solstice?"

Verity sank back into the sofa to better absorb the mindblowing surrealness of what had been intended to be a casual social visit. She anticipated comparing her day with Keith's later, convinced that the other-worldliness of these life-lessons would eclipse his. Here was her cousin, a broke, jobless weed smoker and pirate radio DJ on a council estate in Barton, spouting more knowledge than many of the professors of the revered Oxford academia just a few miles away would ever be capable of.

Drew was off again. "Also, 216 is the sum of six times six times six."

"Damn, boy! Now you're saying I carry the Number of the Beast?"

"There's nothing inherently evil about the number 666, V. True, the number has been co-opted and used by Satanists, but it states in the Book of Revelation that it's the number of a man, not a beast, or 'the Devil'.

Drew paused to light another pre-rolled joint. "I woke up with a voice in my head this morning," he continued. "I wrote it down." He pulled a screwed-up Rizla rolling paper from his jeans pocket. "It said, 'Everything here today is exactly as you decided you wanted it a long time ago before you came'.

"See, we start out in the spiritual realm before we consent to descend into matter and incarnate into this physical dimension, and so much of what we experience here is pre-determined by our higher selves. Sometimes we line up little pointers along the way to remind us of this.

We're not forced into these lives and these bodies. We choose them. We also choose the people we're going to interact with as family members, friends and adversaries. We meet all the people we were always meant to meet. It's all by mutual consent. And the day we'll die – even though we never really 'die' – is already written."

"So, you're saying that everything we undergo is pre-determined? But that would just make us like robots, going through the motions, not in control of anything." Verity became aware that she had slipped into Lux-like interview mode.

"No. Like Consent, Free Will is at play too, and our experiences here involve an interplay between the two. So the basic framework of our lives can be pre-determined – what part of the world we'll be born into, whether we'll be male or female, who our family members will be. But along the way we're presented with Free Will choice between right and wrong, and we'll reap the results of which way we choose to go whenever we're presented with one of these scenarios. Both individually and as a species."

Verity frowned as Drew took a deep toke and continued.

"See, this physical realm, and everything natural within it – including all the animals – is a kind of schoolhouse, where our souls come to learn lessons and evolve and grow. Nature," (he raised the spliff in his right hand,) "and other living things, are here to test our morality. Will we learn to co-exist with them peacefully and do no harm, or will we choose to dominate them through ego, arrogance and assumed superiority?"

Verity took a few seconds to absorb and reflect on Drew's words. "This is your deepest lecture yet, cuz!"

"Yah man!" Drew grinned back. "Knowledge is a beautiful ting!"

# CHAPTER 15

## Saturday 12th May 1990

*"But you're gonna have to serve somebody,*
*Yes indeed, you're gonna have to serve somebody.*
*Well, it may be the Devil or it may be the Lord,*
*But you're gonna have to serve somebody."*

*Bob Dylan: 'Gotta Serve Somebody.'*

Back at Blackbird Leys Community Centre, Max Zeall concluded his lecture shortly after 5pm. The enthusiastic applause was loud enough to have come from a crowd twice the size. As most gathered together their personal effects and headed for the exit, a few flocked quickly towards Zeall as he moved away from his lectern, eagerly shaking his hand and bombarding him with urgently arising questions. Keith and Phil remained in their seats observing the spectacle.

"Wait 'til the scrum's cleared and we'll go up and say hi," said Phil. A few minutes later, as Zeall finally became free, Phil strode towards him, his hand extended.

"Max, awesome information as ever, my brother."

"Phil," said Zeall, meeting his handshake. "Good to see you again."

"This is my good buddy Keith," said Phil. Zeall shook Keith's hand also as pleasantries were exchanged.

"Max, I don't know if you have to rush off, but Keith has very much got into your work, and I know he'd love to have a chat with you if that's all good?"

"Sure, sure," replied Zeall as he began the task of removing his 35mm slides from the venue's carousel projector and placing them in his backpack. "I usually head over to the Blackbird pub next door. Keith, you want to join me for a drink there?"

"Yeah, if it's not putting you out, that'd be great," Keith replied, not having anticipated this turn of events, silently grateful to Phil for the introduction, but remembering his promise to Verity that he'd be home straight after the lecture. He fumbled in his pocket for a 50p piece. "I just need to nip over to the phone box and put in a quick call home and I'll be right back."

"You joining us, Phil?" asked Zeall.

"Off to play cricket in University Parks while there's still a few hours of daylight," Phil replied. "I know you two will have a lot to talk about."

* * *

"You know, sometimes I have to stop and wonder how my life came to this," said Zeall, relaxing back into his bench seat at the Blackbird pub as Keith placed two bottles of Hobgoblin Ale on the stained and chipped wooden table, right beneath a poster advertising a reggae jam hosted by Sir Sambo Sound. "Spending my whole Saturday repeating information that should be taught at infant school through the obligation I have to Creation to communicate these truths, instead of so many other things I'd prefer to be doing with my time."

"What would have been your ideal way of passing today?" queried Keith with genuine curiosity. He'd absorbed so many of the teachings of this man to the point that he could now probably give one of his lectures himself, but knew very little about his personal life and day-to-day affairs.

"If I'd had the choice, I would have spent the day honing a couple of songs I've been trying to get finished for several months, and I'd have booked a session in Warehouse Studios, (he gestured in the general direction of Kennington with his head,) "to get something laid down on tape."

"You're a musician?"

"I play the Stratocaster and write songs. Have done since I left college. My day job was an engineer, working on sound boards for Solid State Logic in Hanborough, but I was in a couple of bands too. The second one was doing well. We were due to be signed to a major. They told us they were going to make us the next Clash."

"What happened?" enquired Keith, taking a long sip from his Hobgoblin and happy that he seemed to be stripping away the public exterior of this personal mentor.

"The price to be paid was too much of a heavy one." Zeall looked Keith square in the eyes as he clutched his bottle. "The manager – extremely well-known in the record industry – wanted the lead singer to give him a blowjob in exchange for securing the contract."

Keith ceased drinking in shock. 'I . . . take it he refused?"

"Let's just say he made it *very* clear that wasn't his kind of party," said Zeall, leaving a couple of seconds for his statement to sink in. "This was in 1977. I was 20. It was the end of our chance to make it big, and the beginning of my awakening to what's *really* going on in this world, and who's *really* calling the shots in every aspect of Organised Society.

"That event created a domino effect for me as I delved into the true nature of the corporate music industry. What I now know would shock most members of the public to their very core. Most would just flat out deny it could be taking place, because it's easier to dismiss it than to have to take on any kind of personal responsibility to oppose it. It completely destroyed the sense of wonder and reverence I had towards all my rock music idols. Learning how they were all controlled and serving agendas, I could never trust any of them again.

"But I'd always rather know. Better have the rose-tinted nostalgia of your youth completely blown to pieces than spend your entire adult life living under a delusion designed by somebody else."

There was a pause as both men glugged from their bottles, and Keith wondered how to phrase his next question to coax more information out of Zeall.

"What sort of things did you discover?" he asked, disappointed in his lack of inventiveness.

"That the industry is run by Satanists and Luciferians," said Zeall, emphatically and without hesitation, beginning to slip out of social pub chat and back into professional lecture mode. "Most are Freemasons and many are also paedophiles. It's that way in every walk of life and every aspect of Organised Society. Popular music is used for mind-control. They cast spells on master tapes of recordings. They embed occult signs and symbols into record sleeves and music videos to be subliminally absorbed by buyers without their knowledge. They routinely place subliminal messages backwards into audio recordings.

"ANY big-name music act that's all over TV and radio has sold their soul in order for their career to be gifted to them by those that can make these things happen. Artists are required to engage in depraved sex rituals before they can become household names. Many are blackmailed into co-operation as a result.

"Many undergo trauma-based mind-control programming to ensure they can be shaped and moulded to do the bidding of their industry overlords. Many familiar names are only in the public eye because of the families they come from. The music industry was set up by, and is still controlled by Military Intelligence agencies, which were behind all of the early record labels. Key artists can never retire, and they do what they're told by their handlers for the rest of their days.

"How 'bout that?" Zeall sought to assess the impact of his words through studying Keith's facial expression.

"But not every group in the industry, surely?" countered Keith. "I like a lot of Punk and New Wave stuff. Those groups are expressing anti-Establishment sentiments."

"They *appear* to be, but that's part of the mind-control. All artists will put out a song from time to time to make it *appear* that they're on the side of the masses – 'just like us' – because it gets them more enthusiastically accepted, so that the *real* impact of their output can continue.

"Keith, deception and duplicity exists in this world on a scale that few are capable of believing. Saying that you acknowledge that the entire industry is corrupt and satanic, but that, somehow, *your* favourite band just managed to slip through the net when no-one was looking, and *they've* remained organic and pure and outside of the clutches of the controllers, is like..." (Zeall paused to consider an appropriate simile.) "...It's like having a commercial airliner where everyone on board has paid for a ticket, except just this one person, who managed to slip through every passport and every ticket check and blag themselves a free seat without the airline noticing. That's how ridiculous the claim is.

"You know, it's the same thing with religions, where someone who clings to one of the orthodox faiths will insist that everyone who doesn't go along with what they do is misguided and deceived, and all these other false gods are wrong, but somehow *their* religion is the absolute truth. Then you'll meet somebody from another faith who will claim exactly the same things about *their* chosen (or enforced) belief system!

"And these same dynamics are present everywhere else in human society because, ultimately, it's the same groups and networks that control everything from the top down. And it's all steeped in dark occult religious belief systems that get strictly adhered to.

"I used to be an Atheist, but not any more. As soon as I discovered that all this stuff was very real, I took on a very profound understanding that there is a higher power, and that this physical domain represents a constant battle between good and evil, with the manifested outcome being determined every step of the way by the choices we make.

"Coming to an understanding of this is what prompted my studies into Natural Law, and the responsibility that comes with this knowledge is why you'll now find cassettes and VHS tapes of my lectures all over the place instead of copies of the albums I had dreams of recording when I was 20 years old."

At the table next to them, two elderly black men nursing glasses of rum looked up from their game of dominoes, alerted by the intensified energy field surrounding Zeall's table. This was not the average Saturday evening discussion in the Blackbird.

# CHAPTER 16

## Friday 15th June 1990

*"Us, and them.*
*And after all, we're only ordinary men."*

*Pink Floyd: 'Us And Them.'*

At Thames Valley Police's St. Aldates station, there was an indication that the normally vigilant and attentive Detective Chief Superintendent Nomas was stressed by the slight gap in his office door, which would normally have been carefully pulled shut. As Constables Rissey and Alves walked up at precisely 1.55pm, five minutes prior to the time for which they had been summoned, they stopped in their tracks at the sight of the ajar door and the sound of Nomas' voice coming from behind it. In spite of their obedience to protocol and decorum, natural curiosity got the better of them. Looking at Alves, Rissey put his index finger up silently to his lips.

Nomas was on the telephone. It was unclear from the broken soundbites who he might have been talking to. The Constables listened hard for his words, trying to piece together a likely conversation in their minds.

"Yes, it is concerning...We may need to undertake some kind of damage limitation...as a matter of fact I do have an idea who, but I'll need to see you face to face. It's a long story."

Alves' eyes darted about as he strained to hear the words, landing on the engraved name badge on the top-centre of the door. It read: *Chief Superintendent C. C. Nomas*. With the voice on the telephone now paused, Alves cupped his right hand around Rissey's ear and whispered, "what do you think the C.C. stands for?"

"I can hazard a guess," replied Rissey. Alves immediately placed his hand over his mouth to stifle a laugh. Rissey fixed him a piercing stare and returned his index finger to his lips.

It was from behind the door that a laugh did come. Nomas snorted derisively at whatever his phone opponent had just said. "No, believe me, he's totally clueless...Right...I've already sent him on a couple of wild goose chases, and I'll put him on to something else temporarily, just to let the heat die down a bit...I have to go. I have business to attend to any minute.

*"Per furtim prosperabitur."*

As it became apparent that Nomas was finished on the call, Constables Rissey and Alves took a couple of paces away from the door, straightened their posture, and instinctively brushed their hands down the front of their uniforms. The clink of a heavy ring against a drinking glass was heard from behind the door, then a glug, followed by the sound of a chair being pushed back and footsteps pacing the uncarpeted wooden floor towards the door. There was a brief pause as Nomas surveyed and considered the slightly-open door. Suddenly, it was yanked fully open and Nomas found one of the Constables on either side of it, as if keeping vigil. "Gentlemen," he bellowed, seeing from his watch that it was now precisely 2pm. "You're right on time. Come in."

"Sir," the pair said in unison, following Nomas back into his office. Positioned on their side of the large, marble-topped desk were two cheap wooden visitors' chairs. Nomas beckoned for them to take a seat as he paced around to his side of the desk and returned his backside to the burgundy leather chair with ergonomic design features. Several variously-coloured manila folders secured with paper clips were piled methodically in the centre of the desk. Either side of them were stacks of steel letter trays full of typewritten papers. In front of the right-hand stack was a black Bakelite rotary-dial telephone, of which type the Constables were used to seeing. Next to that was a less common red telephone of the more modern push-button design, sitting at a slightly skewed angle.

Had the Constables been close enough to the antique oak bookcase on the left of the office, they would have been able to survey Nomas' expansive collection of books. Tomes on police procedures and classic crime cases, including several on the Jack The Ripper murders, sat above two rows of works by writers whose names the Constables wouldn't have known, even if they could have seen them: Aleister Crowley; Albert Pike; Manly P. Hall; Aldous Huxley; H.P. Lovecraft; Kenneth Grant; Robert Anton Wilson; Kenneth Anger; Anton La Vey.

"So, gentlemen," said Nomas, tossing a yellow manila folder to each of his guests. "Let's discuss your performance appraisals since we pulled you off of speed trap duty."

\* \* \*

W.D.C. May Pearce knocked lightly before walking through to Detective Inspector Neil Lowe's office.

"You wanted to see me?" she asked.

Her words caused Lowe to look up from the document he was reading. "Yeah, preferably naked," he thought, working hard to ensure the words didn't get articulated. It wouldn't be the first time he'd made that gaffe.

Outside of the window to the back of him, the top decks of two red buses rolled past. To the right of the window were three framed photographs, the first a black-and-white picture of the Queen meeting Ugandan student Zarina Bhatia at Sommerville College in 1968. Behind the pair, on security duties as one of three Constables, stood a 23-year-old Neil Lowe, the buttons on his uniform almost popping off as he puffed out his chest with pride, a smile etched on to his lips.

Next to it, from 1983, a black-and-white photo of Lowe proudly shaking hands with Home Secretary Douglas Hurd at Oxford Town Hall, shortly after Margaret Thatcher's second Conservative election victory. The third was from the opening ceremony of Lux FM the previous September, and showed Lowe and Nomas mingling with Jess Hewitt, Rose Cross and the remaining three directors of the station.

May quickly surveyed his desk, fully expecting to see the remnants of a bacon sandwich, a hot dog, or similar such meat-based snack somewhere among the debris. There were none, though she thought she detected a faint savoury smell in the air.

"Any further word on the slaughterhouse murder?"

"Not really. The appeal is still out for witnesses."

"Right. Superintendent Nomas may well ask for a progress report over the next couple of days. I'll need you to liaise with him, as I'm going to be occupied with something else." As Lowe spoke the words, he puzzled for a moment over why Nomas had ordered him to oversee this case – hardly the territory of his job title – when the Herzlos and Iiblis murders were still hot.

"Oh? Right," replied the W.D.C..

Lowe's eyes surveyed her beadily from over his reading glasses.

"You might as well just ask what it is, 'cause I know you want to."

"Just exercising my copper's naturally enquiring mind, Guv" she answered diplomatically, getting the impression that he'd planned to tell her either way.

He had.

"Word is there's one of those raves set to take place on Milton Common Saturday night. You know all about these, right?"

"Sure. I've heard about them. Not my idea of a party, though. I'm too old for all of that."

"You sure?" Lowe retorted. "I can just see you at one of those."

"I'm 26," May replied. "Born about a decade too late."

Lowe regarded her for a few seconds.

"Well, either way, we've got word that it's happening on our patch. The organisers have been flying under the radar. Flyers just say somewhere in the South East and advertise an 0860 number to find out the meeting point. Trouble for them is they're new kids on the block."

He paused, assessing May's response.

"Oh?" she replied, knowing what he was implying, but not sure of his reaction if she let on.

"Meaning they're not 'approved' promoters."

May followed through with the obvious question. "So what is an 'approved' promoter?

"Well," said Lowe as he leaned forward, removed his reading glasses and folded them up, happy that she had asked. "Do you ever wonder where all the drugs, the 'e,' comes from at these big raves, and how it all just started appearing overnight when the scene first got going? This isn't stuff being cooked up by a few random chancers as a cottage industry, you know."

"It's coming from corporations?" May enquired.

"It goes a bit further than that." Lowe seemed to be enjoying getting the story off his chest. "I've seen all this before. In the late 60s, with all the hippie Flower Power stuff. I'd have been a few years younger than you are now back then. Used to go up to the Countdown Club in London to see Pink Floyd play in the days when they'd just put Syd Barrett in as their lead. Couple of years before he fried his brains on LSD. Later it was the Marquee. And the free festival in Hyde Park in '68."

May smiled to herself at the irony of the lane outside of the police station being named Floyd's Row, as Lowe continued on his nostalgia fest.

"The Floyd were the Cambridge set. Oxford hadn't produced any bands to rival them at that point. The track record's not that great still, is it? What, Supergrass, Radiohead and Mr. fucking Big?"

Lowe began to sing. Badly. "Over Bridges of Sighs, to rest my eyes in shades of green. Under Dreaming Spires. To Itchycoo Park, that's where I've been."

"What's that?" asked May Pearce innocently.

"You've never heard *Itchycoo Park* by the Small Faces? You need to get a musical education, Constable. Particularly as the opening lines are about getting high around the iconic sights of Oxford. Same places Lewis Carroll was doing opium a few decades before. *Alice In Wonderland* is the biggest acid trip ever.

"Anyway," said Lowe, getting back on track. "There was LSD fucking everywhere. All this E shit is just the modern equivalent of that. It's all cooked up in laboratories. Same thing that was going on over in the States with all the hippie festivals, all these psychedelic rock concerts,

Woodstock and the like. Well, it wasn't just America. The Swinging Sixties that you hear so much about wasn't just about Carnaby Street and Twiggy and Mary Quant. The acid was getting eaten up like Smarties here too."

May wasn't sure Lowe had thought through the wisdom of sharing all this with her, but she was glad he was. She remained quiet for fear of anything she might say interrupting his flow.

"Well, where d'you suppose it was all coming from, and why d'you suppose the supply lines weren't shut down immediately? It wouldn't have been that difficult for a committed police operation to identify the drug barons, seize all their gear and put them away. Sure, you saw the odd low-level street dealer get thrown under a bus, same way you do now with some of these little scrotes selling E. But it's only to give the public the perception that 'something is being done'."

Lowe dropped the punchline.

"The LSD was coming from the security services and was being planted into the scene by their foot soldiers. The CIA was doing it in the States, and MI6 was doing it here. They wanted all these kids to get hooked on psychedelics – on sex and drugs and rock 'n' roll. They wanted them to feel this was 'their' scene and to put them at odds with their parents' generation."

"But ... why?" May couldn't avoid the question.

"You know, I've been giving thought to that question since about 1966. I sometimes think it's all been nothing more than a massive social experiment, just to see what would happen if these kids could all be turned into drug-taking, degenerate freaks with no respect for authority. How society would collapse and crumble. The people who pull off stunts like this seem to get off on chaos and disruption.

"Either way, we've got just that – a wasted generation of bums and drop-outs with no values, no morals. Degenerate monkeys. You wouldn't catch my kids at one of these hellholes."

"Oh, you have kids?" May asked, already knowing the answer, but coercing Lowe into elaborating.

"Son and a daughter, 19 and 17. They've been raised with proper respect for authority," said Lowe, apparently seeing no contradiction between this statement and his earlier admission of himself having dropped acid and smoked dope at Pink Floyd concerts in the '60s.

"So," he said, getting back on track, "that's why there are these raves and these dealers that are 'approved,' and there are those that are not 'approved.' The skanky little chancers running this one on Saturday night, so the word has come down the line, are not 'approved.' That's why we're taking them out.

"You're going?" asked May?

"Am I fuck! 2.30am Sunday morning I'll be tucked up in my bed. So will you be, hopefully." Lowe corrected himself. "I mean ... "

"It's OK," May half-smiled. "I know what you mean."

"Right," said Lowe, getting up from his desk. "Can't stand here chatting forever. Friday's my Aunt Sally night."

# CHAPTER 17

## Sunday 17th June 1990

*'Gonna dance to the music all night long,*
*Gettin' high, gettin' happy, gettin' gone.'*

*Primal Scream: 'Don't Fight It, Feel It.'*

It was a far cry from the previous weekend, where the only human activity had involved the usual array of dog walkers, a few ramblers, and a gaggle of teenagers sharing a two-litre bottle of Dry Blackthorn and a spliff over by the bushes. Now, at 2.21am on a fully moonlit Sunday morning, shortly before the Summer Solstice, Milton Common had been transformed into a wild circus of hedonism and debauchery.

Ten thousand years earlier, revellers in this very spot might have been chanting as they danced around a fire, sacred icons and motifs carved into trees and rocks around them, as they banged out rhythms on animal-skin drums, and underwent consciousness changes through plant-medicine 'teachers' administered to the tribe by a shaman. Here, in 1990, the very same primal states were being expressed – just in ways more suited to the times.

It wasn't the crackling embers of a bonfire that was illuminating these scenes. That job was taken care of by the banks of strobe lights, powered by the loudly humming portable generators, their jagged patterns zig-zagging through the sky like lightning, creating a random, haphazard display of unsacred geometry.

There was no absence of signs and sigils. Whereas this contemporary tribe's prehistoric ancestors might have inscribed depictions of animals, rainfall, bountiful harvests, or other things they wished to bring into physical manifestation through applying their will and intent, in 1990, the image most commonly seen was a rudimentary smiley face that might have been drawn by a five-year-old, against a yellow circular background.

Occasionally this was depicted with a splattering of blood over the left eye, as had been the emblem of the 'Watchmen' graphic comics series of a few years before, and seen more recently on the sleeve of Bomb The Bass's chart hit *Beat Dis*. If an onlooker had asked the 5,000-plus revellers what the significance of this emblem was, however, no-one would have been able to give any kind of meaningful answer beyond, "it's Acid House, man! Don't fight it, feel it!" More loose-fitting white T-shirts and hoodies bore the Smiley than didn't, in many cases hand-painted by the wearers.

The Smiley appeared on multiple paper flyers for other, upcoming events, which were scattered wide across the common, and mostly trampled into the mud by hundreds of pairs of dancing trainers. It also constituted the focal point of home-made fabric banners and flags, waved wildly by groups of wide-eyed youths as they danced.

It wasn't the only motif on display, however. A 12-foot wide projection screen situated to the left of the DJ rig, flashed split-second subliminals directly into the subconscious minds of those in its wake. Anyone able to pause the show frame-by-frame and note its contents would have identified an eclectic mix of black-and-white spirals and checkerboard designs, depictions of Jachin and Boaz, the twin pillars of Freemasonry, spotted designs in primary colours, teddy bears and dolls, occasionally with an eye, arm or leg missing, the Eye of Providence of Freemasonry and the Eye of Horus of Egyptian mystery school teachings, the number 666, and shattered mirrors.

When it wasn't any of these, ideas straight out of New Age spirituality traditions was being flashed – planetary conjunctions and alignments, the rising and setting sun, phases of the moon, zodiacal ages. Completing the mix was a dose of UFO and alien symbology – flying saucers, 'motherships' and ET-like 'greys,' including scenes from the alleged 'alien autopsy' at Roswell. Unlike their ancestors of several millennia previous, none of those in attendance would have been able to answer the question as to why any of this was there. This went for the party organisers themselves who, having experienced these motifs at previous raves, had merely accepted that this was the done thing and had replicated them blindly.

The contemporary take on the animal-skin-drum rhythms came from a new style of music which would have sounded completely alien as recently as three years previous. This was the new breed of electronically-produced sounds crafted with the specific aim of being danced to, and to accentuate interaction with various mind-altering chemicals. They were the sonic expression of the frantically flitting strobe lights, most of them the output of British-based producers, influenced initially by House and Techno sounds coming out of Chicago and Detroit, and latterly by each other.

A connoisseur in attendance with the presence of mind to record such things, would have noted GTO's *Pure*, *LFO* by LFO, Joey Beltram's *Energy Flash*, 808 State's *Cubik*, Together's *Hardcore Uproar* and N Joi's *Anthem* among the new sounds, with Wood Allen's *Airport '89*, Raven Maize's *Forever Together*, Stakker's *Humanoid*, FPI Project's *Rich In Paradise*, and Rhythim Is Rhythim's *Strings Of Life* among recurring favourites from the previous year's 'Second Summer of Love.'

The Beloved's *Sun Rising* was less than three hours away from its obligatory appearance. The first wave of British Acid House records that had emerged two years previous, distinctive for their burbling, 'squelching' synth sound modelled on Phuture's *Acid Trax*, had already given way to a new sound, much more energetic and slightly less dark on first impressions. '88 was old hat. The sound of '90 was where it was at.

The remaining throwback to ancient times was the altered states of consciousness. Whereas in previous epochs, (and in present ones in other parts of the world,) ethnic communities underwent these deeply personal journeys of spiritual exploration under the close mentorship of an experienced guide, here, in the last decade of the 20th century, there were no such formalities.

The spirit of anarchy reigned supreme, even if, ironically, this was also on somebody else's terms. Somebody – or some organisation – of which the young, free-spirited partygoers could have had no comprehension. The ayahuasca, peyote and psilocybin mushrooms of ancient times, had been replaced by a new stimulant in the form of laboratory-produced pills, now seemingly in unending supply. Its chemical name was MDMA, but these new Children of the Revolution preferred to call it Ecstasy, or just E. The hippies and Flower Children of their parents' generation might have had their narcotics of choice, but this one was theirs.

Wasn't it ironic, one youth of the 5,000 or so assembled on the Common, a little over ten miles from from Oxford reflected, in his newly-expanded conscious state. Everything in his experience that magical night was deemed "illegal" by the Establishment control system, yet here they were in the political regime of Thatcherism, which advocated private enterprise and entrepreneurialism.

And wasn't that exactly what the event promoters, the DJs, the E distributors, the sound and lighting engineers, and the art designers were doing right here, right now? Many would have been on the dole and dependent on the system just months before, yet here they now were making more money than their parents did. And yet, the youth had it on good authority from the underground grapevine, a new piece of legislation to be named the Increased Penalties Bill was due any day now, raising the cost of organising an 'illegal' rave to £20,000 and 6 months imprisonment. "But only if the bastards catch you," his mind told itself silently.

The 19-year-old's musings were stopped in their tracks by an assault on his conscious state in the form of a hand clasped firmly on his shoulder. "Ted! What's going on, bruv? Wicked rave, or what? You feelin' it?" Two young men and two young women of his own age, from whom he'd become separated some hours earlier, had found him again.

"Might be the best yet, geezer," replied the youth, to whom these same friends had allotted the nickname Ted the previous year. At first, he wasn't particularly flattered that this had been inspired by the term 'Acid Ted,' to describe a fan of the scene who had become a cartoon stereotype, clinging nostalgically to the fashions of those early halcyon days. To be fair though, here he was sporting his red spotted bandana, denim dungarees over the oblig-atory smiley face T-shirt, and with a baby's pacifier hanging on a lanyard around his neck, ready for chewing when his jaw started chattering as the chemical onslaught of a new pill took effect. So maybe they had a point.

"Can't beat last year's," challenged his mate. "Carl Cox on three decks as the sun was coming up?"

"Yeah ... unlike you," retorted Ted.

"Yeah, right!" He let the significance of the statement sink in.

"C'mon, though. That was special. This one's pretty good though. Who's on at the moment?"

"Jumping Jack Frost, I think." Ted squinted and strained his eyes, trying to see all the way through the darkness to the stage from his vantage point on the hillside.

"Where's the next one?"

"We're going up Barking for the next *Raindance* if you wanna come. There's that *Beetle Bash* one at Santa Pod Raceway next month. And we're going down to Brighton to see Coxy at *Storm* in a couple of weekends."

"Count me in for all of those, bruv," said Ted.

"Safe, man." His friend hugged him like a long-lost relative. The others followed suit. As she was released from his grip, the petite red-haired girl asked, "you sorted?"

"You got some?" replied Ted.

The girl slipped a small polythene bag containing three pills discreetly into his dungaree pocket. Forty-five quid's worth, Ted calculated.

"You can owe me," she said, kissing him full on the lips.

"Sorted," Ted called after her as the group left to embark on whatever adventures they could find in the remaining couple of hours or so before sun-up.

Alone – or as alone as he could be factoring in the thousands all around him, Ted – not so discreetly – examined the new contents of his pocket. Three doves. These were supposed to be beasts. He picked up a half-finished bottle of Lucozade that somebody had discarded, necked two of the pills, and washed them down with a swig. After a minute, he hauled himself up and walked down the hillside towards the place from which the assault on all of his senses was emanating. A tsunami of arms in silhouette flailed wildly amid the strobes.

The 19-year-old battled his way through the sweating, gyrating bodies towards the front stage. He squinted at the figure behind the decks who was controlling the throng with every twist of a dial, with every clap of his hands. Another irony flashed into Ted's head; in a few hours, the parents of many of these kids will be assembled in a different type of gathering, receiving a different kind of message, delivered from a pulpit rather than a DJ booth, by a different kind of evangelist. That's their world, he thought. *This* is ours.

As the chemical onslaught on his brain began to take effect, Ted closed his eyes to enjoy the rush more profoundly. But no sooner had he done so than the rapturous experience came to an abrupt halt. The pulsating rhythms suddenly stopped.

Opening his eyes and looking to the DJ stage, the terrible truth emerged. Where there should have been a sonic sorcerer bouncing on his feet and waving his arms in the air, there was instead a gang of coppers. Two were involved in a physical altercation with the DJ and the event promoter.

"Shit! It's a raid!" said someone next to him, as the collective consciousness of the crowd turned to panic.

The cops at the DJ booth were far from the only ones in attendance. Turning in all directions, Ted could see scores of uniformed officers, many armed with dogs, and many getting into spontaneous scuffles. Youths were desperately discarding their bags of pills as quickly as they could retrieve them from their pockets. The party was over, and many would be paying a heavy price for having attended.

But Ted would not be one of them.

# INTERMISSION

*The following are a set of photos, all taken by The Author, showing many of the real locations around Oxford that appear in the story's narrative. All can be traced and visited for any reader who wants to live the full TCATC experience!*

*Scene from aside the Radcliffe Camera: the City of Dreaming Spires.*

*The fabled Eagle and Child tavern on St. Giles, where the literary society known as The Inklings — J.R.R. Tolkien, C.S. Lewis and others — held their informal meetings. The snug where Nomas meets Lowe, is to the left of the front door. Nomas pins the unfortunate traffic warden against the tree in the foreground.*

*The Great Tower of Magdalen College, from which the seven-minute Hymnus Eucharistus has been sung at 6am every 1st May for generations.*

*The balusters of Magdalen Bridge, from which, as per the age-old tradition, students have leapt into the murky waters of the River Cherwell below as part of the annual May Morning ritual.*

*St Aldates Police Station. Nomas, Lowe and May Pearce work from here. This was also the HQ of Colin Dexter's Inspector Morse character.*

*The Randolph Hotel, bearing some architectural similarities to New York City's Dakota Building, opposite the Ashmolean Museum in Beaumont Street.*

*The lobby to the Randolph Hotel where attendees of the Rotary Club ball assemble before retreating into the restaurant to the right.*

*Fox FM's radio headquarters, (now long-gone,) on the Horspath Industrial Estate. An original photo from Summer 1990. The on-air studio was to the front-left of the white reception desk.*

*Studio B, the production and back-up studio, in Fox FM's radio headquarters. An original photo from 1990. All technology in sight is analogue.*

*The Author in Fox FM's on-air studio, pictured circa 1992.*

*The former Fox FM building 30 years on, home to a race simulation company and a fire and stove retailer.*

*The Chequers Inn in Horspath, scene of many a Lux FM boozy extended lunch.*

*Looking out over Port Meadow, from the Binsey side of the River Isis. Verity and Keith swim across the river on the hottest weekend of the year, and dry out on the bank on the other side. Famously, the Reverend Charles Dodgson, better known as Lewis Carroll, is said to have rowed this section of the river with three young girls on his boat, one of whom, Alice Liddell, became the focal point of his Alice in Wonderland stories.*

*The 17th-century Perch Inn in the village of Binsey. The walk-through to the river and Port Meadow is to the rear of the building.*

*The Old School pub, formerly the ticketing office for Gloucester Green bus station and according to legend, built on the site of a former plague pit. Verity and Keith meet with Max Zeall in here.*

*The Grapes public house in George Street. Verity works temporarily as a barmaid here when she loses her radio job.*

*The second floor on the left houses Herzlos' laboratory in the University's (fictional) Bio-Chemical Research Division, where he meets his end.*

*The oak door on the side of Brasenose College through which the participants in The Order's monthly meeting enter.*

*Brasenose College exterior, looking upwards from the main entrance.*

*The Chequers pub in the High Street, with intriguing design.
A legend persists of an arcane underground tunnel linking it
with the Mitre Inn on the other side of the road.*

*The window out of the cellars of The Mitre Inn into the last
avenue of the Covered Market, through which the assailant
escapes after navigating the underground passage
from Carfax Tower.*

*The entrance to Carfax Tower.*

*Pegasus Theatre in Magdalen Road, from which Max Zeall delivers his seminar early in the story.*

*Blackbird Leys Community Centre, home of Zeall's talks after he gets kicked out of the Pegasus. He delivers his lectures from the meeting room on the very right of the picture.*

*Looking towards The Plain roundabout from the Magdalen Bridge end of the High Street. Molly emerges from the far right of the picture to the scenes of the May Morning celebrations, ready to peddle her wares.*

*University Parks, looking South-West to the area where Charlie and Molly are accosted by the plain-clothes police officers.*

*The clump of bushes from where the officers observe the youths' activities.*

*216b Abingdon Road, (to the left,) the rented home of Verity and Keith.*

*The back alleyway through which their night-time visitor gains access to Verity and Keith's house.*

*The (now overgrown) back yard entrance to Phil's ground floor flat in Preachers Lane.*

*The apartment block just into North Way on Barton. Verity's cousin Drew lives here*

*The site of Neil Lowe's favourite cafe on Barns Road, from which the proprietor, Olive, serves him his all-day breakfasts and steaming mugs of tea.*

*The Port Mahon public house in St. Clements. A paranoid Charlie awaits the arrival of his enterprising sister Molly here.*

Mark Devlin

*The ditch to the side of the A41 near Blackthorn, into which the unfortunate Army Sergeant Rob Chance's Vauxhall Astra flies when ambushed. The assailant escapes through the fields towards Launton, to the left of the picture.*

*The view along the High Street from the top of Carfax Tower.*

# CHAPTER 18

## Monday 18th June 1990

*"Coming up next on Lux Gold, hold tight for songs from three national treasures. We have 'Let It All Hang Out' from Jonathan King and 'I'm The Leader of the Gang (I Am)' from Gary Glitter. But first, here's Rolf Harris, with his 'Two Little Boys.' Goodness gracious. Nor 'arf!"*

*Dean Daniels on Lux Gold, 4.15am*

Neil Lowe tossed his copy of the previous day's *Independent on Sunday* on to the wooden table he was occupying at the White Horse pub in Headington. The headline loomed large on the page:

*Arise, Sir Jimmy: Knighthood for nation's favourite Savile. Article credited to Lynne Barber.*

Lowe noticed May Pearce eying the page. "Ow's about that, then?" he said cringingly, in an embarrassing attempt at a West Yorkshire accent. "Bloody well deserved. It's his second time, too. Queen gave him an OBE in 1972 and all."

May skimmed the opening paragraphs.

*"Do you want to see the gear?" he asks . . . The folder encloses the letter from the Prime Minister offering him*

145

*a knighthood, the envelope it came in, some bumf about keeping it secret till the proper date and then – proudest of all – telegrams from Charles and Diana, from Prince Philip, a handwritten letter from Angus Ogilvy, and a very sweet homemade card with a stuck-on snapshot of Princess Bea, from the Duchess of York. He is almost bursting with pride as he shows them off."*

"I always found him creepy," May said with a slight shudder, childhood memories of Saturday evenings watching *Jim'll Fix It* over sandwiches and cakes flooding back. "Something not right about him."

"Bollocks!" replied Lowe. "The guy's a national treasure. What about all that great work for charity? Why d'you suppose he supports all these hospital units?"

"There's always been rumours that he's a wrong'un, though." May was getting uncomfortable flashbacks of her awkward Jack The Ripper comment back at The Randolph. She repositioned herself in her seat and crossed her legs the opposite way.

"Yeah, just that – rumours. Good job people don't pay attention to some of the stuff that's been said about me over the years, 'else I wouldn't be a friggin' D.I., that's for sure. I dare say we could rake up some tittle-tattle about you if we tried."

As Lowe spoke, May continued to scan the page. She found the section she was looking for.

*"There has been a persistent rumour about him for years, and journalists have often told me as a fact: "Jimmy Savile? Of course, you know he's into little girls." But if they know it, why haven't they published it? The Sun or the News of the World would hardly refuse the chance of featuring a Jimmy Savile sex scandal. It is very, very hard to prove a negative, but the fact that the tabloids have never come up with a scintilla*

*of evidence against Jimmy Savile is as near proof as you can ever get.*

*"...Still, I was nervous when I told him: "What people say is that you like little girls." He reacted with a flurry of funny-voice Jimmy Savile patter, which is what he does when he's getting his bearings: "Ah now. Sure. Now then. Now then. First of all, I happen to be in the pop business, which is teen-agers – that's No. 1. So when I go anywhere it's the young ones that come round me."*

"Do you imagine for a minute if there was anything dodgy about him, the Queen and Charles and Mrs. Thatcher would have anything to do with him?" continued Lowe. "Nah, the guy will be remembered as a hero. Trust me."

Lowe's chair legs scraped across the wooden floor as he hoisted himself up and pushed the remnants of his burger lunch across the table. He carefully folded his copy of *The Independent* and put it under his arm. May noticed him make the switch from casual to professional mode that he tended towards when he sensed he was being contradicted or questioned.

"That's why I'm a D.I. and you're a W.D.C. Right. Back to work. What have you got on?" Lowe worked to remove thoughts of his colleague's underwear that had just come into his mind following his last comment.

"Those thefts at the Oxford Union Library to look into. Better get along there now."

* * *

As she manoeuvred the police pool car, an inconspicuous black Austin Metro, along Oxford High Street, W.D.C. May Pearce instinctively baulked at the sight of a troupe of women all dressed in pink T-shirts, shorts and trainers, deely-boppers bouncing from their heads, marching in unison and waving banners proclaiming 'Together We'll Beat Cancer!' A sense of deep resentment came as memories of her mother, who had died 20 months earlier of an aggressive form of breast cancer following several bouts of chemo and radio-therapy, inevitably returned. "May mourning," she mumbled to herself, with morbid wordplay.

Equally resonant were recollections of what her brother Will, devastated by their loss, had subsequently told her he had discovered from his own dogged research. She recalled his very words; Cancer is an industry worth millions, and entire businesses and careers depend on a never-ending supply of new customers; Its 'success' is not judged by how many people it cures, but by how many more people it's treating for cancer this year than it was last year; The last thing this industry ever wants is to find a cure, but it has to keep perpetuating the myth that one day it will find one in order to prolong its existence, and to guilt-trip the public into giving endless funding to ensure its ongoing profitability.

Natural cures for cancer have always existed, and the pharmaceutical cartels have always known, but have worked together to deliberately suppress them. (Research the Cancer Act of 1939, Will added.); The pharmaceutical industry works in league with medical doctors, often incentivising them monetarily, to ensure that its own drugs and surgery treatments are endlessly promoted as the only options for cancer treatment, and natural cures are brushed aside as 'quackery' and 'pseudo-science.'

May additionally recalled Will's claim that Oxford's pharma giant Clive Tuns had campaigned the government to introduce harsh fines and prison sentences for any holistic health practitioners claiming to offer effective alternative treatments, and that a local investigative journalist who had been poised to present his findings in the matter to BBC Radio Oxford, had conveniently died in a late-night car crash on the A420 when the brakes had failed on his car.

She suddenly felt nauseous as these thoughts, which she generally worked to keep tucked away in the back of her mind, all came rushing back to bother her – a confusing combination of grief at the loss of her mother, anger at the idea of her brother's claims being true, crushing disappointment in her own lack of investigation into their validity through not wanting to derail her own career – of which her mother had been so proud – and dismay at the nature of a world in which any of this injustice could be allowed to happen in the first place.

Putting the women in pink out of mind as they disappeared into the rear view mirror, May worked to keep the chatter out of her mind and stay fixed in professional mode. After returning the car to the St. Aldates station car park and signing the requisition form appropriately, she set off by foot towards Carfax Tower and straight over into Cornmarket Street, left into Frewin Court and toward the Oxford Union Library, earning herself a wolf-whistle from an overhead scaffolder on the way.

This world-famous seat of debating had recently reported a series of thefts of ancient and valuable books from the library shelves, mainly titles concerned with Wicca magic, paganism, druidic rituals and other occult practices. May had been charged with investigating – a diversion from the ghastly nature of the Herzlos and Iiblis murders which, if she were honest with herself, she welcomed.

Exiting from the oak-beamed office of the principal, after gathering as many details as possible about the theft, the Woman Detective Constable made towards the main library. Her reaction of awe at the grandly-appointed room, with its two storeys of bookshelves, decorated domed roof, intricate murals and other ornate decor, was usual for anyone experiencing the spectacle for the first time. Fifteen minutes later, she had completed a series of notes and sketches concerning the thefts, (she was bemused to find that even the police were forbidden from taking photographs in this place,) her detective's eye scanning the room's intricacies to try and work out what may have occurred, and how.

Glancing at her watch and considering her workload for the rest of the afternoon, she decided to take up the principal's offer of lunch in the Union members' bar before returning to St. Aldates. She surveyed the room, half-full with students and lecturers, considering a suitable place to sit and peruse the menu.

As her gaze landed on the left-hand corner of the room, it registered familiarity. Three figures were huddled around the circular table – two men and a woman. The men had their backs to her, but she could see the face of the wild-haired woman, whom she had noticed a few weeks earlier at the Randolph charity ball. Though the men's faces were obscured from view, she'd had enough experience of Detective Chief Superintendent C.C. Nomas to recognise his stocky frame and balding head from the back. The plumes of cigar smoke wafting out from his right hand served to confirm her observation.

May's first instinct was to introduce herself to the group. Something didn't seem right about the way the three were conducting themselves, however. They carried the air of a guilty party with something to hide, obviously with need to converse, but doing so guardedly. Giving only passing thought to any potential consequences, and reasoning that her days as a copper were probably limited anyway – whether by her own hand or that of others – she made the potentially unethical decision. She would attempt to eavesdrop by occupying the table on the other side of a waist-high barrier housing a flower trough. Nomas was the only one of the three who might recognise her, and he was still facing away.

Seconds later, she had discreetly moved to the table, seemingly without drawing any undue attention to herself. Positioning her seat as closely to the barrier as possible, and holding a menu on her lap, she strained to determine how much of the trio's conversation she could hear.

The woman spoke louder than the men but said very little. Of the other two, she made out more of Nomas' bass-heavy tones. The other man's words were largely drowned out by the ambient noise of the room. She heard enough to be able to determine his identity, though. This was clearly Solomon Schwartz, CEO of Clive Tuns, the very pharmaceutical monolith which had supplied the drugs and radiation that, if her brother's accounts were correct, had helped speed up the death of her mother. Some of the earlier anger returned.

The wiry-haired woman spoke again. "I'm not going to let one loose cannon bring unwanted scrutiny to a group that's remained hidden from public view for over four hundred years. Being invisible to outsiders has been our strength all this time, and it's going to stay that way. There's too much at stake if any kind of heat comes our way."

"Nothing to worry about from the media?" May could make out Schwartz's words for the first time.

"Everyone's on board. Though from what I hear, Jess has an over-inquisitive newbie reporter who may have to be kept an eye on.

"And I know I don't have to worry about any unwanted attention from Oxford's Finest?"

Nomas spoke.

"No cause for concern there. I've got the right man on the job, ... if you follow me."

Nomas leant still closer to his companions.

"I also have a fairly clear idea who our rogue operator might be."

The woman seemed to consider his comment for a few seconds before replying. "Not here."

A waiter appeared at May's table asking to take her order. As she responded by asking him for another couple of minutes to decide, she heard the wiry-haired woman speak again.

"*Per furtim prosperabitur.*"

With that, the trio stood up and went their separate ways.

# CHAPTER 19

## Thursday 21st June 1990

*Dean Daniels: "And the Paul McCartney World Tour resumes
on Saturday with three UK dates. And I'm very excited to say
I'll be seeing him at the first one at Glasgow's SECC Arena.*

*Caller: "Well, you won't."*

*Dean: "Of course I will! I've got the tickets."*

*Caller: What I mean is, it won't be Paul McCartney that
you'll be seeing, Dean, because the real Paul McCartney was
switched-out back in the 60s."*

*Dean: "Not that again! I should have known it would come
around at some point! Listen, I've been hearing that story for
the past 21 years. The odds of them being able to find someone
who looked and acted enough like the original McCartney and
being able to carry it off right in front of the public's noses are
about as likely as . . ., as . . . let's say, . . ."*

*(He glances down at his running order to pick three artist
names at random.)*

*Dean: " . . . let's say, David Bowie, Prince and George Michael
all dying in the same year!"*

*Dean Daniels' Late Night Phone-In, Lux FM*

Drew's words kept repeating in Verity's mind. 'Your name and birthdate are no random accident. And the day you will die is already written.' Apart from wry amusement from recalling Keith's incisive comment that he'd been "Verified" the first time she got intimate with him, she found herself wondering – assuming Drew's insights were correct – what other aspects of her life were pre-ordained by some higher force?

How much of her future was written, and how much would be determined by the free will decisions she made along the way? Was it like this for everyone? Him, for example, she wondered, catching a glimpse of the skinny young tech-op archiving news stories from a reel of tape in the production area. What would *he* be doing with his life 30 years from now?

The stillness of her momentary musings were shattered by the sound of Colin Cole beginning to hammer away at his typewriter next to her, and she snapped back into a full awareness of her surroundings. All was normal in the newsroom – though stuffier and more humid than usual in the absence of any air-conditioning – except for the empty desk where her friend Amy Noble would usually have been sat.

The dust-caked television on top of the red filing cabinet by Mateo's desk silently displayed the news head-lines from BBC2's *Ceefax*. Jess ripped a sheet of paper from the IRN printer and placed it down on Tom Atton's desk, alongside her freshly-typed scripts of the local news ready for that evening's *Lux Report*. Atton perused the stories:

*Massive earthquake kills an estimated 50,000 in the region of Manjil-Rudbar in Northern Iran.*

*Shooting of New York man Larry Parham believed to be the fourth attempted murder of the city's Zodiac Killer.*

*Parliaments of West and East Germany acknowledge Oder-Neissegrens border between Germany and Poland.*

*Police clash violently with hippies over Stonehenge Solstice gathering.*

*Oxford East MP Simon Opps proposes jail terms for poll tax protestors.*

"Unbelievably tragic, that earthquake," commented Verity, shaking her head as she glanced over at the script on Tom Atton's desk.

"What?" said Atton, looking up briefly from his typing. "Oh, that. Well, it was only Iran."

Verity had to pause to confirm to herself that the words had actually left Atton's lips before replying. "Are you for real? Tell me you're just winding me up."

"No, I'm not," responded Atton without a hint of humour or irony. "That kind of shit happens in that part of the world all the time. If they're not dying in earthquakes they're blowing each-other up with bombs. It's never going to end. It'd be a different matter if that earthquake had happened in Britain. Besides, we've got enough problems of our own here."

"So, because it was Iranian people who died and not Brits it's OK? Iranian people don't feel human emotion like British people? Iranian people don't have families that they care about like British people?"

"Oh, you're looking to fill the bleeding heart liberal vacancy now Amy's gone. Got you!"

With hawk-like vigilance, Jess Hewitt glanced up from the intricate task of changing the ribbon in her typewriter, anticipating another conflict. Colin Cole, seated beside Atton and adjacent to Verity, had anticipated it also, and made his own attempts at diffusion.

"I feel we have to remain dispassionate in these matters," he said. "We're like the police that have to knock on someone's door and tell them their daughter's been found murdered. Our duty is to just report what's going on. We can't get involved emotionally, and we certainly can't change anything."

"So, why did you want to become a journalist, Colin?" asked Verity, grateful for his interception, and knowing that her conversation with Atton was likely to have gone the same way as Amy's of the other day otherwise.

"To provide a journal of record. To document what's going in in the world, but certainly not to get involved in any of it.

"What about you, Tom?"

"For the prestige," Atton replied without any need for reflection. "This is a respectable profession, particularly if you can reach Trevor McDonald or Reggie Bosanquet level. And there's shitloads of money to be earned, too. After Uni the options were banking, law or media. My parents would have been happy with any, but the first two would have bored me to death."

Atton lowered his voice and leaned closer to Cole as he glanced cautiously towards Jess' desk. "If I keep my head down here and get a load of *Lux Reports* under my belt, I could be at the BBC by '92."

Her colleague's hubris felt disgusting to Verity as she listened in. Cole provided another welcome relief.

"Why did you get into this game, Verity?"

"Believe it or not, Colin, because I've always wanted to uncover truth. It doesn't matter how unsettling or incon-venient it might be, I always want to know the truth of a situation. I can't actually understand why anyone wouldn't. When I left college and started applying for reporters' jobs, I figured that's what we'd be doing in places like this – digging into stories, asking whatever questions need to be asked, and telling people the truth of what we find out.

"How naive were you?" contributed Atton without looking up.

"You're absolutely right. I didn't realise this job would consist of reading pre-prepared press releases and public relations statements, and regurgitating stories from Ceefax or Radio Oxford."

"Darling, this job is all about maintaining the status quo in organised society. We present the version of events that it suits the Establishment to have the general public believe, and to help cultivate the types of attitudes in the public's mindset that it suits the Establishment for them to have.

"Because of the public perception that we have, we're trusted because we're 'respectable' outlets. We operate within parameters. We can go so far with a story, but there's a line that can't be crossed. And if you try to cross it, you find out about it very quickly. If you didn't realise all of that before you got into this game, you were very short-changed."

"And none of that bothers you?"

"Why should it? It was either this or be a lawyer." Atton rose from his seat and announced his need for a coffee as he headed to the kitchen. With Jess also temporarily absent, Verity walked around the desking, taking a seat at Atton's workstation next to Cole.

"Sadly he's right," said Cole, with a sympathetic expression.

"I know he is, Colin. It's become clear to me through these murder cases."

"What do you mean?"

"I just get the sense that some covering-up is going on, and that we're a part of it without really understanding what we're doing." She paused before her next comment, but went ahead, realising she was now short on trusted allies in the newsroom.

"I think Jess has been instructed from above to prevent any real digging from going on."

"But that's not what we do."

"I know it's not, and this goes back to my earlier comment about why I got into all this. I imagined that in situations like this we'd be out in the field, sniffing around, looking for evidence, seeking out witnesses, asking all kinds of questions and going wherever the story took us."

"That's Sherlock Holmes and Miss Marple. That doesn't happen in the real world."

"But, besides the commendation from Iiblis' imam, we haven't done one single interview on either of these cases, and there's been no follow-up beyond the initial announcements. All we've done is repeat Thames Valley Police statements. What if there's more to know, that they're choosing not to tell us? Why is there just this blind assumption that they're always to be trusted?"

Another distraction arrived, as if pre-ordained by Creation, to alleviate the situation.

"Go girlfriend, it's your birthday!" chanted Dave Vickers and Pete Hollis, hurrying over from the presenters' area, with Hollis brandishing a silver helium balloon with the phrase '21 Again' emblazoned upon it.

"Jess," shouted Hollis towards the now-returned news editor, "please cut this young lady loose and give her a pass to come and enjoy some birthday drinks."

Jess glanced at her watch. Atton was now back at his typewriter. Noting the time to be 5.20pm, and with prepa-ration for *The Lux Report* all but done, she flashed a fake smile and said, "go on then."

"But not the bloody Chequers, though. Let's grab some booze from Tescos and go sit in Florence Park. It's too hot to be indoors. Mateo, you coming?"

"Can't, can I?" said the sports editor from the corner of the room, stubbing out his 37th Benson & Hedges of the day. "It's the England/ Egypt game tonight."

"Looks like we're the only three in this place that don't give a shit about the football then, V," said Vickers. "Too bad you two boring old bastards are tied up with *The Lux Report*," he added, addressing Cole and Atton.

"I believe I'll survive," smirked Atton cynically.

Playing quietly through the newsroom speaker from the studio downstairs, New Order's *World In Motion* had reached the point of England footballer John Barnes' 'rap' section.

"Pure skills," Hollis remarked, striking an exaggerated hip-hop pose.

"KRS One and Rakim must be shitting themselves," quipped Vickers.

Reaching for phone extension 216, Verity put in a quick call to Keith asking him to meet her at the park and headed off with her friends. The drama and seriousness would all still be there tomorrow, she reasoned. If a girl couldn't put such responsibilities aside and enjoy herself on her 24th birthday, when could she?

# CHAPTER 20

## Tuesday 26th June 1990

*"L and an S and a D,*
*Coming in like love, sex and danger.*
*Drop a tab of EE,*
*Mek you rub up with a stranger."*

*E-Zee Posse: 'Everything Starts With An E.'*

In the corner of the downstairs bar of the Port Mahon pub on St. Clements, shuffling anxiously on the wooden seat, sat the youth known to his friends as Acid Ted, and to his family members as Charlie. He had spent the whole of the previous day enduring the comedown from his weekend of chemically-assisted hedonism. A crushing sense of anti-climax and devastating disappointment had been joined by pangs of guilt, regret and self-doubt.

At the root of it all, Charlie acknowledged that the only thing that was giving him a glimmer of optimism amidst the clouds of gloom, was the thought of reliving the entire experience all over again in a few days' time. On the agenda was a session at Storm on Hastings Pier, to which a convoy of at least four or five cars from Oxford was planned. Fabio and Grooverider, Jumping Jack Frost, Carl Cox, and The Ragga Twins in PA. Sweet! There was also the rumour of an allnighter in a farmer's field somewhere off the Southern stretches of the M25, which would serve the partygoers' insatiable appetites yet further on the way back.

Charlie pressed a button to illuminate the screen display on the bulky, black, brick-sized mobile phone on the table in front of him, making a mental note not to leave it behind on this occasion, and to remember to place it back in its charging dock as soon as he reached home. He reached in his pocket for a crumpled A5 flyer advertising the open-air rave and giving the 0860 number to be called on the night to receive full directions.

The locals perched at the bar instinctively turned around as the pub door was pushed open, ready to scrutinise the new arrival. From his own vantage point Charlie did the same, and his anxiety immediately lifted upon the entrance of the frizzy-haired teenage girl.

"Moll!" he called out to her.

The girl hurried over to his table, threw down her backpack, and dropped ungracefully into the wooden seat opposite him. They were a mere three-minute walk away from the antics of May Morning, and it was the first time she had been back to this part of town since.

"You look proper prang!" she exclaimed with a knowing smile.

"Need to get sorted for the weekend. Gonna be a big one."

"So I heard. Sounds like I'll be making a fucking killing, bruv!" She smiled menacingly as she put out her fist to touch Charlie's.

"Better hope it doesn't go the same way as the Milton Common one. And the last Eynsham Barn."

'You know this!"

"So, what you got?"

"Whatever you need. Not here though."

"Is Dad at work?"

"Yeah. Mum's out too."

"Right, let's go get a Mickey D's, then we'll do it there."

# CHAPTER 21

## Friday 29th June 1990

*"The stars, forever unchanging,*
*They guide us on paths unseen.*
*And you were written in my story,*
*Destined to collide with me."*

*Karliene: 'Destined.'*

A path through the grey haze hanging low in the stuffy newsroom air – mainly emanating from the sports desk – got wafted by Jess Hewitt, as she strode swiftly from her desk over to Verity's, placing a typed A4 sheet on her typewriter keyboard as she spoke.

"I've got an interview for you to do later. W.D.C. May Pearce of Thames Valley C.I.D is coming in at two to talk about the latest in the Herzlos and Iiblis murders. We'll get it out on TLR this evening."

"*Is* there a latest?" asked Verity, risking incurring Jess's temper, but unable to temper her cynicism.

Jess was evidently not in the mood for any conflict. "Largely a formality. Herzlos' family have been putting a lot of pressure on the police, asking why there have still been no arrests. I gather this is to placate them. It'll be a standard statement. 'We're investigating all possible avenues.' The usual guff."

At five minutes to two, Extension 216 in the Lux newsroom rang, and Geraldine the receptionist advised Verity that her guest had arrived. Welcoming a reprieve from the stifling, smoky heat, clattering typewriters and inane workplace banter, a fresh reel of Zonal tape and a blue one-minute cartridge in her hand, she ran down the stairs. Heading past the studio area where Dave Vickers was ushering a pair of guests who looked very much like Adamski and Seal into Studio A for an interview, she proceeded to the reception area.

"W.D.C. Pearce. Hello. I'm Verity Hunter. Please come through."

As Verity led her guest through the heavy double doors of Studio B and into its quiet, air-conditioned luxury, her mind raced to recall where she had encountered the police-woman before. Verity was the opposite of Keith, who never forgot a name but was lousy at faces. For Verity's part, she always knew if she had met someone before, or even viewed them from a distance.

"If you'd like to take a seat around the other side of the desk there. Have we met before, by the way?"

The sharpness of Verity's young mind was surpassed by May's.

"We never met, but I saw you at the Randolph charity ball back in May. You were there with Richard Owen, I think."

"Oh, right. Well remembered!" Verity now recalled having seen May standing alongside Lowe and Nomas at the ball, and being especially impressed that she had worn a casual dress of the type she herself would have bought, to a formal function.

"I often hear you on the news," continued May. "It's good to put a face to the name."

Verity proceeded to conduct a brief, by-the-numbers interview, with May reciting a pre-rehearsed routine about the police following every possible lead, detectives working around the clock, and pretty much all else that Jess had predicted. She had re-started the tape a couple of times as May's nervous voice had cracked and faltered.

"Sorry about the jitters," May apologised afterwards. "It's the first time I've done one of these."

"No worries. We got it done. A lot of guests are nervous straight off."

'You've got a great voice for radio. You're a natural."

"Well, thanks. I guess we've all got to be good at something, right?"

# CHAPTER 22

## Tuesday 3rd July 1990

*Dean Daniels: "Coming up on Lux Gold, free-spirited sounds from Buffalo Springfield, The Mamas & The Papas and The Byrds, and a classic to pay tribute to the Rolling Stones' Brian Jones who passed away 21 years ago today. But first, it's this evergreen from The Doors on this, the 19th anniversary of Jim Morrison's departure from this world."*

*(The opening notes of The Who's 'Won't Get Fooled Again' start playing instead.)*

*Dean Daniels, looking confused: "... or is it??"*

"There you go," said Keith, placing a rather unimaginative plate of lettuce, tomato, cucumber and various other salad staples on the table in front of Verity. "I think they have yet to catch on to the general concept of vegetarians here."

"I'm used to it," said Verity, wiping her knife and fork with a serviette. Keith pushed a bottle of ice tea her way, retaining the ginger ale for himself.

They were in the Old School pub at the far end of Gloucester Green bus station, in the building that used to be the ticketing office before the recent spate of city centre gentrification had begun. Keith recalled the stories from his school days claiming the bus station itself was built on the site of an old plague pit dating back to medieval times. Keith had suggested a rare lunchtime date together ahead of Verity's afternoon shift. He had ulterior motives in mind, however.

"So," he began, punctuating his words between swigs of ginger ale in an attempt to make them sound unrehearsed.

"What's the latest on the murder cases?"

"No good asking me. I just work in a 'news' room," said Verity, drolly. "The past few days' local headlines have been about city council cuts, renovations for the Westgate Centre and a Bardwell rare books fair. No time for anything as dull as a pair of brutal killings among that lot."

"Exactly. I know the TVP flatfoots aren't exactly the Met, but even by their standards, don't you think it's a little suspicious that they don't seem to be making any progress whatsoever? Smacks of a cover-up to me."

"Well, it would to you, wouldn't it?" The skin around Verity's mouth wrinkled slightly as she gave the wry hint of a smile, a look that Keith had always found attractive.

"There's more to it, though. Nobody ever asks questions about the occult aspects of such things."

As if taking his walk-on cue in a play, at that moment, a svelte, darkly-bearded man in his thirties appeared at the door and, scanning the tables, began walking towards Verity and Keith's.

"Hey, Max!" exclaimed Keith excitedly upon noticing him, rising to shake his hand.

"How's it going, Keith?" said the new arrival, straining a polite smile.

"Max, meet my lady, Verity. V, this is Max Zeall. I asked him to join us here today because I wanted you two to meet and because I wanted to just chew over a couple of ideas with you both"

"I've heard a lot about you, Verity," said Max, leaning over to kiss her on the cheek.

"I've heard more about you," she replied genially, as he took his seat at the table opposite them. Verity found her immediate annoyance at Keith's deception in inviting an eavesdropper to their lunch date was beginning to turn to curiosity. This man had always been an enigma to her from the glowing terms with which Keith and Phil had spoken of him, so she was at least grateful for the opportunity to be in his presence and experience his aura.

"You want something to eat, Max?"

"No thanks, Keith. Lots of research to wade through back home. I just came here for a quick meet-up, as you requested."

"Well, I'm very grateful for you making the time. I'd just started to explain to Verity that there's more to these two murders than just some random crazed individual, and that there are occult aspects that are being missed – or wilfully suppressed – by the police. Why would that be a surprise, right?"

Zeall was not in the habit of discussing such matters with strangers, but through Phil's vouching, had become as sure as he could be of Keith's sincere nature. Keith's own glowing endorsement of his girlfriend's trustworthiness – despite her profession – was something he would have to take a chance on.

"Well, how far did you get?" asked Zeall.

"I was just about to start on the dates."

"OK, so ...," Zeall began. "Herzlos copped it on 22nd March. Right after the Spring Equinox, on 3/22, in the American way of expressing the date. This is the number associated with Skull & Bones, the secret-society fraternity within Yale University. They're known as Order 322 or the Brotherhood of Death. It's a highly secretive organisation reserved only for specially-chosen 'elite' members."

"We're a long way from New Haven here," chipped in Verity.

"But we're in a University town, and Oxford is England's answer to Yale," contributed Keith. "Herzlos was connected to the University, wasn't he? What if there's a similar secret-society set-up here, and the date that he was done in encodes it somehow?"

Zeall took up the mantle.

"Then we have the Halal guy, who gets his throat unzipped on the first of May, May Day, a date loaded with occult significance in the Pagan calendar. Well, these dates aren't going to be random and accidental. They're tied into the Occult Season of Sacrifice as practiced by various religious systems in the ancient world."

"Synchronistically enough, I was reading about this in a book by a former satanist only this week," said Keith.

"Well, it's clear you don't spend all day doing the cleaning," came Verity's reply.

Zeall continued. "So, the Season of Sacrifice is a 40-day period beginning on or around 19th March and running through to 1st May. The dark occultists of this world, who actually run every aspect of society through their various networks and groups, recognise that the sun is the source of all life on this earth, and actually believe that sacrifices to it are necessary to ensure the continuation of its life-giving forces.

"It doesn't matter if this sounds ridiculous and far-fetched to anyone hearing it for the first time. No one individual's opinion alters the fact that it's true. These rituals have been practiced since time immemorial in countless cultures around the world, and they never actually went away. They just went underground.

"In many cases, the blood sacrifices have been of animals, but human sacrifice has also been involved, and there's always been a huge concentration of them during the period of the year that we're talking about. They're often passed off as 'terrorist events' or 'acts of God' in order to disguise their true nature, but the dates on which they occur always tell you a lot.

"It's also connected to astro-theology, which these groups observe. So the astrological year actually begins as the sign of Pisces transitions into Aries, around 21st March. Forget all this 1st January nonsense, which was an invention of the Romans to throw humans off-track from their natural connectedness to the skies.

"So, the Spring Equinox, meaning equal night and day, occurs around 21st March in what we think of as the Northern Hemisphere. Three months later, around 21st June, it's the Summer Solstice, known as the longest day, when the sun is at its zenith, giving the most hours of daylight. Three months after that it's another Equinox, then around 21st December we get the Winter Solstice, which is a reversal of the Summer one, with the sun this time at its lowest point in the sky and giving the least amount of daylight.

"This event, symbolising the 'death' of the sun and its resurrection after three days to bring 'salvation,' is also the origin of Christmas, which has nothing to do with donkeys, kings and mangers. In what's referred to as the Southern Hemisphere, the process occurs in reverse.

"Then you get mid-points between these four events, which combined, divide the solar year into eight parts. The mid-points are around 1st May, 1st August, 1st November and 1st February. All of these are important dates to the solar-worshipping cults that have existed for centuries and which still do today, through the secret-society networks and cabals that represent the real power structure of the world."

As Verity listened to Zeall speak, she imagined him presenting this information on a radio show or in a lecture, to an attentive and sizeable audience, reflecting on how wasted it all was in a pub on a quiet Tuesday lunchtime.

"Whoever did these killings is broadcasting the sacrificial nature of them to anyone who's smart enough to read the numbers. Unfortunately that wouldn't appear to apply to the rank-and-file members of Oxford's Finest – though you can bet it won't have gone un-noticed to those higher up the chain of command."

Turning to Keith, Verity flashed him one of her curious raising of the eyebrows.

"They'll all be Freemasons, V," he said, as if reciting his line in a performance. "Anyone in any significant Establishment position will be. You can't get to those levels without being part of the Order. And what is Freemasonry founded upon? Oaths of allegiance and the keeping of secrets."

An image of the small group of high rollers at the Randolph ball earlier in the year, and the distinctive rings they all sported, flashed instantaneously into Verity's mind.

"So," she ventured, looking around the pub to ensure nobody was in earshot, and lowering her voice either way, "if the crazy bastard who killed those two is doing it according to the occult season of sacrifice, Herzlos and Iiblis getting theirs represented the beginning and the end of the period?"

"Right."

"So, we can assume that's the end of it?"

"There's a strong chance it's not," countered Zeall. "Once I'd spotted the pattern, I suspected we might get another stunt pulled on the Summer Solstice. But the fact that we didn't doesn't mean we're home and dry.

"It could be that whoever's doing this wanted to let the dust settle a bit before announcing themselves again. Or it could be that they're planning another one on what they consider to be a more significant date. After 1st May, the most important point in the occult calendar would be Halloween, as 31st October goes into 1st November. It would not surprise me at all if, now that the ball is rolling, we get something on that date.

"It's also worth considering the nature of the choice of victims, one being covertly involved in vivisection, and the other in ritual torture and slaughter. We can't discount the possibility that the attacker has been exacting some form of personal retribution, carrying out his own brand of justice – as he sees it. This could dictate the nature of the next victim, if there's to be one. Someone involved in what this person considers to be harmful, or unjust activities within their chosen livelihood."

"Well, you'll be OK," Verity remarked sardonically to her jobless boyfriend. "And I trust he doesn't have any beef with news journalists!

"But seriously, though," she added after a few seconds' thought, "it's obvious the police aren't following this line of enquiry. And even if the upper ranks are suppressing this in some way, as you suggest, we need to talk to the officers running this case about this information – D.I. Lowe and them – so they stand a chance of starting to ask the right kinds of questions."

"NO!" Zeall raised his voice emphatically, a steely and determined glare appearing in his eyes. "I will not co-operate in any way with immoral order-followers!"

The convivial energy of the table had changed.

"Look, I get your objection to authority figures. Keith's spoken to me about it. But from what you've just said, we three could be sitting on information that could help identify the lunatic that's been doing this if it's put into the right hands. Two people have been killed, and from what you say, it could end up being more. We have a responsibility here."

"And each individual has a responsibility to learn truth and morality for themselves, rather than on somebody else's say-so! Any order-follower who undertakes actions on somebody else's instruction – without judging for *themselves* whether that action does or does not put harm into the world and take away other people's rights – is an immoral person.

"Claiming you're 'just following orders,' and then taking a paycheck for it, is a cop-out – forgive the pun. It's the claim of people who don't want the responsibility of making these judgements for themselves. They're too spiritually immature and would rather abdicate that responsibility to someone else, without realising that this is something you *can't* put on to somebody else! To carry out an immoral act because someone else told you to do it, puts you in a far worse place spiritually than to have even made the decision for yourself!

"The police – and military for that matter – are doing the bidding of the Satanists and dark occultists who really run these institutions, whether they realise it or not. And trust me, their overlords, their masters, view them with the contempt and disdain that their lack of morality warrants.

"Do you realise they actually refer to them as their 'dogs' and 'pets'? Why do you think soldiers wear 'dog tags'? Do you realise that the uniforms they make the police wear, with the Masonic black-and-white checker design and the seven-pointed star positioned right over the third eye chakra, are actually mocking their own profanity and spiritual ignorance?

"So, no, I will not have any dealings with any of these people. The outcome is in the hands of fate without me needing to try and influence it. You two must decide for yourselves what you do in all of this, but that's my position, and don't expect me to change it any time soon."

With no instant riposte coming to mind to either Verity or Keith, the table fell into an awkward silence. It was broken again by Zeall.

"Listen, Keith, Verity, I have to go now. I've enjoyed talking with you, and I hope we can speak again soon. I hope what we've discussed has had some personal value to you. Take care. See you again."

Zeall shook each of their hands before striding assertively towards the exit.

Keith and Verity stared at each other for a few seconds as they let the profundity of his protestations sink in.

As Zeall paced towards the pub's exit, a frizzy-haired teenage girl and a tall, slim male wearing a back-to-front baseball cap appeared from nowhere and stepped into his path. The girl swore under her breath as she barged in front of him and through the door. Zeall stopped and looked back, unimpressed. Her male companion managed an awkward "sorry, geez" as he hurried after her.

"Moll, wait up," he called after his sister. "What's the rush?"

"I need cash. Got to get some disco biscuits in ready for the weekend and I'm brassic."

"You're having a laugh! You made a fortune last weekend!"

"Had a load of people to pay off though, didn't I?" Come."

The pair jumped on a bus just about to close its doors and head out of Gloucester Green station.

\*\*\*

Over at Barns Road in Cowley, D.I. Neil Lowe was tucking into the all-day breakfast that Olive, the cafe proprietor, had just placed on the table. The milky tea in his 'Sweeney' mug steamed away next to the plate. The fat pork sausage impaled on his fork shimmered under the cafe's fluorescent ceiling lights as he lifted it to his mouth.

Before he could take his first bite, a hand slapped him hard on the back. "Thought we'd find you in here, you old cannibal!" said the accompanying voice.

"Oh, you two," said Lowe, with no great enthusiasm. Charlie/ Ted and his frizzy-haired sister Molly took their seats opposite him.

"Alright, Dad?" said the girl. "I need a favour."

# CHAPTER 23

## Sunday, 5th August 1990

*'Nobody told me there'd be days like these.*
*Strange days indeed.*
*Strange days indeed.'*

*John Lennon: 'Nobody Told Me.'*

"And lastly the weather. Following in the footsteps of Friday's hottest day of the year, it's sunshine all the way with highs of 32 degrees."

"And it shows," murmured Keith, his eyes obscured by black sunglasses, as he reclined semi-naked in the parched grass.

"Lux FM, it's two pm," continued the voice on the portable radio cassette, before a jingle played, and the first song of Dean Daniels's Sunday afternoon show began – Deee-Lite's by now hugely overplayed *Groove Is In The Heart*.

The couple had spent a blissful day so far – or as blissful as could be enjoyed in temperatures a few degrees above their respective comfort zones.

A light lunch had been taken in the beer garden of The Perch in Binsey, a 17th-century thatched pub that the pair were both agreed was their favourite spot in town. They had then taken the winding, tree-lined footpath that opened out on to the south bank of the Thames at the stretch of riverside common known as Port Meadow.

Having secured the rest of their valuables in the Maestro in the Perch car park, Keith had stripped down to his boxer shorts and waded through the river with his radio, a pair of towels and their sunglasses, placing them on the other bank. Verity had stripped down to her underwear, earning a shocked look from a pair of elderly dog-walkers and a look of self-satisfied pride from Keith himself, and joined him for a welcome swim in the cooling waters.

Now, half an hour or so later, they were laid out on their towels letting the sun dry them and revelling in one of the most unspoilt expressions of nature remaining in all of Oxford. To the rear of them, the vibrant green meadow stretched off as far as the eye could see. Not far along on the river bank, a group of brown cows grazed, while a couple of their number waded in the shallows of the river.

As Keith shuffled uncomfortably on his towel, the intensity of the sun's piercing rays already starting to become too much for his pale complexion, Verity lay still and found herself reflecting on the nature of their location.

This place looked the same here today as it had for the past who-knows-how-many thousands of years, the overhead telephone pylons and the faint hum of the traffic on the A34 being the only features to give away the contemporary setting. She recalled the account she had heard at college of the Reverend Charles Lutwidge Dodgson and a contemporary rowing a boat along this stretch of river in 1862 with three young girls on board – Lorina, Edith and Alice Liddell.

Dodgson became better known as the author Lewis Carroll, and Alice was the muse who inspired his *Alice In Wonderland* stories, published some decades before J.R.R. Tolkien and C.S. Lewis would further cement Oxford's reputation for timeless literature. There was a more unsavoury account of these events, though, and Verity shuddered slightly at the claims that Dodgson was a paedophile, and that his obsession with Alice went far beyond literary inspiration. She laughed to herself at the irony of Dodgson having been a lecturer at Christ Church College, and of his boat having been bound for Godstow. A less Christ and God-like individual in the circumstances would have been hard to find.

She could fully appreciate how Dodgson would have drawn much artistic inspiration from these surroundings, however, as they certainly held some kind of magical quality. She remembered that this stretch of the Thames, as it flowed through Oxford, was known as the Isis, after the goddess of Egyptian mythology. Carroll's *Alice* stories, surreal and hallucinatory as they were, were borne of a mind reportedly fuelled by copious amounts of opium, though Verity could imagine this place holding an other-worldly, almost supernatural appeal all of its own, no entheogens necessary.

As her thoughts drifted back to the present space and time, she found herself becoming aware of the lyrics to the song playing on the radio. The vocal sounded a lot like George Michael.

'*The rich declare themselves poor, and most of us are not sure,*

*If we have too much, but we'll take our chances, 'cause God's stopped keeping score.*

*I guess somewhere along the way, He must have let us all out to play.*

*Turned his back, and all God's children crept out the back door."*

She thought of the high-level strangeness of the times in which she was living, now, in the final decade of the 20th century, and of how different the world seemed compared to just a few months before. The last year had seen the 40-plus-year Cold War and the Communist Soviet regime apparently enter its death throes, poetically symbolised by the dismantling of the Berlin Wall on 9/11/89. The Apartheid political system of South Africa was on its knees following the release from jail of Nelson Mandela back in February. These were events which few of her parents' generation had expected to witness in their lifetimes.

These sentiments of change had only been further exacerbated by the far more worrying contents of the international news of the past few days. On Thursday, it had been reported that Iraqi military troops, under the orders of that country's dictator Saddam Hussein, had, without warning, invaded the tiny, neighbouring, (oil-rich) nation of Kuwait.

This had prompted a predictable response from the United States, with president George Bush mobilising troops into Saudi Arabia, and promising military strikes against Iraq if it did not withdraw its troops immediately. Given America's history of stomping its jack-boots over any foreign nation it considered not to be playing ball with its own self-serving agendas and kowtowing to its demands, the immediate future in the Persian Gulf region was not looking good.

Given that it was only a matter of time before Margaret Thatcher committed British military troops to line up alongside their American cohorts for the cause, things didn't look too great for this country, either. She snorted sarcastically as she gazed over at Keith in his sunglasses, the title of Timbuk 3's song *The Future's So Bright I Gotta Wear Shades* coming to mind.

It felt like everything was changing. Not just in her life and career, and her relationship with Keith, but with world events, and the very nature of reality itself. In a way that she couldn't quite put her finger on, nothing was ever going to be the same again. It brought to mind another, earlier George Michael lyric.

*"There's no comfort in the truth, pain is all you'll find."*

She lifted her sunglasses to peer up at the dazzlingly bright sky overhead.

*"And the wounded skies above say it's much, much too late,"* went the lyrics to the song, right on cue.

*"Well, maybe we should all be praying for time."*

# CHAPTER 24

## Tuesday 11th September 1990

*"Who are these people that keep telling us lies?*
*And how did these people get control of our lives?*
*And who started the violence, 'cause it's out of control.*
*Make them stop!"*

*Burt Bacharach and Elvis Costello: 'Who Are These People?'*

"And, three...two...one." The cameraman gave a hand signal, his forefinger and thumb joined together, the remaining three fingers raised, to indicate that he was now filming.

"Well, today is a very special day for another media operation in the area. Lux FM, the local commercial radio station for Oxfordshire, has been broadcasting for precisely one year this very day. So we at Central News came along to join in the celebrations of our cousin on the radio airwaves."

As many Lux staff as it was possible to fit into the lobby area outside the two on-air studios were huddled together by the far wall and the door to the stairs. Presenters, news crew, sales and admin staff were haphazardly mixed, leaving room for the television camera crew that had come up from Central News HQ in Abingdon. Warren Smart, whom most of the staff were used to seeing hosting the daily show, was strategically positioned outside the glass window to Studio A, so the camera could capture images of Pete Hollis at work on-air. Warren looked shorter and smaller than Verity imagined, before she reminded herself that she only ever saw him seated behind a desk.

Mal Knight was first up to be interviewed. To Verity's mind he resembled a pelican, his bloated chest puffed out with pride. He joyfully strode into the camera's view upon Warren's introduction, flashing a toothpaste grin.

"So, Mal Knight, as Lux FM's Managing Director, this must be a very special day for you."

'Well yes, Warren, it certainly is. One year down the line. we've become a staple part of the lives of hundreds of thousands in the region. That being the case, sometimes it's hard to recall just how woeful the radio airwaves were for the people of this region before our arrival. The only station offering local news and information was BBC Radio Oxford. We've filled the gap by not only surpassing the quality of their news coverage, but by offering a great mix of music, too."

Verity smiled at thoughts of what her cousin would have to say about that assertion.

"Well, thank you, Mal," gushed Warren. "Let's turn now to a couple of the directors and shareholders in Lux, Jeremy Bardwell of Bardwell Books, and veteran writer and broadcaster Rose Cross."

As the camera panned away from Knight, his public-relations grin turned to a look of shock at being side-lined so quickly, and then to one of annoyance, particularly as he himself would have reprimanded any of his own presenters referring to the station simply as 'Lux.'

As Bardwell and Cross recited similarly-rehearsed saccharine lines about Lux FM's invaluable service to the local community, Verity had had enough of the polite formalities and, being on news duty, had a justifiable excuse for leaving the assembled crowd and returning upstairs. There, she found the newsroom deserted apart from Mateo taking a nap, his face obscured by a copy of *The Sun*. The faint clanks of a hired catering team preparing refreshments in the kitchen area, the low-level audio from the on-air monitor speakers, and Mateo's snoring were the only sounds. She took advantage of this unusually calm atmosphere to leaf through the national news updates from IRN.

*U.S. President George Bush to address a Joint Session of Congress in Washington later today. Expected to unveil plans for a "New World Order," and to pledge further U.S. military presence in the Persian Gulf to mobilise against Saddam Hussein's occupying forces in Kuwait.*

Rolling her eyes, she reached for the pile of papers in the letter tray marked 'local leads.' Top of the pile was a press release from Thames Valley Police bearing that day's date.

*Thames Valley Police C.I.D. today announce that they are not treating the recent murders of Professor Gottfried Herzlos and Sharun Iiblis in Oxford as being connected in any way. Chief Superintendent C. C. Nomas remarked that: "there is no evidence to suggest that these murders were committed by the same person, or persons. We are treating these as two entirely separate incidents, and officers are working around the clock to bring the perpetrators to justice."*

Examining the feelings that had just swept over her upon reading the words, Verity identified a hint of nausea, along with slight panic and a sense of trauma in realising that what was going on in this town – and in the world generally – was very different to anything she had consciously registered before. In light of the conversation that she and Keith had had with Max Zeall, this statement – though saying very little on the surface – spoke volumes.

Her peace was suddenly shattered, as the laughing, chattering swarm made its way up the back stairs and burst forth into the news area. The caterers appeared with trays of champagne glasses and canapés, and the open-plan area erupted into the din of unnecessarily loud chit-chat. Random grey clouds appeared as cigarettes and cigars were lit.

Verity got up from her seat and melded into the congregation, seeking out her targets.

Standing some distance from the rest of the crowd was the small group she had expected to find. Mal Knight, Jess Hewitt, Rose Cross and Jeremy Bardwell were huddled in conversation by the photocopier, drinks and canapés absent.

They were joined by two more figures easily recognisable to many in the region, Oxford East MP Simon 'Si' Opps, and Chief Superintendent Nomas of Thames Valley Police C.I.D. Under the guise of making a beeline for the kitchen and toilets, Verity quickly swept past them, smiling pleasantly, and flashing the quickest of glances at however many of their hands she could.

She saw all she needed to see.

# CHAPTER 25

## Thursday 1st November 1990

*'He's the universal soldier and he really is to blame,*
*His orders come from far away no more.*
*They come from him, and you, and me, and brothers can't*
*you see?*
*This is not the way we put an end to war.'*

*Buffy Sainte Marie: 'Universal Soldier.'*

Army Sergeant Robert Chance pulled up the straps to his backpack and bade goodnight to two passing colleagues as he walked towards the personnel car parking area of the Graven Hill base near Bicester. He had just logged off from a 12-hour shift and now, at 2am, was keen to get back to his home in Waddesdon and watch the VHS of *Full Metal Jacket* that he had rented from Blockbuster Video.

The thought of some light relief from his tasks appealed greatly. Training was becoming ever more intensive, the war drums were still banging loudly, and it was surely only a matter of time before it all kicked off in the Persian Gulf and his unit became embroiled in the whole mess.

Chance threw his rucksack carelessly on to the back seat of his white Vauxhall Astra, and wasted no time in climbing into the driver's seat, turning the ignition, and accelerating sharply towards the base's security gate. The guard on vigil waved a sign of recognition, and pulled one of the imposing wire-grilled gates to the side to allow him to pass. Reasoning that he could be at home in little more than fifteen minutes or so at this time of night, he swung the Astra round the roundabout and on to the A41 towards Aylesbury, hitting 60 miles per hour within seconds.

Reaching for the interior light, Chance fumbled around in the box of cassettes that he kept on the driver's seat, pulling out one at random. He turned on the radio. The larynx-strained vocals of Robert Plant from the raucous section of Led Zeppelin's *Stairway To Heaven* blared out.

Dean Daniels's voice was about to relate the conspiracy theories regarding occult backmasked messages in the song on Lux FM's Halloween special. But Chance had no interest in this. As he pushed in the tape, it cancelled out the radio, and he remarked "oh yes!" as the hardcore breakbeat sounds of Colin Faver, recorded off of London's recently-legalised Kiss FM, filled the car. He turned off the light and began nodding his head furiously in time to the frantic tempo of the electronic bleeps.

Chance was too absorbed in his 140 nods-per-minute to notice the dark silhouette of a stocky figure suddenly emerging from bushes to his front right, only slightly illu-minated by his headlights, straight after he had passed the left turn to Launton. Had he seen him, he might have made the assumption that he was some sort of worse-for-wear Halloween reveller, given his all-black attire all the way down to the ski mask. What would have left him in no doubt that this assumption was wrong – had he been paying attention – was the figure running all the way to the central reservation of the road, and swiftly throwing some unidentifiable item down in the path of the Astra, now hurtling along at 70mph.

The 'stinger,' which had been liberated from the back of an unattended police patrol van some weeks earlier, fulfilled its purpose. The upturned metal spikes arranged along the metal strip, tore into the car's front right tyre a split second before the left one whipped the entire device up into its wheel arch. There was an appalling grind of tortured metal as the smell of burning rubber filled the air. The car sped on, but began veering wildly from left to right, spewing thick black smoke in its wake.

The attacker watched with a mix of fascination and concern as it raced on another 100 yards or so, before its lurching sent it way off to the left. Its mangled front wheels dropped into the ditch at the side of the road as the tail end of the vehicle shot up in the air, its still-intact back tyres spinning wildly and depositing debris all around, as smoke continued to spew from the exhaust. The car stereo continued to blast out the frantic electronic music.

The attacker had always been unsure of how this situation would work out; he knew the outcome of a stinger deployment was open to chance. He had also prayed – in his own way – that no oncoming vehicles would be involved. His grievance was with this individual only and he did not wish for anyone else to come to harm. Having said that, the arrival of a concerned witness at this point would severely scupper his mission. No vehicles had so far passed on the Bicester-bound side of the road. It surely couldn't be long before one did?

Pulling his flashlight from his shoulder bag, he illuminated his way along the carriageway as he ran the several yards towards the wreck. Shining his light at the car, he could see that the driver was desperately trying to push open the twisted door on the passenger's side, but that it was hopelessly constrained by the banks of the ditch.

"Please! Help me!" called out Rob Chance in a state of extreme panic, and trying to shield his eyes from the glare of the torch, not quite understanding what had caused his crash, or the true nature of the predicament he was now in.

"I wonder if the children in Belfast cried that when you blew their dads to death with your grenade in the Crumlin Road stand-off last year?"

"Wha…what?" The panic in Chance's eyes had given way to a look of sheer miscomprehension. It dawned on him only now that this figure, far from being someone who might help him, had actually been the cause of the crash. He tried to process the significance of the words that had just been uttered.

"Listen…listen to me." Chance could barely get the words out, the rapidity of his heart rate almost matching the tempo of the music that continued to play out. "I serve my country. I don't make the rules. I follow the orders I'm given. There's collateral damage in any war situation!"

Not that Rob Chance realised it, but it was the wrong choice of words for the occasion, and they were doing him no favours. The attacker was about to tell him so as he reached for an item in his bag, when he stopped dead in his tracks.

Up ahead, two white headlights were piercing the blackness of the night. A vehicle was advancing fast.

There was no more time. As Chance turned towards the headlights, sensing his possible salvation, the attacker reached into his shoulder bag and pulled out a glass whisky bottle filled with a clear liquid. A length of bandage fabric was dipped into the liquid, the rest of it plugging the rim of the bottle.

With the scene becoming ever-more illuminated by the approaching vehicle's headlights, the attacker pulled a cigarette lighter out of his trouser pocket, hastily lit the fabric protruding from the bottle's neck, took a few steps back, and hurled the Molotov Cocktail through the car's broken window.

The oncoming vehicle was almost opposite the Astra. Flames curled up from inside the car as Chance screamed. The attacker leapt over the ditch and, using his torch to light the way, began desperately running through the frozen fields towards Launton. There was a screech of brakes as the approaching vehicle stopped.

Then, the tranquility of the cold, dark winter's night was shattered as an airless whooshing sound was followed by the metal and glass of the Astra disappearing into a bright orange fireball.

# CHAPTER 26

## Thursday 1st November 1990

*'You hot shot, wanna get props and be a saviour?*
*First show a little respect in your behaviour.'*

*KRS One: 'Sound of Da Police.'*

At TVP's St. Aldates headquarters, the scene in the incident room was wearily reminiscent of the one that had taken place exactly six months before. Indeed, exactly the same personnel were in attendance with the exception of Nomas.

Neil Lowe filled his officers in on what details had been gleaned so far from the carnage of less than twelve hours previous. They learned that, miraculously, the occupant of the van that had pulled up alongside Rob Chance's car, had escaped the ensuing inferno relatively unscathed, and had been treated at the John Radcliffe Hospital's A&E department for shock. He reported having seen a figure running off through the fields. Residents of nearby Blackthorn had been awoken by the blast and had called 999, with the first response vehicles arriving at around 3.40am. The mangled stinger had been recovered from the burned-out vehicle's front wheels.

Sergeant Sam Haine was first to speak when Lowe opened up the meeting for questions.

"Guv, I know the official line from TVP, as far as the public is concerned, is that the Herzlos and Iiblis murders were unconnected. But does this new event not change things? What are the chances of *three* killings like this being committed by three separate lone nutters? Is it not far more likely that we're back to looking at one man for all these crimes?"

"No statement to that effect is to be made to anyone outside of this police station, Sergeant. Is that clear? At this stage in the game we do what we always do. We follow up all leads and remain open-minded until the relevant evidence presents itself."

Haine's barely-concealed sigh echoed the sentiments of the other officers in the room. Lowe proceeded to allot tasks to each one and called the meeting to a close.

"Right, let's get cracking. The world keeps turning for the rest of us."

Once Lowe was alone in the incident room, Nomas's head appeared suddenly at the edge of the door.

"Neil," he said, far from good-naturedly. "A word."

* * *

Nomas was now seated behind his large, marble-top desk, with Lowe occupying one of his uncomfortable visitor chairs.

"This is getting fucking embarrassing, Neil. Our force is becoming the laughing stock of the land. You know who I've just had on the line? David Bloody Waddington! The Home Secretary himself, asking how it is that we've now had three murders on our patch, and not one single solid lead, let alone any arrests. He's indicating that an investigation into our methods – or lack of them – may be on the way."

"Well, naturally I feel embarrassed about it all myself, sir," replied Lowe. "I became a cop because I wanted to catch bad guys, and there's not been much of that going on lately. But to be fair, Sir ... "

The words had already left Lowe's lips before he realised he'd made a mistake, and he found himself lacking in imagination to change what he was about to say to something that would stand him in better stead.

"Yes, Neil?" Nomas quizzed.

I've no choice, figured Lowe. To hell with the consequences.

"Well, to be fair, I've been removed from these crimes on several occasions and placed on other tasks at your recommendation, sir, which has been very distracting. And announcing that the first two murders were unconnected could have scuppered investigations, given that my officers are no longer looking for patterns or shared motives. It always seemed far more likely that they were connected, and this new killing seems to bear that out.

"Look at what we've got – a vivisectionist, a slaughterman and an army Sergeant just back from duty in Northern Ireland, and under investigation for frying a group of civilians. Seems to me now that someone has a grudge against what these three did for a living, and in his own sick way is carrying out some form of twisted revenge. And in all cases, whoever did it knew all their movements and habits. Knew exactly where to find them. And always in the dead of night."

Lowe was expecting a characteristic outburst of anger from his superior. Instead, Nomas sat silently behind his desk, not conscious of the involuntary triangle shape that the tips of his forefingers and thumbs were now making.

"We need a result quick. The heat is on."

"I know, but until we get some more evidence ..."

Nomas interrupted. "No, Neil, you're not listening properly." He repeated the phrase, with solid emphasis. "*We need a result.*"

Lowe's eyes squinted as he tried to interpret Nomas's expression.

"You follow?"

"Are you saying ...?"

"Don't be coy, Neil. It wouldn't be the first time."

He leaned forward on the desk as if to give his next words added impact.

"We need a result fast, and you're going to get us one."

# CHAPTER 27

## Friday 9th November 1990

*"Every morning when I wake from my bed,*
*I find I'm yawnin,' just a-scratchin' my head.*
*I face the dawnin', I feel like I'm dead.'*

*James Reyne: 'Fall of Rome.'*

Parkers Wine Bar, (the fashionable tag of the time for any pub which wished to rid itself of the lager-lout throwback image of the 1980s,) was slightly less bustling than usual for a Friday evening, doubtless a consequence of the cold chill and heavy rainfall that had persisted for most of the week. May Pearce wasn't convinced she wanted to be there at all but had dispiritedly agreed at the insistence of her elder brother, Will.

Their phone conversation in the week had revealed their shared dejectedness at the fast-approaching second anniversary of their mother's passing. It wasn't wild partying and drunkenness that Will had suggested, merely the change of scene that the social surroundings would offer – particularly in a spot where he knew she used to like going with her girlfriends – as an alternative to another evening spent indoors. There had been many of those these past few weeks since May Pearce had ceased to be a police officer.

As Will jostled his way to the bar for their drinks, May went into a trance-like state, detaching from her surroundings and reliving the day, back in September, when she was finally sure of her decision, and had announced her resignation to D.I. Lowe. As her vision had kept getting drawn to the sickening photograph of Lowe standing guard to the Queen, a sycophantic smile etched on his face, she had found herself unwittingly recalling the moment at her induction where she had sworn an oath to the monarch and the crown.

At the time she had seen it as a mere formality akin to filling in an application form, but with the benefit of having accrued a couple more years of worldly wisdom, she had found herself uncomfortably ashamed of what she had agreed to. Largely as a result of her elder brother's influence, she had come to accept the gross injustice of one family being elevated to a position of great wealth and apparent dominance over all others, purely by virtue of their genetics.

Had these very same people been born into different families they could have been dustmen, toilet cleaners, or production line workers at the Pressed Steel Fisher plant in Cowley, as her dad had been. So many lay starving and homeless around the world when the grotesque fortune hoarded by this outdated institution could alleviate all that suffering in a flash, if the will and conscience were present. Though her future remained uncertain, she had at least been able to draw a small hint of satisfaction at knowing she was extricating herself from her misplaced pledge.

She had been surprised by Lowe's apparent shock at the news of her intended departure, since she was sure he would have picked up on her demeanour of the previous few weeks. She had put it down to a combination of her continued professional performance regardless of her mental state, and to Lowe being an appalling judge of mood and character.

He had not, however, been satisfied with her generic explanation of "it's just not the career for me," and had at least been intuitive enough to realise that there was more to the story. Regrettably, Chief Superintendent Nomas had been insistent on knowing what these reasons were and had called May into his office for what felt like the type of interrogation that would usually go on elsewhere in the station.

The disagreeable manner of Nomas' persistence had worn away at May's polite defences, and had only served to confirm the validity of her decision, and to remind her that she had little to lose, (apart from her salary and police pension, of course.) As her own patience had waned, she had told him that she had lost confidence in the credibility of the police, and that she had serious moral misgivings about what it was she was helping to facilitate by continuing to be a part of it.

Though given more time to react Nomas might have insisted on more specific detail, his spontaneous reply of, "well if that's the way you feel, you can fuck off right away. Leave your badge and clear your desk and locker. You'll be escorted to the exit," had been far more in-character. She had been relieved of the need to work out her four-week notice period and had not been anywhere near the St. Aldates station from that day on. Nor had she worked in any capacity.

She suddenly became aware of her 'thousand-yard stare' indicating that she was deep in daydream mode, and re-focused on her immediate surroundings. As she glanced around the pub for any faces she recognised, she suddenly focused on one. The slim, shiny-haired black girl occupying one of the circular tables on the other side of the bar seemed familiar. Within a second she had placed her.

Two minutes later, as Will fought his way back with their drinks, he was alarmed to find their table empty. Glancing around, he noticed that May was heading over to the black girl and her companion at the other table.

"Did you see that piece on *The Word* earlier about the video to the new Madonna song, *Justify My Love*?" asked Keith, not waiting for Verity's answer. "They were saying that if you play it in reverse, the lyrics come out as her saying 'I love Satan'!"

Before Verity could respond, a figure had appeared in her vision.

"Hi, it's Verity, isn't it?" May asked, already knowing the answer.

"Yeah. Oh, hey, you're the police officer that I interviewed, aren't you?"

"Well, not any more. It's a long story. Actually, I was hoping I might be able to talk to you a bit about that. If I'm not interrupting?"

"Oh, no, that's OK. This is my boyfriend, Keith."

Keith detected a slight flush in his cheeks as he smiled and greeted May. What neither she nor Verity knew was that he had noticed her when she had first arrived, and proceeded to mentally undress her. Hardly appropriate behaviour on a night out with one's girlfriend, the base aspect of his consciousness was reminded by the more ethical.

Realising she could now do very little by herself, it was May's hope that she might find an ally in this radio reporter. And now that she no longer had any official capacity, she could hardly come into the station to talk to her there. Though she didn't know her, and she would be taking a chance in divulging certain information, it was one she was prepared to take – even with Keith present, whose discretion Verity went to great lengths to vouch for.

"One of the reasons I left the police was … well, I guess you could call it a crisis of conscience. I saw evidence of what I consider to be corruption, and what I can only take to be systematic incompetence."

"I'm assuming we're talking in connection with the three murders here?"

'Yes. It's my belief that it's known, at a senior police level, who has been committing these crimes, but that a cover-up is in place, and officers are being fed false leads, and kept from freely investigating."

"Actually, I've … we've," Verity corrected herself and gestured towards Keith, "been thinking along similar lines, and I've been feeling stifled in my newsroom in not being able to freely report what's been going on."

"I overheard a conversation in the library between three of these heavy-hitters a few months back, where a reference was made to Jess Hewitt having a, what was it? An "over-inquisitive newbie reporter" in her ranks. I'm guessing that would have been a reference to you."

As Keith found his mind reflecting on how disappointing it was that so fine-looking a woman could have chosen to be a cop – but drawing encouragement from the fact that she no longer was – Verity raised her eyebrows in surprise.

"It seems it would. There seems to be a …" she hesitated, partly to bring to mind the right word, and partly to silently study May's expression. She detected only engaged concentration.

"There seems to be a network in place involving many of the senior figures in Oxford Establishment. They're obviously very influential and able to call all kinds of shots. They have control over all areas."

"Are we talking the Freemasons?"

"We don't think so, do we?" Verity gestured again towards Keith, who nodded. "We think this group is something different."

"Do you think they're responsible for the killings?"

'Possibly. Or if not, they'll have an idea of who is."

"Wow."

All three paused briefly for reflection. May looked around the bar to check no-one had been listening. Her gaze caught that of Will, looking concerned. May mouthed to him that she'd be back soon.

As more of Drew's words came back to Verity – "we meet all the people we were always meant to meet" – Keith spoke.

'You know. We three and Zeall might be the only four people in Oxford outside of that society – whatever it may be – that have any idea that this is going on.

"So the question becomes – what the hell do we do about it?"

# CHAPTER 28

## Friday 9th November 1990

*"You may be the stronger now, but my time will come around.*
*You keep adding to my numbers as you shoot my people down.*
*I can feel the future trembling as the word is passed around.*
*We are going to stick up for what we do believe in,*
*And we're prepared to be shot down."*

*Richie Havens: 'What About Me?'*

No more than a mile across town, Chief Superintendent C.C. Nomas had narrowly avoided colliding with an elderly Asian couple who were hobbling across the entrance to Floyds Row. The brakes to the imposing black Mercedes screamed piercingly as he slammed his foot down on the pedal, before winding down the window to hurl a racial slur at the pair. The elderly man shook his fist as he shouted something back in a language Nomas could not understand.

Regaining his composure, the chief raced the car along the alley, and lurched wildly to the left into his designated parking space. Turning up the collar of his black overcoat as some measure of shielding from the cold November air, he walked briskly to the station entrance, pushing the main door with sufficient force to cause it to knock out a small chunk of plaster as the handle smashed back on the wall. His arrival alerted the two Constables on duty on the main desk.

"Evening, sir. You're in late," said one, unimaginatively.

"Is Detective Inspector Lowe in?" snapped Nomas, ignoring the comment.

"Oh, ... haven't you heard, sir? He's pulled in a suspect in the Rob Chance murder. He's interrogating him in room one now."

Nomas's eyes narrowed as he took in the information.

"How would I know when nobody thinks to tell me?" he spat, making his way towards the main body of the station.

"Pure stress. I hear the Home office are giving him major grief," said one of the Constables to the other when he was sure his superior was out of earshot.

\* \* \*

"I don't answer questions."

Neil Lowe had lost count of how many times the phrase had now been uttered.

"Well, it makes a change from 'no comment,' I'll give you that. But it's going to take more than that to get you off the hook here, me old mate. Your contempt towards serving members of her majesty's armed forces is a well-known fact around town."

"I especially don't answer questions put to me by order-followers doing the bidding of their psychopathic, satanic overlords, and who need to take orders from others because they lack the intelligence, moral fortitude and BALLS!" (The detainee of Interrogation Room 1 slammed his fist down on the empty desk as he screamed the word,) "…to decide for themselves between right and wrong! So you can take your questions and go fuck yourselves, SLAVES!"

Neil Lowe turned to face Detective Sergeant Sam Haine, to his front right. "He doesn't believe in making things easy for himself does he?"

"I reckon he's after unlimited free bed and board at Her Majesty's courtesy. He looks a bit homeless, come to think of it."

"Well, he's going the right way about it."

"Maybe we can get him a cell near to the infirmary. What with it being handy for 'injuries' and 'accidents' and that type of thing."

As the detectives prepared to move to the next phase of their tried and tested routine, the door to the interrogation room was yanked violently open. The three occupants quickly averted their gaze to the doorway, now occupied by the figure of C.C. Nomas.

More than familiar with the room's standard arrangement, Nomas's eyes went straight to the figure seated in the uncomfortable plastic chair behind the desk, adjacent to the one-way mirrored wall.

The Superintendent shook his head, his eyes now registering incredulity.

"No, Neil. No, no, NO! Not HIM!"

Lowe's expression was one of genuine confusion, his anticipation at being praised for his efforts dissipating rapidly into a realisation that he had misjudged yet another situation. His look put Nomas in mind of a family cat who had brought in a half-dead bird as a gift for its owners, only to get scorned and derided for doing so.

"Not HIM! That's not what I…Just…Get out. Leave this to me now."

"But Guv, we're making progress here. We'd just . . . "

"Did you not hear me, Detective Inspector? Your superior officer has just issued you with an order. Now leave the room and take Detective Sergeant Haine with you."

Confusion still reigned on Lowe's face, and an identical expression was now being displayed on Haine's. But the officers knew their place, and the fearsome aura that Nomas was exuding affirmed that this was no time for arguing. Wordlessly, they pushed back their chairs, and slowly walked out of the room, looking back contemptuously at their detainee as they went.

"Your owner has spoken, BOYS," he taunted, a tone of deep sarcasm in his voice. "Now, do as he says and if you're really good and roll over, he might just tickle your tummies and throw you a biscuit."

Nomas stared intensely into Max Zeall's eyes as the interrogation room door closed. He pulled up the chair that had been occupied by Lowe and leaned forward on to the desk.

"We both know we're on a different level to those two."

"Oh, so you claim to know me and my work?"

"I know everyone of any note in this town."

"So where does that leave me, when I've been accosted against my will, taken from my place of work and brought here, under duress? And just so you know, it took three of your house slaves and a pair of handcuffs to get me here. Nothing else would have done it. They – *you* – had no right. And I'm not talking about police 'rights.' I'm talking about *real* rights in Creation."

Zeall leaned closer to Nomas.

"But you know what I'm talking about, don't you, Superintendent? You know."

"It's *Chief* Superintendent."

203

"Oh, you're a chief all right."

"Like I said," repeated Nomas, the faint glimmer of a smile coming to the corners of his lips, "we're on a different level to those two."

"I'm not on your level. I have no interest in being on your level. I serve Creation and Truth and nothing else. Certainly not what you serve. I know what you represent, and best believe, your days are coming to an end. I'm going to do everything in my power to see to that."

Zeall rose from his chair and made towards the door of the interrogation room. Nomas made no effort to stop him. Instead, he fixed him a gaze, a tone of mockery in the nuance of his words.

"I wish you luck!"

Zeall snorted derisively. He pulled open the door, pausing just before exiting.

"Oh, and Superintendent."

Nomas stared.

"You might want to do something about that."

Zeall gestured towards the wall-mounted cassette machine, the illuminated red light indicating it was still in 'record' mode.

"You'll find two officers intimating violence towards a detainee on it. You wouldn't want that getting on the Lux FM evening news. Not with all the problems you already have."

Now alone, his hands in another involuntary triangular arrangement in front of him, Nomas reflected momentarily on the evening's events. He let out a huff of laughter as he rose from his seat. Before leaving the room, he pressed the stop and eject buttons on the cassette recorder, and carefully placed the tape in his top pocket.

# CHAPTER 29

## Monday 12th November 1990

*"You had your time, you had the power,*
*You've yet to have your finest hour.*
*Radio, (radio.)"*

Queen: 'Radio Gaga.'

Her nonchalant 'hello' to Geraldine the receptionist was a robotic afterthought as Jess Hewitt hurriedly made her way through Lux FM's reception. She took the quickest route to her desk, being greeted by the usual assault on the senses – the clattering of typewriters, the hubbub of telephone talk, the grey fug, the unnecessarily-inflated heating – as she made through the news area to her corner desk.

Staffing the newsroom were Tom Atton, Richard Owen and Verity, the latter collating scripts ready for the 11am news bulletin that she was due to read. While the national and international stories were provided, as ever, by IRN, Verity had been entrusted with reading a couple of local leads.

Jess removed her jacket and hung her handbag on the edge of her chair, sighing as she prepared to lay into the pile of letters and papers that lay strewn across her desk, not relishing the thought of having to transcribe a story over the phone from the *Oxford Mail* that one of its reporters had promised to share. She glanced at her watch. 10.57am. She became vaguely aware of Verity rising from her chair, scripts and cartridges in hand, and making her way down to the studios.

"What's IRN's lead?" Jess called out to no-one in particular a few minutes later.

"Something about that thing called the, what is it, the Worldwide Web or something?" replied Atton. "Some guy called Tim Berners-Lee has put forward a formal proposal for it."

"It'll never catch on," came Mateo's voice, as he typed up the results of Oxford United's home game at The Manor from the weekend.

"Local lead?"

"Yeah, how about that? The shadier side of 'respectable' Oxford, huh?"

"What do you mean?"

"You know, the killings possibly being some ritualistic aspect of some arcane secret society. It's like something out of Sherlock Holmes."

"What . . . What are you talking about?"

"Verity's story at the top of the last hour. You didn't hear it?"

"Shit!"

Jess surprised her colleagues by moving faster than they'd ever seen her before, sending Richard Owen's plastic letter tray stack crashing to the floor as she banged her hip into the edge of his desk in her haste. Before he could register what had happened, the door to the stairs had been flung open and frantic steps could be heard descending.

As Jess emerged at the bottom of the stairwell, she registered the words coming from the on-air monitor speaker outside studio B.

" ...as the 125th emperor of Japan ... "

Inside Studio B, Verity registered the few seconds of audio left on the cartridge that was playing, listening for the outro phrase, and preparing to read the next script.

"Local news now, and ..."

She turned, mid-phrase, to the studio door which had just been pulled open – a strict breach of radio protocol during a live link. Within a second her near-hysterical news editor had reached forward and wrenched the script out of her hand.

The commotion – being broadcast live to the whole of Oxfordshire – caught the attention of Pete Hollis in the next studio. His training kicked in as he hurriedly reached for the nearest cartridge – a promo for *Lux Gold*. He slammed it into the cart player and quickly switched live studio output from the one next door to his.

Emotions ran high in studio B.

"What the hell do you think you're doing?"

"My job! You've just interrupted a live bulletin, Jess. What's going on?"

"That story you were about to read. Who approved that?"

"No-one approved it, but you gave me autonomy to research and present the local lead. That's what I did."

A light began flashing on the desk console. It was a silent indicator that the 'XD Line' was ringing. This was the emergency telephone number – independent of the regular call-in lines – that was reserved for sole use by members of senior management.

"Stay right there!" Jess ordered Verity as she picked up the receiver and pressed the button to answer the call.

"Yes. It's Jess...Yes, Mal. Listen, I've had an emergency situation here...I know it is...I know...Look, I'll explain more when you get here...OK."

Turning back to Verity, and now sweating profusely, Jess continued her questioning.

"Where did you get information about a secret-society being involved in those murders?"

"I have a source, but I vowed that I wouldn't reveal it."

"Who the bloody hell do you think you are? Carl Bernstein? You're a staff reporter on a local radio station, and you're way out of your depth, Missy. You WILL reveal who gave you that information. This is far from over."

Pete Hollis was so engrossed in the entertaining sight through the studio glass that he almost missed the fade-out of Phil Collins' *Another Day In Paradise* as it came to an end. As he dutifully began reading the weather, he became aware of Jess Hewitt, now through the window on the opposite side of the studios, heading past a bemused-looking Geraldine into the 'racks' room, as it was known, behind the reception desk.

Breaching another aspect of radio protocol, Jess pressed the Stop button on the VHS video recorder that had been logging the station's audio output since 4am and recording it on to a four-hour video tape at half-speed. Plugging in the pair of studio headphones that hung on a peg to the right, she pressed rewind on the tape. She stopped it again after a few seconds and began stopping and starting the tape until she reached the recording of the previous hour's news bulletin. She listened intently to Verity's voice, timed at 10.02am.

"Local news now, and a source close to Thames Valley Police has indicated a possible connection between the three murders that have taken place in Oxford this year, and a covert secret-society network operating within the city's civic Establishment.

"According to information that has been shared with Lux FM, the killings may have been carried out by a member of an arcane organisation in line with its traditional occult rituals. The name of the organisation remains unknown, but membership of its ranks are said to be comprised of some senior figures within the city's academic ranks."

Pulling off the headphones, she clasped the palm of her hand to her forehead.

\* \* \*

Fifteen minutes had passed. Jess Hewitt was seated opposite Mal Knight in his office. A damage-limitation exercise was underway.

"So you're certain she concocted this alone? I mean, no collusion with anyone else in here?"

"As sure as I can be. Tom and Richard didn't seem to know anything about it."

"What about the logger tape?"

"I erased it."

"Right. It goes without saying that this story will never go to air, or even be acknowledged ever again."

"We just have to hope that nobody out there recorded it."

"If asked about it, we go into denial mode. If really challenged on it, we'll have to resort to saying we were mistaken and it was fake news."

"Do the others know?"

"Of course. I've already been admonished. And your loose cannon?"

"Has been cut loose."

\* \* \*

216b Abingdon Road now housed two unemployed occupants. Verity Hunter had ceased to be a reporter for Lux FM earlier that afternoon when she was dismissed for breach of professional protocol by her news editor. She was due a month's pay, but was asked not to return to the station building.

As little as a month earlier she would have been devastated by the outcome. In the event, she had been fully prepared for it, and would have been more surprised if things hadn't panned out this way – particularly in light of how her friend Amy Noble's career had been abruptly aborted through her straying from politically correct territory.

Verity and Keith had spent the whole weekend deliberating on the move. A handful of factors had affected her decision to embark on the gambit – inspiration from May quitting her police post as a matter of principle, Verity's growing discontent at the blatant cover-up of the three killings and the apparent evidence of her news editor and managing director's collusion, and – not least – her growing sense of commitment towards doing the right thing. Keith's influence had been paramount on the latter point. The couple had resolved themselves to having to give their landlord a month's notice and to move back in with their respective parents for the foreseeable future. Later in the week, the search for a new career would have to begin.

"If all else fails you could always be a teacher," laughed Keith, in reference to the endless commercials that had aired on Lux calling for new school recruits.

"Or if the worst came to the absolute worst, *you* could go and find a job."

"Sacrilege!"

Keith shuffled closer to his girlfriend on the sofa and gave her a reassuring hug.

"Things will work out. If you align yourself with Truth and what you know to be the right thing, the Universe will take care of the rest. I'm proud of you. That was a brave move."

"We had to do something, right?"

"Well, it should have smoked them out. You can be sure the whole group will have heard the story. Now they know that someone's on to them, but they won't know how far it goes. They can stew away assuming it goes way beyond a lone radio reporter on a personal agenda."

"What's the best we can hope for now?"

"At the very least, no more killings."

# CHAPTER 30

## Thursday 6th December 1990

*"Everybody's looking for the answers,*
*How the story started and how it will end.*
*What's the use in half a story, half a dream?*
*You have to climb all of the steps in between."*

*Prince & The Revolution: 'The Ladder.'*

There wasn't another living soul in sight as the shiny steel doors to the elevator parted with a ding, and Verity stepped inside.

The walls and ceiling were mirrored, but the light inside was so dim that it was hard to make out any detail. As the doors slid shut again, the elevator began to ascend, there having been no need for Verity to select a level.

Though there was no display to indicate her elevation, she was fully conscious of movement, and as it gradually progressed through the levels, the darkness inside the box seemed to slowly lift. There were no electric lights inside the capsule and no obvious sources of light right here in the central core of the building where the lift shaft was situated. Yet undeniably, it was slowly becoming brighter.

There had been none of the sounds usually associated with a lift journey—no dings as it passed each floor, no whirring of the motor or clattering of metal from the shaft. Suddenly, however, without warning, there was sound. The faint strains of an elevator muzak-style version of *Santa Claus Is Coming To Town*, then, over the music, the voice of Verity's mother, Joy, filled the capsule. She was reading from one of her most recited Biblical passages.

*"...and behold, a ladder was set on the earth with its top reaching to heaven; and behold, the angels of God were ascending and descending on it. Genesis 28:12."*

Verity looked around for the source of the sound, but there was no evidence of a speaker. The lift was featureless apart from its mirrored edges, now reflecting the brilliant light which was being radiated all the more with every passing second. The voice continued.

*"Your eye is the lamp of your body. When your eyes are healthy, your whole body also is full of light. But when they are unhealthy, your body also is full of darkness. See to it, then, that the light within you is not darkness. Luke 11:34-35."*

The light that filled the lift—white and dazzling—was now almost blinding. Her own image loomed back at her from every mirrored edge. The voice had stopped, and Verity sensed that the lift was slowing down. Though there was still no mechanical noise, the sensation indicated that it was encountering some resistance in pressing on upwards.

Within a couple of seconds the straining seemed to disappear, and the upward motion continued smoothly. Presently, the God-given senses to detect motion with which she'd been endowed told Verity without a doubt that there was only stillness.

With a ding, the mirrored doors slid smoothly open. Directly in front of her was a plaque on the opposite wall, indicating that she had reached the 33rd floor.

The same dazzling light that filled the lift was also engulfing the corridor as she stepped out and turned towards the right. After a few steps, she instinctively looked up to see a narrow trapdoor embedded into the white, marbled ceiling.

It looked simple enough to pull open, with an arched handle sitting invitingly in the centre, and she realised that she could reach it quite easily. More of the intense light radiated out as she peered up. Noticing that the floor seemed to have raised her, Verity reasoned that the inlet was just wide enough for her body to slip into, and that she could pull herself into it with little effort.

Guided by faith, and feeling no trepidation or fear, she placed her arms at either side of the opening and, pausing only for a moment in suspension, hoisted her body up into whatever lay beyond. Again, the voice of her mother.

*"After this I looked, and behold, a door standing open in heaven! And the first voice, which I had heard speaking to me like a trumpet, said, "Come up here, and I will show you what must take place after this. Revelation 4:1"*

Still blinded by the light, she moved her body away from the opening and along the edge of the new surface. Moving instinctively towards the right, she tilted her head upwards again. The dazzling light abated enough for her to make out the shape of a single eye, blinking momentarily.

There was now a new sound; a soft jazz saxophone. Verity thought she recognised the recording. Wasn't that *Courtney Blows* by Courtney Pine from the latest Soul II Soul album? Everything in her vision was blurry, and the white light had now become red.

As she continued to stare at the flashing red eye, the detail, now different, became clearer. The flashing was coming from the two red dots in the centre of two illuminated figures. To the left of the dots, a 2, to the right, a 16.

The radio alarm clock was dutifully reporting the time. 2.16am on the morning of 6/12.

As she turned her gaze away from the clock and back into the darkness, she ran her mind back over the potency of what she had just experienced. Though nonsensical on the surface of it, she knew that it held some profound meaning, the validity of which, she reasoned in her half-awake state, may make more sense later as the day dawned properly – if only she could recall the detail.

Either way, she told herself, it made a change from the recurring dream that she had experienced endlessly over the past year of being in the radio studio, live on-air with the microphone open, but of being frozen to the spot and unable to speak. Something about confronting a deep-rooted fear of not being good enough, or not being able to complete an obligatory duty, Keith had told her, assuming amateur psycho-analyst mode. This was not something she would have to worry about any more. Lord only knew how he would interpret this latest one.

Keith suddenly stirred next to her and, in the faint red light from the flashing alarm clock, turned his face towards her. He smiled as he reached to embrace her under the covers. "Everything will be alright," he mumbled, before drifting off back to sleep.

# CHAPTER 31

## 1991

*"Live each day as if it were your last.*
*It's written in the stars, your destiny is cast.*
*And that hourglass runs too fast, no doubt.*
*For the sands of time are running out."*

*Elvis Presley: 'Wisdom of the Ages.'*

The period which housed the transition from 1990 into 1991 certainly hadn't disappointed when it came to local, national and international stories for the Lux FM newsroom to get stuck into.

Most tumultuous of all events had been the full-scale military invasion of Iraq – what the media had chosen to dub 'the Gulf War' – ordered by U.S. President George H. W. Bush. 'Operation Desert Storm' had been preceded on 16th January 1991 with an aerial bombing campaign. Naturally, Britain had followed obediently in the footsteps of its superpower cousin, consigning hundreds of thousands of its troops to the Persian Gulf region, as did 30-plus other 'ally' nations of the West.

The rain of firepower fell on Iraqi targets for the next 42 nights, reaping untold numbers of both military and civilian casualties, (the latter group referred to by the handy catch-all media tag of 'collateral damage,') and occasional deaths by so-called 'friendly fire.' Ground-based action had begun a few weeks later. Iraq's retaliations resulted in the launching of scud missiles on to targets within U.S.-friendly Saudi Arabia and Israel.

An iconic image which quickly came to distinguish this 'war' (Keith preferred the word 'genocide,') was that of the raging fires engulfing the thousands of oil wells in the Kuwait desert. The official account was that these had been deliberately set on fire by Iraqi forces retreating from the region in defeat – a last-ditch middle-finger to the coalition forces given that, according to many political commentators, the U.S. and its allies only ever took an interest in the affairs of the Middle East due to the endlessly-profitable reserves of oil that stood to be plundered from there.

The petrodollar was very much the God of nations in 1991. Unsurprisingly, the view of Keith, shaped from the protestations of various alternative researchers, was that the oil wells had been ignited by U.S. Coalition forces them-selves, the resulting media spectacle serving to further demonise Saddam Hussein in the eyes of the world, and justifying further attacks on Iraq whenever they might be needed.

In what was intended to be only a temporary situation, but had already lasted several weeks, Verity had gone back to working shifts as a barmaid at The Grapes public house in George Street. The income had at least allowed her and Keith to continue living at Abingdon Road. Though Keith had been right and the Universe was providing, one way or another, her notion that she was living in some kind of end times – or at the very least, a time of great transition of human consciousness – was exacerbated by the TV's Apocalyptic visions of the blazing infernos bellowing choking black smoke into the skies, rendering untold levels of resources, infrastructure and labour completely redundant. This must be the closest thing to Hell on Earth, she surmised. At the very least, it all felt so anti-life and anti-nature, and not the way that human beings were ever supposed to live.

'The Highway of Death' was another convenient catch-all tag that caused Verity's heart to sink every time she heard it referenced on the radio news. It referred to the overhead bombing of a convoy of around 1,400 vehicles containing Iraqi military, which had attempted to flee Kuwait on the main highway north on the night of 26th February. The convoy fell under attack from Saudi aircraft. The mass slaughter resulted in a 60-mile stretch of road being strewn with corpses, incinerated vehicles and other debris.

By this point, Kuwait had been declared as free from Iraqi domination, and the defeated Saddam Hussein was ranking alongside the likes of Hitler and Stalin as a universally reviled Public Enemy No. 1 – a dynamic facilitated in part by government spin, but predominantly by the nature of reporting through the mainstream media.

While the likes of Jess Hewitt and Tom Atton took positive delight in the events of the Gulf War weeks, working round the clock to secure stories with a local slant, and with a Sony Radio Award and a spike in Rajar listening figures never far from their minds, the affair proved perplexing for certain presenters.

Jess arrived at work one morning to find Dave Vickers and James Cody arguing passionately with Pete Hollis, the latter having received instructions from the Lux board to avoid making reference to the original names of two music acts. Bomb The Bass, currently on the playlist with *Love So True*, were to be referred to by the name of the group's frontman, Tim Simenon, until the military strikes were over. Similarly, Massive Attack, making great strides with their groundbreaking *Unfinished Sympathy*, were to have the 'Attack' bit dropped from their name.

"It's so as not to offend any listeners with terms that might remind them of military attacks during these delicate times," stated Hollis, merely recounting what Mal Knight had told him as spokesman for the board.

"So, let me get this straight," said Cody. "*References* to dropping bombs are now considered more offensive than *actually* dropping bombs?"

'It's fucking ridiculous!" Vickers protested with added bluntness. "It's just a thought, but we could always just NOT drop bombs on foreign nations and kill innocent people to protect oil interests, THEN we wouldn't have to change the names of groups with songs in the fucking Top 40 so as not to make people feel all uncomfortable over their Cornflakes in the morning. Like I say, just a thought. But what do I know? I'm just a fucking DJ." (Vickers and Cody were already perplexed enough that the Christmas Number One spot of 1990 had been taken by Cliff Richard with *Saviour's Day*, making him the first and only artist to achieve chart-topping singles in the 1950s, 60s, 70s, 80s and 90s.)

Zeall's reaction to unfolding events had been to hastily arrange a series of rallies at the Blackbird Leys Community Centre. Leaving the geo-political analysis to the many others who liked to think of themselves as authorities in such areas, he – as usual – took the road less travelled and used the events to focus on the moral and spiritual repercussions of military action. The main crux of his observations was that if *all* soldiers, ("soul-die-ers," as he expressed it) in their mass numbers were to refuse to engage in murderous activities upon somebody else's say-so, there would be no war.

"I don't know if anyone's noticed," he remarked wryly at one event, "but you never see the politicians and generals who give the orders for war out there on the frontline doing all the dying – or their sons, for that matter. No, they leave all that to the expendable cannon-fodder from the general population – those that *don't* come from important family bloodlines. It's worked immaculately for centuries, so there's no reason to assume it's going to stop working any time soon."

Not that it would have made any difference to the playout of the country's involvement either way, but the Gulf War weeks saw the UK under the nominal leadership of John Major as Conservative Prime Minister. After eleven and a half years at the helm, Margaret Thatcher had tearfully resigned at the end of November, having been effectively ousted by a coup staged by senior members of her cabinet.

Although it was commonly stated that the resignation of her deputy Geoffrey Howe over economic issues had set the ball rolling, bringing to the surface the contempt towards Thatcher that had been bubbling away for years, some pundits suggested it was her disastrous Poll Tax scheme, and the widespread public opposition it received which ultimately sealed her fate. Drew Hunter was amused to note this issue appear in the lyrics to *Devotion* by Nomad, which he heard on heavy rotation on London's Kiss FM, MC Mikee Freedom declaring, "'Cause a frightenin' nightmare can terrorise, Poll Tax came and up went the rise ... Maggie came but now she's slaughtered."

Big news for Oxfordshire had been the opening of the new stretch of the M40 to the North, now providing a continuous motorway link between London and Birmingham, with Oxford at the mid-point. For the first few weeks, every single member of Lux staff driving in from the East neglected to make the new turn-off that was now necessary for Oxford, and found themselves forced to go ten miles out of their way to the next junction at Bicester and then retrace their steps.

It was inconceivable to Verity that, all the way to 1991, motorists heading from Oxford to Birmingham had to take the tortuously slow and winding roads through towns like Kidlington, Banbury and Stratford. The county's jubilation at getting its first motorway was temporarily dampened on 14th February, when a lorry breaking down in thick fog caused a calamitous pile-up of more than 100 vehicles, and one death.

Extreme weather had also hit hard on 8th December when the region endured an onslaught of snow, inevitably plunging the roads into chaos, causing power failures, and rendering many remote locations inaccessible. Mal Knight quickly saw the PR opportunities of the situation, and ordered any member of staff who could make it in to man an emergency *Snowline* from the Lux HQ. Jess pitched the idea of using the food supplies left over from the last Lux Box charity appeal, and to get these sent out to vulnerable members of the public via emergency vehicles. Everyone was sure there were several boxes of Lemon Scampi Fries in the hold, but none were found.

Drew's challenges were far more trivial. The departure of Pete Tong from London-only Capital FM to national BBC Radio 1 in January, meant that many of his customers who had previously relied on him for their weekly tapes were now able to listen and record the new show themselves. His trade in tapes taken from London's Kiss FM and Choice FM, both of which had been granted 'legal' status the previous year, remained lucrative, however.

The news of the imminent opening of a new nightspot that Spring, The Park End Club, had been greeted with great anticipation by the city's clubbers – particularly as it promised to be operated with a maverick, independent spirit in contrast to the glut of soul-less corporate spots, and to place emphasis on bona-fide House and Dance music.

Drew had been far more interested by rumours of a 'back room,' however, which would be the domain of black music, and had planned to put in a pitch to become one of its resident DJs. Molly was equally excited about the club's imminent arrival as she sought to widen her customer base.

Finally – absurdly – there was still no progress in the three murder cases which now hung like a sword of Damocles over Oxford C.I.D. Officers had routinely questioned all animal rights activists, current and former members of white supremacist hate groups and anti-war demonstrators, but no arrests had been made.

Nomas received regular correspondence from the Home Office concerning an internal investigation into TVP's failings, yet no progress had been made on that front either. And wouldn't for months yet, Nomas reasoned, being well used to public sector red tape bureaucracy delaying intended tasks for many months.

# CHAPTER 32

## Monday 18th March 1991

*"Selfish desires are burning like fire among those who hoard the gold,*
*As they continue to keep the people asleep, and the truth from being told."*

*The Last Poets: 'E Pluribus Unum.'*

As dusk began to descend, the two tall, slim figures hurried off the High Street into St. Mary's Passage, then into Radcliffe Square. Their profiles were illuminated by the street lamps that had been there since the Victorian era – then lighting the way by gaslight, now through bulbs triggered by sensors to come on whenever the daylight finally retired.

Both might have been from a bygone era, dressed as they were in all black, he in a long overcoat, minus a top hat, and she in an ankle-length dress and overcoat, teetering slightly as her heeled boots negotiated the uneven cobbles. The urgent pace of their strides suggested their lateness for an important engagement.

Heading towards the iconic Radcliffe Camera, then taking a sharp left into Brasenose Lane, they reached a heavy wooden door acting as a side entrance to the 16th-century Brasenose College. The hordes of American and Japanese tourists that descended on the grounds daily had dissipated a couple of hours before. At this hour, the door would ordinarily have been locked, but on this occasion, the man was able to turn the ridged metallic ring, of the type that had given the college its original name, and push it open with a groaning creak.

Closing it carefully behind them, the pair moved through the courtyard that lay beyond, the vapour of their breath still showing in the crisp early Spring air, to another door leading back into the main part of the college.

They moved along the stone-walled corridor to a third door on the right. Outside this one, a lone gatekeeper – a Tyler – whose solemn, fixed expression might easily have found him employment as a Beefeater at Buckingham Palace, stood vigil. His purposeful expression implied that getting past him would be no easy task without the correct authorisation.

With no prompting, the tall man cupped his hand to the guard's ear and whispered a phrase that would have been inaudible to any eavesdropper, had there been any in attendance. Promptly, the guard stood aside and opened up the door, allowing the couple to pass freely through.

As they entered the room that lay beyond, a familiar sight loomed before them. The room itself looked largely the same as it had for the past 440 years. High, church-style arched windows were embedded into the two outside walls, each with metallic mesh stretched tautly across them. The high ceilings were adorned with dark oak beams.

Arranged around all four walls at various heights were portraits of distinguished looking individuals. Most were men of middle age and beyond, adorned in regalia suggesting affiliations to royalty, aristocracy, or high position within one of the University colleges. In several cases, the men had been painted concealing their right hand within their jackets. The few women on display wore distinctive jewellery, particularly necklaces engraved with talismans.

Positioned in the dead centre of the South-facing wall was a landscape-format tapestry, now yellowing with antiquity. Woven into its fabric was the emblem of the fraternity – a slithering adder, the only venomous snake native to the British Isles, a zigzag design running along its back. Above the image, at the top of the tapestry, sat an inverted five-pointed star. Below it, in black italic writing, was the phrase *Scientia Potestas Est*. Below the emblem was weaved another.

*Profana Patiatur In Sua Manu*.

Positioned perfectly dead-centre underneath the tapestry was an imposing wooden table, large enough to seat 33. All but two of the places were already occupied. All present had a silver goblet placed directly in front of them. Upon the arrival of the pair, all of those seated turned in their direction. Satisfied that the couple were indeed who they had been expecting, all eyes turned back to where they had previously been facing.

At the far end of the table, a decanter of water and a black clipboard and pen in front of him, alongside the obligatory goblet, sat a man who, it was clear to see, was the Chairman of this meeting. The two new arrivals dutifully offered their apologies for their lateness. "Noted," replied the Chairman, beckoning them to take their places in the two remaining seats to his right.

Had names been in liberal usage at this particular gathering, someone might have referred to the couple by their first names of Theo and Sophie. But there were to be no names uttered here this evening. There was no need, as everyone in attendance was already familiar with everyone else's identity and status. Similarly, there was nothing to identify this group by name other than the colloquial reference to 'The Order' that its members used amongst themselves.

The tradition of this group holding its meetings on every first Monday after a full moon had been going on so long that no accurate record of when it had first begun was in known existence. The current Chairman had been its *de facto* leader for the past 23 years. It had been his birthright, and his taking up of the role upon the passing of his father had never needed to be a point of discussion. His ancestors had held the same position within The Order for the past several generations. All had held outwardly respectable positions within the city's infrastructure – Lord Mayor, Chief Magistrate, Dons of various colleges. The current Chairman's role of Chief Superintendent of Thames Valley Police C.I.D. was the latest in a long line of such professions. It merely became a question, with each new generation, of which field the new representatives of the bloodline would be ushered into.

Seated around the table were those held in similar high esteem within Oxford society. The current Lord Mayor and Chief Magistrate were present, along with two judges, the Dons of three university colleges, an archbishop, an Imam and a Rabbi, three lawyers, two surgeons, an army general, and the CEO of a large banking conglomerate.

From the corporate world, the managing directors of four of the most prominent local industries could be found, along with Solomon Schwartz, CEO of Clive Tuns Pharmaceuticals. Representing the media were two of the directors of BBC Radio Oxford, two from Central Television, and the chairman of the Oxford Mail group.

Their number was completed by the presence of Mal Knight and Jess Hewitt, Managing Director and News Editor respectively, of Lux FM. Esteemed veteran writer Rose Cross was in attendance, as were Jeremy Bardwell of Bardwell Books, and local Member of Parliament Simon 'Si' Opps.

"Well, now that we're all here," Nomas began, fixing a glare in the direction of the two new arrivals, "let us begin. I have various housekeeping points to address, namely, the election of a new society treasurer, the confirmed dates of our meetings for the next six months, and the new location in which these will temporarily be taking place until the issue that I will address shortly has been resolved.

"As we have striven to remain true to our motto for the past four centuries, I have no intention of allowing us to be subjected to unwanted scrutiny by an occurrence that has been largely out of our control. This will shortly be resolved, however, and it is this which it is my duty to share with you all this evening."

As the Chairman spoke, his fingers subconsciously joining together in a triangular arrangement, all seated around the vast table trained their gaze directly upon him, paying close attention to his every word. Having covered his housekeeping points, Nomas proceeded to the main topic of discussion.

"As many of you will already know, the identity of the individual who has been running amok over the city has been established. This person's father will have been known to most of you. Our best guess is that this individual has been carrying out these killings to avenge – as he sees it – the fate of his father, and to assuage his long-standing grudge against The Order. It's unclear just how much this individual knows about the true circumstances behind what happened to his father.

"Either way, it seems he thinks he knows enough, since his intention would appear to have been for the finger of blame to eventually be pointed towards The Order, and for us to have become exposed to the glare of attention. Witness the zigzag line painted on the floor of the laboratory and our motto daubed in blood on the wall of the slaughterhouse. Fortunately neither of these details have been released to the press or the public. If these events really had occurred at our hand, of course we would have cryptically pre-announced them. You all know our tenets of disclosure.

"Clearly, this person has deep knowledge of our fraternity. Assuming the killing of the soldier was committed by the same person – and there's no reason to doubt that it was – we can only assume that he didn't have the opportunity to plant any clue implicating The Order. Or that if he did, things didn't go to plan and it was destroyed in the car fire. Whatever the case, you don't need me to tell you that this is becoming a very real potential threat to our number.

"Unfortunately for our man, he seems to have under-estimated the reach of our organisation in being equipped to counter such measures. Though we did have a couple of close shaves with a nosy radio reporter," Nomas glanced surreptitiously in the direction of Jess Hewitt and Mal Knight, "and a meddling junior police officer. We don't expect any further trouble from either, but they will be carefully monitored for a period nonetheless."

As Nomas paused to take a breath, Solomon Schwartz, nervously twitching as he sought an opportunity to break the protocol of the meeting and ask a question before being invited, took his chance.

"What measures are being taken to neutralise the individual of whom you speak, this perpetrator?" he quickly chipped in.

"Questions will be taken at the end of the address," affirmed Nomas.

A visibly anxious Schwartz was not in the mood for formalities.

"This affair has threatened the profitability of my company and has caused me great personal hardship," he persisted. "It became personal to me the moment Herzlos was taken out. I need to know ... "

Nomas interrupted him. "If you had allowed me to continue, I was about to outline the solution that has been decided upon." He glowered at Schwartz who, reminded of his place in the hierarchy, relented in his insistence.

The Chairman continued.

"Prior to this meeting, the senior council of The Order," Nomas nodded almost imperceptibly in the direction of the six members seated to his extreme left, "elected unanimously to negate the threat. Our psychological profiling of this individual, combined with his *modus operandi* and his apparent agenda to implicate The Order in his activities, indicated he would most likely strike again on the Spring Equinox. It would be too much of a temptation for him not to. Therefore, The Fixer has been assigned."

The air around the table shifted at the mention of the name. The emotions of surprise, regret, relief and reassurance all merged into a melting pot of auric frequencies.

"Given that the Equinox is only three nights away, the deed is set to be done within the next 48 hours," Nomas continued. "You should all remain vigilant and keep a close ear and eye on the output of our colleagues." He gestured towards the Lux FM, Central Television and Oxford Mail representatives as he spoke.

"I will now take any questions."

Rose Cross was quick off the mark.

"If The Fixer has been assigned, should our bothersome reporter and disgraced Constable not be removed from the scene at the same time, given that they appear now to have direct knowledge of our organisation?"

"The senior council has decided against this," came the reply. "Once the perpetrator has been removed – efficiently and discreetly as is always the case – we expect the matter to quickly die down. Particularly if it becomes eclipsed by other news of a sensational nature to divert public attention elsewhere. Besides, it would be too risky and messy for all three to disappear at the same time. There's only so much I can cover up."

One of the white-haired University dons was next with a question – though he could already guess at the answer.

"What methods are to be used in removing our perpetrator?"

The Chairman did not disappoint.

"It's not necessary for these details to be divulged at this stage, except to say that his body will not be found. If it did, it would inevitably lead back to his father, and threaten to expose his affiliations with The Order.

"This individual will disappear into obscurity, and the Unholy Trinity of Oxford murders, as the media is to dub them," again, he nodded in the direction of the radio, TV and newspaper personnel, "will remain unsolved and pass into legend, just like the Jack The Ripper killings of 100 years ago. That'll help bring the Japanese tourist money into the city for generations to come."

A query from the judge immediately followed.

"Might I address the question of the Home Office investigation into your department, which I understand is ongoing? Given our enthusiasm for discretion, and in line with our founding motto, this is hardly in keeping with how we have always sought to conduct ourselves."

Had the query have come from a member of more inferior social standing, Nomas would have become hostile. He, however, like all others around the table, knew his place, and replied with appropriate cordiality.

"This too will diminish in time – particularly if some new sensation comes along to set tongues wagging. A political sex scandal, perhaps? We're probably due one of those by now."

For the first time since the meeting convened, an air of humour introduced itself, as a few dry laughs broke out around the table. Nomas permitted the lightheartedness to run its course. A quick glance at his watch revealed the time to be four minutes to nine.

"Let us drink."

Upon his command, the 33 each lifted up their goblets. At once, in unison, they chanted "*Per furtim prosperabitur,*" and took a swig of the contents of their cup.

"Now, our business here is concluded. Let us all convene to the altar room. It is time for the ceremony."

The 33 rose up wordlessly from their chairs and headed, in ritualistic fashion, towards the two portable wardrobe rails positioned to the left side of the Great Hall's main door. Hanging on each rail were 20 long, thick robes in black silken material, with deep red inner lining. All the robes were hooded. Each of the 33 claimed a robe, put it on over their regular clothing, and followed the Chairman out of the main hall and past the still-attendant Tyler.

At the end of the cold, stone corridor, the procession took a left, and headed down a stone spiral staircase that led to the ancient and cavernous basement area beneath.

# CHAPTER 33

## Wednesday 20th March 1991

*"Every generation blames the one before,*
*And all of their frustrations come beating on your door...*
*So we open up a quarrel,*
*Between the present and the past,*
*We only sacrifice the future,*
*It's the bitterness that lasts."*

*Mike & The Mechanics: 'The Living Years.'*

As hundreds of thousands of others within the Oxford Ring Road attended to their regular commercial activity, so it was another day at the proverbial office for Molly Lowe. Now having passed her eighteenth birthday, her ambitions to become – and remain – the area's top dealer in recreational narcotics was shaping up well.

When coming up against the inevitable competition in her line of business, she had learned to play the vulnerable female, manipulating the sensitivities that existed even in hardened street dealers. Their sense of empathy towards what they perceived to be a naive, feeble underling – albeit severely diminished from that which might be expected from a more regular member of society – was, she reasoned, their weakness, and she fully intended to exploit it.

Any book she had ever leafed through in the Personal Empowerment section of Bardwells had advocated this hard-headed, ruthless approach to business. If this was how those who were hailed as heroes of the corporate domain had got there, then why shouldn't the same tactics be employed by those of her ilk? Her father's slow, subservient plodding through the ranks was not for her. She craved quicker rewards.

Not all of her competitors were as accommodating, however, as she had learned the hard way in an encounter at an all-night rave on former military land near Bicester the previous New Year's Eve. There, she had earned herself a slash to the side of the face as a warning, and which she'd had to attribute to a carelessly-handed hairdresser by way of explanation to her parents. That event had led to her commissioning her own security for any occasions she deemed of a similar high risk. A couple of her regular customers had been happy to take on the protective role for an appropriate share of the night's takings.

This afternoon at the cricket scoreboard in University Parks, however, uncharacteristically warm for the time of year, no such precautions were necessary. Following a successful weekend doing the rounds at Boodles, The Coven and Downtown Manhattan, this was her light work, dealing Es and weed to students. There were no threats among this group. Plus they paid more.

Along to assist her in her enterprises was her elder brother. Charlie Lowe was nursing his own small stash in the pockets of his puffa jacket – hardly essential wear for such a sunny day – servicing those students whom he now knew by sight.

Had the pair not been so engrossed in their affairs, Molly through her sharp observational skills and Charlie through his off-the-meter paranoia would almost certainly have noticed two figures who had been observing their activities, sat beside the clump of bushes to the east. Presently, the pair stood up, briefly conferred with each other, then separated. One started walking towards the cricket pitch as the other began tracing the perimeter path of the park.

With most of their expected clientele having already been served, Molly and Charlie took advantage of a quiet spell to check the time and to survey the rest of the park.

"We'd better think about jetting," said the girl, pushing a wad of cash deep into one of her dungaree pockets, and her remaining merchandise deep into the other one.

\* \* \*

Verity paced the last few steps to house number 216b, the two heavily-laden Sainsburys carrier bags dragging on her arms. In the weeks since her departure from Lux she had taken to walking around the city as far as possible and felt much fitter for it. Being able to wear trainers everywhere instead of the punishing high heels that had been a staple part of her newsroom wardrobe had made the simple act of walking a whole lot easier too.

Some metres along the road, separated by an old lady with a shopping trolley, a young mother with a pram and a couple of baseball-capped youths smoking cigarettes, doing their best to blend in to the scene and remain inconspicuous, were two middle-aged men, one tall and slim, the other plump and squat. Keeping a similar distance, they had been tailing Verity since she had left her house over an hour earlier, quietly observing and noting her activities. As they regarded her walking to her front door, turning the key and disappearing inside, they remained confident that they had been unseen throughout, as they paused, one of them taking a notebook and pen from his inside pocket.

Inside 216b, the curtain of the upstairs bedroom fluttered momentarily. From behind it, Verity's keen reporter's eyes peered down at the two men. Though they had no idea of the simple fact, the watchers had become the watched.

\* \* \*

Across Folly Bridge and into the city centre, another Oxford resident had just arrived home and was preparing to go inside his lodgings.

Phil Meritus, in a sweat-soaked tracksuit, had just returned from his latest gym workout. He had stepped up the frequency of these visits to almost obsessive levels in the past few days, as evidenced by the increased muscle tone in his forearms. As was his regular habit, Phil neglected to enter his unglamorous ground-floor flat in Preachers Lane through the front entrance, having settled on coming and going by way of the back yard. Walking over the patch of grass, he clicked open the tall wooden gate and stepped into the area beyond, fumbling around in his tracksuit bottoms for his door key.

He tensed. His senses, sharpened considerably by the events of the past few months, warned him that danger was imminent. Sure enough, as he turned, he was just quick enough to catch a flash of movement as a figure appeared in the corner of his eye, and to register the glint of a blade being thrust in his direction.

With no time for anything other than primal instinct, Phil raised his right foot and kicked out in the direction of the threat. His trainer connected with the hand that was holding the knife, sending it upwards, alleviating the immediate danger, but only temporarily. The attacker had not let go of the knife.

As Phil steadied his stance, he assessed this new situation as effectively as he could. His attacker was tall and svelte. He wore black gloves on his hands, and a grey zip-up hoodie on his torso, the hood pulled over his head. The bottom of his face was obscured by a black scarf pulled up over his mouth from beneath the hoodie.

His right hand continued to grip the blade. Phil's reptilian brain, at the very base, went into its programmed fight-or-flight mode. His attempt at kicking the knife away had already constituted an attempt at the former. Though he had removed the immediate danger to his person, the attacker was still armed. Had he not been, Phil would have faced him off.

He already knew who had sent this man, and why he had come. What he didn't know was whether he was alone, or whether there would be further danger waiting inside his flat even if he were able to overpower this man. All these thoughts raced through his mind in mere fractions of seconds.

Lacking the chance to properly think through his options, flight mode kicked in.

As the attacker prepared to lunge forward again, Phil swiftly reached to the side, grabbed one of the round metal dustbins, and sharply pulled it over into the wake of the man. As the garbage spilled out, he yanked the wooden gate back open, sprinted out, and took a sharp right along the paved area that lined Thames Street.

The attacker had cursed as he had tried to jump over the horizontal bin, misjudging it, losing his footing, and hurtling back painfully into the sea of trash. By the time he was back on his feet and had yanked back open the gate, Phil had taken advantage of a merciful break in the traffic.

Once across the road, he continued on into Butterwyke Place, not daring to look back, but the sound of screeching brakes and an angrily-hooted horn back at the main road was enough to tell him his attacker was not far behind.

# CHAPTER 34

## Wednesday 20th March 1991

*"No man is invincible, no plan is foolproof.*
*We all must face our moment of truth."*

*Gang Starr: 'Moment of Truth.'*

It had been far from the straightforward operation the plain-clothes officers had hoped for to bring the two youths into custody. They had first considered posing as potential buyers, but given that all of the previous customers had been half their age, realised they would have stood out and most likely warned off the savvy young entrepreneurs. A more direct approach was required. They had photographic evidence of their subjects' transactions from the high zoom-lens pictures they had surreptitiously taken, so there was justification enough to bring them in. They had decided that advanced constraint methods and handcuffs would be needed.

The rest of their approach was far from elegantly executed, emerging as they did from either corner of the cricket scoreboard, and aiming for one target each. The hastily contrived plan fell flat on its face when the girl's razor-sharp reactions kicked in. Upon the first swish of the officer darting into view, she adopted a defensive stance like a deer having spotted an approaching predator. Quickly grabbing the straps to her rucksack, she was on her feet and running in less than two seconds, shouting a warning to her brother to do the same.

Charlie, now just short of his 20th birthday, was less responsive than his sister. Years of chemical assaults on his cognitive functions had taken their toll and had numbed his reflexes. He too adopted a stance befitting a wild animal, only his was more like a rabbit caught in headlights as he stood frozen to the spot, trying to acclimatise to this new scenario. Panicked, he called out, "Moll! Wait!" to his fleeing sister. The ensuing officer noted the name.

By the time it had finally occurred to Charlie to start running, the officer had launched himself into a rugby-tackle, and brought the youth crashing to the ground, knocking the back-to-front baseball cap from his head, and sending a wad of £10 notes and a bag of pills flying on to the grass. The other officer, realising he had lost his prey, ran to join his colleague. As he did so, the girl paused in her escape, viewing the situation with angst, and hollering in the direction of the officers.

"You're making a big mistake there, mate. You two must be rookies. You ought to do your research better."

She continued to shout similar taunts as the officers hauled the youth to his feet, one of them administering the handcuffs and reciting his well-worn monologue, while the other gathered the evidence strewn around. As they dragged the youth towards the car parked near the Southern gate, his protestations began.

"Bro, did you actually hear what she just said?" The youth's local accent was heavy.

"Don't think she's bullshitting. You two are in serious shit. She's right, you must be newbies."

"Shut up, son. You're the one who's in big trouble here," retorted one of the officers.

"Alright, alright,' replied Charlie. "Wait and see."

\* \* \*

The pursuit of Phil Meritus by his unnamed attacker had now reached Albion Place, as fortune had allowed him another free passage across busy Speedwell Street. As he continued to sprint along the pavement, he permitted himself a glance back to judge the distance between him and his pursuer.

The hooded man, clearly in top physical shape, was keeping up his pace. He had seemingly concealed the blade. The occasional pedestrian they encountered stopped in their tracks to gawp at the chase and wonder if it was good-natured playfulness between two friends, or something more warranting of concern.

As Phil turned to gain another glance behind him, he failed to notice a courier carrying boxes who had emerged from his van on the other side of the road. Phil barged violently into the courier, sending the boxes flying, then crashing to the ground. Phil and the courier tumbled haphazardly over each other. The courier let out a string of expletives.

Lacking the time for cordiality, Phil scrambled desperately to his feet and resumed his flight, limping for the first few strides, but quickly picking up speed. He heard the still-grounded courier cursing at the attacker as he breezed past him.

The tall, svelte man with the scarf and the hoodie was known within the company that he kept as The Fixer. This was far from the first mission of this type with which he had been charged. Having undergone a lifetime of trauma-based mind-control treatment from the age of three, he wasn't so much a free-minded human being as a programmed machine, or what many researchers into the subject would, in future years, come to refer to as a 'super soldier.' Through the rewiring of the neural pathways that normally responded to such factors, he was able to withstand levels of pain, fatigue and sleep deprivation that would disable an ordinary man.

Though Phil was keeping up his pace as best he could, exhaustion was setting in. The Fixer had caught him at a severe disadvantage as he had already undergone a punishing gym workout that lunchtime. Phil already knew the true nature of who he had behind him; The Fixer's reputation preceded him.

As he navigated the left-hand bend in Albion Place, reasoning that he would be out of sight for a few seconds, he looked around for a potential reprieve. Immediately identifying one, he headed for the car park of the Oxford Deaf & Hard of Hearing Centre and laid out full-length behind the short brick wall that separated the car park from the pavement.

These were quiet back streets and he had not been seen. He would be out of sight to The Fixer when he rounded the corner any second, he reasoned, and he could sure use a lie down. If only he could conceal the giveaway sounds of his heavy breathing for long enough.

He detected the footsteps, with no break in rhythm, continuing around the bend in the road. They suddenly stopped. The Fixer was considering the options. After four or five seconds, Phil heard the footsteps start up again as The Fixer bore left into Littlegate Street.

Considering the danger to have temporarily abated, Phil worked to regain his breath and enjoy the minute or two of rest that he was able to afford himself.

\* \* \*

The front door to St. Aldates police station was flung wide open, the handle making a further indentation into the wall plaster that had been started by Chief Superintendent Nomas' entrance some weeks earlier. The two officers prodded at the youth named Charlie, coercing him towards the front desk. The Sergeant on duty registered an expression of shock as he scrutinised the officers' suspect.

"This one's been arrested on suspicion of dealing drugs in University Parks," said the arresting officer. "His pal got away, but we have her on film. What cell can I put him in to cool off?"

The Constable avoided the question. "Do you know who you've got there?" he asked instead.

"I don't know," answered the officer. "Who have we got here? You got a name, boy?"

"Oh yeah, I've got a name, mate," replied Charlie.

"Well?"

"Well, for now it's Mickey Mouse."

"Very bloody funny. Well, let's see what a few hours in the cells does for your memory, shall we? Cell one, Sergeant?"

"Before you do, I need a word," insisted the Desk Sergeant, looking perturbed.

"Let's get this one under lock and key first. I don't trust him." the arresting officer replied, pushing Charlie in the direction of the cell block.

\* \* \*

Detective Inspector Neil Lowe arrived at St. Aldates front desk. He had just returned from Cherwell School where, as part of the police-community liaison duties for which he had volunteered some years ago, he had been lecturing the secondary school pupils on the perils of recreational drug use and reminding them of the harsh penalties that existed for dealing in them.

The angst displayed on the Desk Sergeant's face hit Lowe immediately.

"What's up, Carl?" he asked.

"Sir. There's been a ... I mean, there's something you need to know."

Minutes later, an apoplectic Neil Lowe stormed into the corridor that housed the cells, a bunch of heavy keys jangling in one hand. His arrival alerted the attention of the Constable on cell block duty.

"Hello, Sir. Can I help?"

"Yeah, you can step aside and stay out of this," Lowe snapped back at him, fumbling with the keys to find the appropriate one for the door.

"But Sir," the Constable continued to insist.

Lowe had already entered the cell, slammed the door and locked it behind him.

# CHAPTER 35

## Wednesday 20th March 1991

*"Everything is everything,*
*What is meant to be will be.*
*After Winter, must come Spring.*
*Change, it comes eventually."*

*Lauryn Hill: 'Everything Is Everything.'*

After no more than three minutes' reprieve, Phil Meritus had raised his head with extreme caution over the top of the brick wall of the Deaf Centre. A woman pedestrian across the other side of the street was glaring unapprovingly. No-one else was in sight. Most importantly, there was no indication that the Fixer had returned following his futile path along Littlegate Street.

It was painfully clear to Phil that returning to his home was no longer an option – this afternoon, or at any other time. The available possibilities for survival raced through his mind as he pulled himself up from the bed of dry brown leaves in which he had been lying and began walking briskly towards St. Ebbes in the direction of the city centre. His immediate chances of safety were better there than in these quiet streets, he figured.

Keeping up a steady pace, he smiled wryly as he glanced over to the right and the passageway that afforded a clear view of St. Aldates Police Station. "We'll give that way a miss, me old mate," he whispered to himself, attempting to maintain some semblance of humour in these most testing of circumstances.

A young Asian man was approaching on the pavement. As the man drew closer, Phil studied his expression. His face seemed to show some consternation at what he saw behind him. Phil instinctively turned.

No more than ten paces behind him was The Fixer. He was no longer concealing his blade, but clutching it ready for action in his right hand.

The young Asian hurriedly crossed the street. Phil broke into a sprint and headed past the Royal Blenheim pub on his right and the entrance to Sainsbury's on his left, his sight fixed on Bonn Square ahead. There, in the hustle and bustle of Queen Street, his furiously racing mind told him, he stood some chance of losing himself in the crowd ... if he could only out-run the psychopath in this next crucial section. Phil registered the sound of The Fixer's trainers slapping on the ground as he sought to match Phil's pace.

As he reached the junction with Queen Street, a pair of shoppers newly emerged from the Westgate Centre suddenly appeared in his path. Phil ploughed into them, sending the woman and her shopping bags flying. He was able to maintain his own stance, and, veering to the right, kept running.

The plight of the shoppers was of no concern to the pursuant Fixer. It had, however, been witnessed by two police Constables who had been conversing with the tramps gathered in Bonn Square, and a third officer was now running out of St. Ebbes Street to join them, having been informed by the young Asian man of The Fixer's knife. One of the officers began radio-ing for back-up, while the other – uselessly – shouted at Phil and The Fixer, both still sprinting madly from them – to stop. Neither took any notice.

They were now in the midst of the busy crowds that Phil had anticipated, and he dodged and weaved his way through the bodies. As he reached the doorway to Baedeker's restaurant, he permitted himself a glance backwards. The Fixer had gained on him and was making no attempt to conceal the blade. Passers-by were gasping and recoiling in horror. A few steps behind him, the two police officers were giving chase, one gesticulating wildly as he ran and continued to shout at them to stop.

There was something else behind The Fixer too, though he didn't know it.

With an elderly couple directly in his path, The Fixer lurched out to the right to avoid them. As he did so, he put himself directly in the path of the Thames Transit double-decker bus that had rounded the corner at the Westgate Centre and was on its regular path to the High Street. Though adequate for negotiating the hordes of pedestrians, its speed was sufficient for the figure that had jumped into its path without due care or attention to be knocked off his feet, plummeting with a sickening thud into a crumpled mess on the tarmac road in front.

The screech of the bus's brakes were drowned out by the screams of terror from onlookers as the knife, having been knocked from his hand, landed on the pavement in front of the entrance to the Clarendon shopping centre.

As the traumatised bus driver sat frozen to his seat, the crowds parted as one of the Constables ran over to the now-motionless body of the man known within very closed circles as The Fixer, while his colleague continued his frantic pursuit of Phil who, having witnessed the full horror, had more reason than ever to keep running.

Now lacking any kind of plan or direction, Phil pressed on, encountering confused onlookers who had just missed the carnage with the bus by seconds and had no idea what was going on.

Almost at the junction with Carfax Tower, he paused as his attention was caught by the flashing blue lights of a police patrol car heading towards him from the High Street.

With the harsh reality of how limited his survival options were only too apparent, with little thought, he careered to the side. As the officers in the now-stationary car, and the Constable behind him all repeated their panicked instruction to him to stop, he dashed into the entrance to the tower, ejecting the shocked member of staff on duty into the street, and slamming the heavy wooden door behind him.

* * *

The drama unfolding in the St. Aldates cell block had now attracted a crowd of several officers. Two of them had been trying in vain to open the door, frustrated to find that it had been locked from the inside. A Constable had been despatched to fetch the spare set of keys from the cabinet at the end of the corridor, while another had dashed off to alert a senior officer.

Peering through the horizontal slat two thirds of the way up the door, Detective Sergeant Sam Haine was able to get a view of the happenings inside the cell. There, his senior, D.I. Neil Lowe, had the upper half of his son Charlie's body in a headlock. Charlie's nose and upper lip were bloodied. His own nose bloodied and left eye swollen,

Lowe grunted as he struggled to maintain his grip on his flailing son.

Suddenly, the youth lunged his elbow into his father's groin area, and Lowe shrieked with pain, instantly releasing his grip and putting both hands towards his crotch in a desperate attempt to ease the agony.

"No more brothers or sisters for me now, eh, Dad?" yelled the youth. At that moment there was a jangling of metal as the cell door was pulled open, revealing several open-mouthed officers, aghast at the sight and unsure of quite what to do.

Lowe continued to clutch his groin, grimacing, as Charlie spat a mouthful of blood on to the concrete floor.

"Shameful. Just shameful. You're a disgrace," croaked Lowe, attempting to regain his composure, removing one hand from his groin to brush down his blood-splattered shirt.

"I'm what you made me, 'Dad'," Charlie over-exaggerated the latter word. "I'm the product of my upbringing. I'm what happens when you place your career first. I'm what goes wrong at home when you're out all hours trying to sort other people's problems out through some misplaced belief in 'duty.' I'm what happens when you think more of the Queen and the Prime Minister than you do your own flesh and blood. I'm what happens when every other kid in my class gets a family holiday every Summer, but I never did because you were always working overtime."

"You always were a disappointment," Lowe growled back, apparently oblivious to the accusations. "To think, I once held out hope of a career in the force for you. And look what you turned out to be instead."

"Well then, you need to prepare yourself for more disappointment, mate. You want to know who the biggest dealer of E in Oxford is? 'Cause it ain't me. I'm just a gopher for the real key player. Shall I tell you? You sure you're ready for the truth? You want to sit down on that bench? It's your daughter! Your own daughter!

"You ever wonder what she's doing with herself all that time she's in her room? 'Cause it ain't reading *Just 17* or *Smash Hits*! She's up there counting out her stash and hiding wads of cash in sports socks, and you have absolutely no idea it's going on. Not really much of a 'detective,' are you?"

Lowe stood in the centre of the cell, lost for words at his son's revelation. Charlie moved past him towards the door, where Sam Haine clasped a hand on his shoulder. "Just wait a second there, son. We'll take your dad upstairs and then we'll get everything sorted out." Turning back towards Lowe, Haine saw that he had begun sobbing uncontrollably. He turned back towards the Constables who had been waiting outside the cell, looking for one to take charge of Lowe, only to notice that all but one had dispersed.

"What's going on?" asked Haine.

"Major drama in Cornmarket Street, sir," the Constable replied. "It's all hands on deck."

# CHAPTER 36

## Thursday 21st March 1991

*"I hope you got your things together,*
*I hope you are quite prepared to die.*
*Looks like we're in for nasty weather,*
*One eye is taken for an eye.*
*Oh don't go 'round tonight,*
*It's bound to take your life,*
*There's a bad moon on the rise."*

*Creedence Clearwater Revival: 'Bad Moon Rising.'*

The chimes of midnight rang out from the bell tower of University Church of St. Mary The Virgin. Activity in the High Street was now down to a minimum typical of the time of night. Only an hour earlier, it had been bustling with drinkers exiting the pubs around the Covered Market, some stumbling and hollering boisterously as they went, others clambering into taxis.

Now, a small handful of pedestrians, some alone, some in small groups, went about their way on both sides. The smell of burning flesh filled the air as the two rival kebab vans which always competed for business at this time sat in their usual spots, only 50 yards from each other. Local taxis and buses were a familiar sight at this time, but tonight, several police patrol cars were in evidence on this route, slowly slinking up and down both sides of the High, their occupants peering eagerly in all directions.

Within the past half-hour the staff of the Mitre Inn, just to the right of the Covered Market and to the left of the entrance to Turl Street, had cashed and locked up for the night. The interior of the pub was now silent, the faint illumination from the street lamp outside and the red blinking of the alarm system the only sources of light in evidence.

Down in the dank, ancient cellars the darkness had the place entirely to itself. It was not, however, devoid of movement.

Aside from the scratching and scurrying of a couple of rats among the beer barrels, the silence was suddenly broken by a series of hollow bangs, then the slow grinding of metal against concrete.

For the first time in more than a hundred years, a cast iron manhole cover in the cellar floor was being slowly pushed from the inside. A dull beam of yellow light exuded from the space below and was hastily shone upwards and in all directions around. After a few seconds of stillness, the cumbersome cover got heaved to the side some more.

Another pause; a hand reached out of the blackness of the hole and placed the torch that had been projecting the light on the top of the manhole cover. Two hands then appeared at the edge of the hole, and with a series of grunts and groans that he was unable to contain, a figure used every last vestige of strength he had to hoist himself up out of the hole.

The torch continued to shine its rapidly diminishing beam as the sound of tiny scurrying feet around the beer barrels intensified. Had the electric bulb to the bowels of this archaic tavern been switched on, it would have revealed the sight of an exhausted and bedraggled man, filthy with the grime, dust and cobwebs of ages, utterly relieved that the latest stage of his ordeal was now over, no matter what further ones may lie ahead. The dirt covering his face provided some ready-made concealment of his identity. His ripped and blackened clothes were almost unrecognisable as the tracksuit that they once were.

Phil Meritus continued to shine the torch beam, its batteries now on their very last legs, around the cellar, orienting himself with the layout, and most importantly, searching for the exit door. Having located it, he allowed himself a few further minutes of repose as he reflected on the events of the past few hours.

He had just become the first human being in at least 100 years, probably a lot longer, to have traversed the High Street by means of an antiquated underground passage, the existence of which had only ever been known to a small select handful through the ages, and now, in the 1990s, probably to a number so small it could be counted on two hands. Phil benefited from the distinct advantage of having been schooled in aspects of Oxford's history that didn't appear in the tourist guides – or indeed in any of the academic text books. This was esoteric knowledge for chosen ones, not exoteric information for the masses.

No-one was entirely sure when the passage in question was dug, but it had been the subject of legends for centuries. Among the various tales that Phil had heard in his childhood was the account of a tunnel linking the Mitre with the equally antiquated Chequers Inn on the other side of the road, which had been carved during the Middle Ages. According to the story, during the Dissolution of the Monasteries, soldiers acting for Henry VIII had driven a group of monks into the tunnel and bricked it up at both ends. A story which had just proven to be far more useful to him, was an extension of the tunnel leading all the way from the cellars of the Mitre Inn to underneath Carfax Tower.

Hours earlier, he had had no confirmation of the existence of the tunnel – or, if it had once existed, whether it was still physically possible to navigate its length. As he had rushed into Carfax Tower, hurriedly thrown out the man attending the admittance desk, and barricaded the door as best he could with a fire extinguisher, he knew that only arrest and life imprisonment, or death awaited him on the other side of that door. The only other option available was to take a chance on hidden knowledge to which he had been privy being able to serve him now, in his time of desperate need.

Intense survival instinct kicked in. He pulled open the wooden door to the right of the main one. Finding it containing janitorial equipment and a toolbox, his eyes scanned the floor frantically. There, embedded in the concrete, was a cast iron manhole cover.

Outside of the tower, it had taken no more than a couple of minutes before eyewitnesses had reported to the officers that Phil had been seen running in – a fact confirmed by the rudely removed desk attendant. The officers had encountered little resistance from Phil's makeshift barricade in busting open the door, but had earned themselves a soaking from the fire extinguisher pipe spraying water wildly in all directions.

The diversion had given Phil the time he needed. Luck – and the mists of time – had been on his side as he had been able to prise open the metal cover with the assistance of a screwdriver from the toolbox. Praising his habit of having always carried the pocket torch with him wherever he had gone over the past few weeks, he had unclipped it from his belt and shone it into what lay beyond.

The dark, damp depths that loomed underneath were far from inviting, but he could at least see that the bottom was only four or five feet below. Having already reasoned that he had nothing to lose, and being well-trained in making spur-of-the-moment survival decisions and sticking to them, he had dropped down into the abyss, pulling the manhole cover back into place as best he could from the other side.

Convinced they had their prey cornered, the officers – once they had tempered the wayward extinguisher – had reached into their sodden pockets to radio for armed back-up. Within minutes, two patrol cars that had forced a path through the hordes of tourists, shoppers and gawping onlookers in Cornmarket Street, had pulled up on the pavement outside Carfax Tower, sirens and blue lights blazing.

The occupants had flown out of the car, and as two officers had remained at the one-way-in, one-way-out door to the tower, two others, guns poised, had started up the spiral staircase that ran to the top. Confusion was reigning by the time the officers had realised that their suspect was nowhere to be found. The roof area had been searched thoroughly, the assailant clearly hadn't jumped, and multiple onlookers had confirmed that he had not come back out the way he had gone in.

A few feet below them, and several feet along, Phil Meritus had begun his fateful journey along multiple yards of pitch-black, dank, stinking underground passage, armed with nothing but a pocket torch, a digital watch and a screwdriver. He had found himself trudging through some kind of soft, sludgy material, but didn't dare to look down to see what it might be. He had become aware of the high-pitched squealing of rats all around him, and a faint rumbling sound from above – undoubtedly the vibrations of the buses traversing the High Street a few feet above his head. He had constantly swept away the spiders' webs that had caked his face. This place was the closest thing to Hell that he had ever experienced – whether or not the skeletons of walled-up Monks lay in the immediate vicinity.

His only instinct had been to keep moving forward. And he did, until he could move forward no more, his path blocked by bricks. His torch beam had revealed the tunnel to branch off to the right, but, shone upwards, it had also revealed a covering embedded into the ceiling of the tunnel above him.

He had lit up his watch. It would now be a waiting game of several hours, and an extreme test of endurance. To pass the time he had settled upon reliving a habit of his late childhood. One by one, he had recalled his favourite pop songs and had silently recited the lyrics in real time in his mind. Once this distraction had outlived its appeal, he had chosen to embrace the darkness and the silence, experiencing full sensory deprivation. Only once before had he ever been so devoid of sensual stimulation in an awakened state, when he had visited West Kennett Long Barrow on a school trip and had gained a few moments in the timeless chambers all by himself.

\* \* \*

Now, at 12.30am, he finally felt able to make his move. Having carefully ascended from the Mitre cellars, donning a donkey jacket he had found on a hook en route, and having passed a warren of corridors, he found himself at a small window, at about shoulder level.

The glass was misty and ingrained with dirt, but he was willing to take a chance that this opened out into the last avenue of the Covered Market. Having confirmed to himself that the handle was seized up and that the window hadn't been opened for decades, he realised his only option was going to be to break it. The screwdriver that he had carried through the tunnel would have to do the job.

Within a minute, as noiselessly as possible, Phil had stabbed away the bulk of the glass, giving just enough space for him to haul his body through, the donkey jacket absorbing the stabs from the jagged shards.

As he had suspected, he found himself in one of the alleyways leading into the market. Looking back out towards the High Street, he detected flashing blue lights and the muffled sound of radio dialogue. He stifled a chuckle at the thought of the bungling flatfoots still standing vigil outside the tower just a few feet away, as if expecting their man to magically reappear out of oblivion at any moment.

Phil pulled up the collar on the donkey jacket. Slowly, and with cautious precision, he walked out of the alleyway back into the High Street, fixing his gaze on the ground. Without incident, he made a quick left into Turl Street.

# CHAPTER 37

## Thursday 21st March 1991

*"I'm just a soul whose intentions are good.*
*Oh Lord, please don't let me be misunderstood."*

*The Animals: 'Don't Let Me Be Misunderstood.'*

All was not as still as it should have been in the front bedroom of 216b Abingdon Road. While Verity Hunter had been asleep for the past couple of hours or more, no such repose was coming easily for Keith Malcolm. To her right in the standard-sized double bed, his head rested as ever on his outstretched right arm and his face turned towards the wall, the same thoughts were bothering him as had been the case for as many weeks back as he could remember.

Though he was sometimes able to get to sleep within an hour or so, tonight was proving one of the more frustrating, though familiar scenarios. He was at least happy that Verity seemed to experience none of his troubling insomnia, and he rarely reported any of his anxieties when she asked him how he had slept. The past few weeks had been a test of his conscience that he had never expected to be faced with; a true dilemma of morality with plenty of challenging questions, but no easy answers. Not immediately apparent ones, at least.

As he glanced at the digital alarm clock, revealing it to be 2.33am, he was suddenly alerted by a dull thump which seemed to come from the downstairs level of the house. Keen to confirm that his senses weren't playing tricks on him and he wasn't further into pre-slumber than he had thought, he tensed and strained for any further sounds to be heard. Seconds later, there it was again; an intermittent knocking, followed by a dull thud.

The possibilities raced through his already overworked mind. It certainly wasn't the boiler kicking in, and it was a still night, so was unlikely to be the wind. The innocent explanations disappearing by the nano-second, glancing over at his still-sleeping girlfriend, Keith reacted in the only responsible way he could and switched into defence mode. His swift movement of throwing back the sheet and blanket, springing up and swinging on to his feet was enough to disturb Verity. Coming to and instinctively rubbing her eyes, she mumbled to Keith, "what time is it? What's going on?"

'It's OK," he whispered, putting his finger to his lips, though Verity couldn't see it in the dim light and through the haze of her watery eyes. "I thought I heard something downstairs. I'm just going to check. You stay here. It'll be fine."

He found himself assuming protective alpha male mode and wished he could be so sure himself of what he had just conveyed to his woman. As he became conscious of another thud from underneath the bedroom, he glanced around for anything that could be employed as a makeshift weapon, settling on a metal towel rail propped upright in the corner that he had been intending for weeks to get around to fixing to the bathroom wall.

Verity was now sat upright in bed and had no intention of following Keith's advice of going back to sleep, even if she'd been able to. Through the semi-darkness, lit subtly by the street lamp outside, she watched him carefully opening the door and creeping out. In only a white T-shirt and boxer shorts, the towel rail brandished in hand, he began slowly creeping down the old wooden stairs, cursing as every other one creaked under his weight.

Hoping for the best but steeling himself for the worst, with no idea what he would find the other side of it, Keith's tiptoeing stopped as he reached the threshold of the living room. Reaching noiselessly for the handle, he suddenly yanked it down and wrenched open the door.

"Don't turn on the light," said an urgent voice. A voice Keith instantly recognised.

In the centre of the room where there should have been nothing, there was a dark figure, the profile of which also had an instant familiarity.

"Phil? What the fuck?"

"Hello Keith. You can put that down. It's a novel variation on a baseball bat, I'll give you that."

To Keith's mind, this was hardly the occasion for chit-chat and light humour.

Still brandishing the rail, Keith's eyes darted around the room. The curtains to the front window were fully drawn as they had been when he had gone to bed earlier. It was a different story with the window that led into the back yard, however. Here, the curtains had been yanked open and with the aid of the moonlight, Keith could make out black smears over the outside of the glass.

"Glad I didn't have to break it," said Phil quietly. "And apologies for the state of me. It's a long story. It's been quite the night to remember!"

Keith moved his eyes from the window back to the figure of his old college buddy. Here he was, standing inexplicably and without invitation in the dark, in the centre of his living room, at half-past-two in the morning. He regarded the thick donkey jacket, the collars to which Phil still had pulled up around his ears. His bottom half told a story all of its own. Phil's tracksuit bottoms were caked in filth as were his once-white trainers, now blackened with indescribable grime.

"Hello, V."

Phil nodded a greeting to the doorway behind Keith. He turned around to find Verity standing at the room's entrance wearing just the bra and panties she had been sleeping in.

Phil repeated what he had said to Keith. "Don't turn on the light. And please, don't be alarmed. I know I've got some explaining to do. If you'll allow me, I'll tell you everything."

"You'd better," was the only response Verity could find.

As the three stood in their respective positions, adopting defensive stances and unsure of what was going to happen next, they might have been the three characters in the Mexican stand-off scene at the end of *The Good, The Bad & The Ugly*, particularly as all three began taking calculated paces. Phil had his eyes on an armchair, being in desperate need of a seat, and began moving towards it. Keith stepped backwards. Verity took paces towards the telephone on the table in the hall.

Phil slumped down into the chair with relief, the grime from his lower half already beginning to rub off into the fabric.

Keith and Phil kept their eyes fixed firmly on each-other. In the six-plus years they had known each-other, there had never been an occasion remotely close to this one. The unquestionable sense of camaraderie with which Keith had always considered his friend had now been replaced with...what even were these emotions, he struggled to establish? Hostility? Trepidation? Fear?

Phil's eyes closed with exhaustion. Keith broke the silence.

"What's all this about not putting the light on?"

"I came in through the alleyway from Green Place and the back gardens. The house is being watched." Phil addressed the question wearily without opening his eyes.

"I know," said a third voice. Verity had re-entered the room, now in a white towelling dressing gown having become conscious of her semi-nakedness. "I've been getting tailed for days."

"I can explain all of that," said Phil. "Just give me a few moments."

Keith wasn't in the mood for waiting.

"I know." He projected the phrase, loaded with gravity, in Phil's direction.

"You know...what?" asked Phil, still with eyes closed.

"Phil. I know." repeated Keith. "I know what you've done. I know it's been you."

Phil's eyes suddenly opened. There was puzzlement in his expression, though the others were unable to detect it in the dim light, but no request for further clarification. And no denial.

The puzzled expression turned to one of apparent calm. "Well, that'll make explaining things a whole lot easier."

"What the hell are you two talking about?" Verity demanded with vexation in her voice. "You'd better start talking pretty damn quick, Phil!"

Keith answered for him.

"Phil's the one that's been committing the murders, V. The Unholy Trinity."

There was inevitable silence as an open-mouthed Verity struggled to comprehend the situation. There was no attempt at a denial from Phil.

"So…," Verity's voice now sounded like she might break out crying any second, "you're telling me that a mass-murderer is right here in front of us in our living room, and we're just standing around calmly? And that you KNEW ABOUT IT?"

"I was never sure until now. Look, V – we're not in any danger. He's not come here to kill us, for fuck's sake."

"Have you? Tell her." Keith turned his head back to Phil.

"Of course not. V. He's right. You're not in any danger. Please just sit down and let me explain everything. At the end of it, we can all figure out what we do next."

Preferring to remain standing, and with the hallway telephone in the corner of her eye, she remained in the doorway. Phil exhaled deeply as he considered the best way to get his story across.

His future fate for the rest of his days was wholly dependent upon the ultimate reaction of the two people in the room alongside him.

# CHAPTER 38
## Thursday 21st March 1991

*"It's the terror of knowing what this world is about.*
*Watching some good friends screaming, 'let me out!'"*

*Queen & David Bowie: 'Under Pressure.'*

It had been the most difficult, morally-testing and surreal conversation that any of the three had experienced – not that there was much competition in the circumstances. Phil had spent several hours in the punishing darkness of the tunnel rehearsing how he was going to relate his story, but his first opportunity to convey it engagingly that night had not gone the way he had planned. He didn't imagine that this one would be any different, so he began blurting out his words with little regard for eloquence or finesse. He opted for some semblance of chronology, and so took his audience of two back to his past.

"My Dad was a Freemason. You already know that, Keith. It's been in the family for generations. It was expected of me to take up the mantle at the right time. He also belonged to another fraternity, though. One that's very old and specific to Oxford. They refer to themselves as The

Order. They have their own dark religion and they basically run the whole city. They have its entire infrastructure in their grip – all the top positions. They've had centuries to get it that way.

"I knew about Dad being a Mason from very young, but he kept his place within The Order hidden from me and Mum. I found out when I was 15 and I'd stumbled across some documentation that he'd stashed away. When I challenged him about it, he didn't deny it, but he swore me to secrecy. When he was sure he could rely on my discretion, he let me in on their doctrines. Clearly, he left out some of the detail of exactly what goes on in their rituals, though.

"It seems that being able to tell me was kind of…cathartic to him, having had to keep his association concealed from anyone who wasn't a part of the group. He seemed to have developed something of a conscience about it – about the darker aspects of what they do. It's like he'd been under a mind-control spell his whole life, but turning 40, he seemed to be regaining something of his…his true humanity."

Phil paused to sigh as he evoked difficult memories and uncomfortable home truths.

"In college, I got to know this guy who was studying journalism, but who was also into the occult and secret societies. You never knew him, Keith. He'd got wind of the existence of The Order. He wanted to include them in a book he was planning to write. His Dad owned a publishing house and had offered to put it out.

"Well, I mentioned this guy and what he'd said to me in passing to my Dad. I thought he might advise me to warn this guy off, but instead he offered to meet and talk with him, and to fill him in on aspects of The Order. He welcomed an opportunity to out them so long as his name wasn't mentioned. So they met."

Keith sat in silence, letting the truth of this new take on his reality sink in. His mind leapt ahead in the storyline, anticipating what Phil would tell him next.

"You know the rest, Keith. Dad didn't last the week after that meeting. I doubt he expected to, truth be told. He'd broken the oath of secrecy which is a cardinal sin. He would have known that. Me and Mum got a call from his work saying he'd been discovered slumped over the desk in his study after suffering a 'heart-attack.' Quite coincidental timing, don't you think? You already know that these things can be induced. And when the crooked coroner is a part of The Order – naturally – the whole thing can be neatly tied up with a bow."

"What…what happened to the student guy that he'd met with?" asked Keith.

"Your guess is as good as mine. Disappeared, the day after Dad had his 'heart-attack.' Never heard of from that day to this. His parents took out a missing person's case, not that was ever going to do a blind bit of good. It's another of their specialities. Making people 'disappear.' That and 'car accidents.' Like the writer who was set to publish an exposé of Clive Tuns and how they've been systematically suppressing natural cures for cancer, then decided to become James Hunt on the A420 late one night. What's the betting they used the same goon to take him out as they got to try and stab me yesterday."

"Right…where does all his lead to you becoming a serial killer?" Keith was all out of patience.

Phil paused again to consider the most appropriate way to convey the story.

"We're fast-forwarding a few years now to when I first discovered Zeall's work. When I first got up on true spirituality. Natural Law. The Hermetic Principles. When I first came to truly comprehend the concept of spirit becoming matter. Of what our lives here are for."

"I know all about that," Keith interrupted. "You're preaching to the choir. You were about to explain how you became a killer."

"The more I studied the Principles, the more I realised that this world is a shithouse slave plantation only because humanity has collectively chosen for it to be that way. That would-be dominators and controllers like those demonic fucks in The Order only have the power that they do because we allow it. That made me mad. And looking around me, all I saw was immorality. Towards other humans as well as other living beings."

"OK. Now we're starting to get there," Keith interjected again.

"Towards the end of '89 I was beginning to lose my mind with all this stuff. I was at breaking point. I kept it well-masked from you and everyone else. I guess I got it from my Dad in terms of how to be one thing behind closed doors and another to everyone else.

"I wanted to make an example of some of the worst offenders and enact some rightful retribution. I did a lot of homework in selecting who I did, studying them for weeks to get to know their habits. I figured if I went about it in the right way – choosing occult dates, leaving clues behind – I could make it look like these were actions taken by The Order. If I could get them exposed, it would go some way towards avenging my Dad."

Verity spoke this time. "But who did you think you were going to expose them *to*, Phil? They run the whole city. Anyone that might have been able to do anything is already a part of it."

"I realise that now, V. As I know you do. But I'd under-estimated their reach when I started out. A harsh lesson I've learned is that The Order doesn't like *not* being in control. It only became apparent that no-one was going to be allowed to properly delve into them – the police, the media – after I did that fat slaughterman. And trust me, every minute of pushing weights at the gym paid for itself to get him up on that hook.

"When your radio station announced that the police had said the two killings weren't being linked...well, I guess you could say that was when the penny dropped. You and that WPC, Pearce, seem to be the only two who noticed – or cared. I was already in too deep by that point."

Keith interjected. "But it still didn't stop you killing the third one. The soldier."

"Oh, you mean the order-following boy whose blind faith in his psychopathic overlords resulted in him blasting a family to death with a grenade just because someone with more stripes on his uniform told him to? Honestly, who other than his sorry-ass family is going to mourn the removal of an immoral piece of trash like that? I'd set out to do three, and I finished the job. You could consider them...how do the military put it...'collateral damage?' They're no great loss to Creation."

Keith eventually broke another incredulous pause.

"What you said earlier. You mentioned 'enacting some rightful retribution.' Just who do you think appointed you judge, jury and executioner in all this? Why, in your sick mind, do you get to enact that retribution on behalf of the rest of society?"

"Because no-one else has the *balls* to, Keith! Most of the dumb, McDonalds-eating, *Blind Date*-watching golems don't even realise there's anything wrong in this world. Can you imagine actually thinking that everything that goes on here is in any way 'normal?' I mean, just imagine that for a second! These people have no concept of morality, or else they feel it's just subjective, and their view of what's acceptable behaviour is just as good as the next man's. They think the world is basically just fine, and we can all carry on leading our self-centred, godless, immoral lives with absolutely no consequence in terms of the playouts that it will lead to, both in their own lives and those of everybody else. *Someone* had to take a stand."

"But you've appointed yourself God in this matter, Phil. If any of these three people had done something to harm you personally, or posed an immediate threat, you would have been within your rights to enact the Self Defence Principle. But that's not what happened here. *You* instigated the violence against *them*."

"Oh, you really feel they were doing no harm? Torturers of animals? A murderer of other people's children? Really?"

"But it wasn't *your* place to murder these people on that basis! It wasn't *your personal* responsibility. The Universe has mechanisms in place for dealing with these scenarios. Karma is real. And these situations happen for reasons. For every Cause there's a Cure. It doesn't make a difference whether we get to witness it or not. We can just trust that it happens. Those people would have paid the price for their life choices on a soul level without you having to intervene."

"Keith, those people deserved to die."

"Maybe so – but it was never your place to decide how and when. The Universe takes care of these things. It always has."

There was a contemplative pause.

"The Universe is structured that way, Phil. Our souls need these tests and experiences in order to evolve and learn. It can seem haphazard and chaotic to us, but there is a divine plan at play. You know all this! It's been going on for as long as this place has been here!"

"Maybe this is all part of my life experience then. Maybe this is what *my* soul needs. Maybe I was cursed to live this life. Maybe I was always meant to pay the price."

Keith paused, Phil's unexpected words slowly sinking in.

Verity took the opportunity to move back into the hallway, something she had been anxious to do for several minutes. Moving over to the front door, she crouched down and carefully pushed open the flap to the letter box. Peering outside, she saw the short, squat man, one of the two figures that had been tailing her for the previous two days, underneath the lamp post across the road.

She became conscious of her increased heart rate. She could only guess as to whether the goon knew Phil was in the house. If Phil had been as careful as he'd claimed in entering via the back gardens there was no reason to assume the goon did. Either way, it had been a strategic move not to have put the light on. For all the goon knew, she surmised, she and Keith could still be asleep in bed.

"You know how it all works, Phil," Keith said, as Verity moved back to her position in the door frame. "You've read the same books as me, and you've been listening to Max Zeall lectures for long enough."

A wry smile crossed Phil's lips, though the others were unable to perceive it in the 3am darkness. He let out a derisive snort. "That's funny, Keith. That's what he said."

"What do you mean? When?"

"Oh, about an hour ago. I went round his first, before I came here."

Keith was incredulous.

"You've broken into my house and you're sitting here in my living room scaring my girlfriend, and I'm not even your first port of call? This just gets better and better, Phil!"

"I didn't want to have to involve you in any of this, Keith. I'm only here because I have to be."

"So what did Zeall say to you?"

Phil snorted again. "Pretty much the same as you're saying to me now. That I got it all so wrong."

"You did, Phil! Can't you see that? How did you get it so twisted?"

Verity interjected. "And what do you mean, you're only here because you have to be?"

# CHAPTER 39

## Thursday 21st March 1991

*"Are you a man? Can you stand alone like a man has to sometimes?*
*(Yes I can.)"*

*Jeru The Damaja: 'Ya Playin' Yaself.'*

"I need your help. You two are the only ones I can turn to. I can't go home ever again. They'll be waiting for me there. I wouldn't last five minutes. I need to disappear."

A tone of desperation had crept into Phil's voice.

Keith had anticipated the request.

"Phil, we can't shelter you. We'd be accessories to murder in the eyes of the law. I know that's Man's Law, but even under Natural Law, this wouldn't be Right Action in the circumstances. Plus I'd be putting Verity's safety in jeopardy, and what kind of man would that make me? You're on your own. You have to be."

Phil stared blankly ahead as he absorbed the words.

"You come into this world alone, you go out alone, right?"

"Something like that."

It hurt Keith to have to harden his heart. Though he knew this was the only stance he could adopt, memories of good times shared with his friend of the past seven years came flooding into his mind. It went against all his instincts not to help out the closest person he'd ever had to a brother – particularly since he knew Phil was hardly exaggerating when he talked of being alone. An only child, when his mother had died of leukaemia almost three years before – strongly suspected to have been triggered by the stress of losing her husband – he had been left with no immediate family members, and no partner.

Keith attempted to console his nagging guilt by telling himself that this would surely make Phil leaving town so much easier than if he had any close ties to keep him here. But then he reflected that he couldn't imagine the turmoil of being in such a situation himself. His cognitive dissonance was completed by momentary thoughts of the gruesome methods by which Phil had despatched his three victims. He worked to clear the thoughts from his mind and stand firm in his convictions.

"Keith, I have no money. I have only the clothes I'm in – if you can even call them clothes. Even this donkey jacket isn't even mine. I've got no hope of retrieving my passport. What am I supposed to do?"

"You should have thought that through," Verity said.

It only occurred to her after the words had been uttered to wonder whether Phil intended to force them to help him, rather than accept their refusal. But Phil was all out of physical and emotional energy. Slouched before her in the armchair was a broken shell; a husk of a human being.

Keith spoke.

"I can't condone what you've done."

"Are you going to turn me in?"

"I'm not going to turn you in. I have no love for the police, you know that. Besides, turning you into them is the same as handing you over to The Order, right? Either way, your life expectancy would be very short."

"Sounds about right."

Keith and Verity exchanged glances as best they could in the dark. There was more silence as all three contemplated what needed to happen next.

"You have to disappear, Phil. You need to be far away by daylight. V and I can't be involved in this. You were never here."

"How far do you think I'm going to get with nothing?"

"I can't give you anything. My conscience has to be clear. Now if you were to break into the jar in the sideboard and take the savings I keep in there," Keith nodded subtly towards the unit in question, "then head out the back door and through the gardens, there's nothing I could do about that. That would be on you."

"What happened to us? We were like brothers." Phil's voice was beginning to quaver.

"What happened is you got it all so, so wrong, Phil. You woke up, and you gained an understanding of Cosmic Law that so few ever do. You came so close. But you got it all so wrong."

He had been ready to crack for a while, but at last, Phil's melting-pot of high emotions overwhelmed him. Abruptly, he let out a wail of desperation, put his still-filthy hands to his head, and began sobbing uncontrollably.

"My life is cursed," he uttered through his tears, repeating his earlier sentiments. "I've always been cursed."

It took all the steely resolve that Keith could muster and went against every instinct not to come to his best friend's comfort. But he knew he couldn't. Words were all he could continue to offer.

"You have Free Will. Free agency. You know that. Nothing is a done deal. It all gets determined by the choices we make. God knows I'm very far from perfect myself. I'm a deeply flawed being with a long way to go. But I try every day. As long as you continue to try and you really mean it, that's the important part. You've made some terrible decisions, but you can still do the right thing and start making better ones. You just have to do it on your own.

"This is my will, and I apply it. Remember what we always used to say?"

"As it is willed," croaked Phil agonisingly through a faceful of tears and grime, "so shall it be."

Verity turned away from the violation of her sanctuary from the madness of the world – her living room – and walked back into the hallway. She dropped to her knees to peer again through the letter box. The short, squat man who had earlier been observing the house from across the street was gone, which might be either a good or bad sign.

She stood back up. As Phil's sobs of remorse began to abate, she felt warm arms around her waist. Keith pulled her body tight to his and she nestled her head under his chin. He began to feel the same magnetic attraction he had when they had begun to fall in love. They swayed gently from side to side as they prolonged their embrace for as long as they had ever done.

From back in the living room there was movement. They recognised the sound of the door to the sideboard unit being pulled open, and the scrape of a jar being displaced, and the lid opened. Neither of them turned around to see, but, within a minute or so, there was the swish of air as a tortured soul-made-flesh moved past them and into the kitchen.

Two words were heard, before the key was turned in the lock, the door opened, and then closed again.

"Goodbye, Keith."

Keith closed his eyes and pulled Verity closer still in his embrace.

"Bye, Phil."

# EPILOGUE

## 1996

*"But just as you get what's coming to you,*
*Everybody else is going to get theirs too."*

*Gang Starr: 'Moment of Truth.'*

The blood-red curtains parted, and the light oak coffin slowly moved along the rollers into the space that lay beyond.

As its occupant had requested in life, *Walking On The Moon* by The Police began to play over Barton Crematorium's PA system. On the table in front of the curtains was a framed photograph. It showed former Detective Inspector Neil Lowe shaking hands with then-Home Secretary Douglas Hurd.

As the curtains closed, the attendees slowly rose from their seats and made their way towards the exit door, to the sounds of sniffles and stifled crying. First onto the concourse was the newly-widowed Di Lowe. One of her sisters was either side of her, doing their best to ease her grief.

Neil Lowe had died a week before following a long battle with cancer of the colon. Although his brother-in-law had suggested he might look into some alternative and holistic cures that he had read about, Lowe had insisted on remaining with the programme of radio- and chemo-therapy supplied by pharmaceutical giant Clive Tuns, that his GP had prescribed. He had been cut loose from Thames Valley Police when he was no longer able to leave his house. When his doctor had given his professional opinion that he wouldn't see out the week, Lowe had requested his wife bring a sirloin steak to his bed so he could enjoy one last favourite meal. He could only manage three mouthfuls.

Before her sisters led her to the waiting cars, there was one thing remaining for Di Lowe to do.

Three men had been the last to exit the crematorium building. The two on either side were solemn-faced prison officers. In the centre, in handcuffs, was her son, Charlie, on compassionate day-release from his three-year stretch at Bullingdon Prison for supply of Class A drugs. Di Lowe burst into tears as she threw her arms around her remorseful son and held him in a tight embrace.

Seated at the back of the service had been a congregation from TVP's St. Aldates HQ. Among them had been Sam Haine, now a Detective Inspector, having been promoted to Lowe's former position. Next to him were former Constables Rissey and Alves, now Sergeants.

Absent was former Chief Superintendent CC Nomas. He had taken early retirement following an internal investigation commissioned by the Home Office back in 1992, which had found his department to have been grossly negligent in addressing what had entered common parlance as 'The Unholy Trinity' of Oxford murders.

The killings had been attributed to the individual known as The Fixer, who had died a short time after being hit by the bus from a blood clot to the brain. A fake identity and history had been invented and fed to the local media. Dead men tell no tales. Taking up Nomas' old position was Doug Redgrave, a DCI drafted in from TVP in Reading. He had forewarned Mrs. Redgrave not to make any social arrangements on any first Monday after a full moon. Nomas himself could generally be found knocking back brandies in the Eagle & Child or muttering incoherently to his plants in his back garden.

It was five and a half years since May Pearce had ceased to identify herself as a WPC. After much soul-searching and encouragement from her sympathetic brother, she had followed her long-held vision of becoming a distributor of plant-based natural health products, vitamins, supplements, herbs and long-life organic foods, and now ran a small shop, Bona Dea, on the Cowley Road.

She had established a solid and appreciative customer base, many of whom were cancer patients exasperated by the lack of effective treatments being offered by the city's hospitals. May had spent many a long night lamenting her poor career choice of a few years before but consoling herself with the knowledge that she was now on her true life path. On average, she got asked out on a date by nervous and blushing male customers around once a month, but remained contentedly single.

Drew Hunter remained in his Barton flat and as a keen consumer of a different type of herb. His DJ residency in the back room at the Park End Club was now into its sixth year, and he had followed his dream of operating his own radio station, serving the local community by playing all the styles of music that Lux FM wouldn't, by establishing his own pirate station, Anarchy FM.

He and a group of friends from the estate had cobbled together the equipment for the studio, run from a back garden outhouse, and had pooled the cost of sourcing and installing a transmitter, which broadcast the station's output from the roof of one of the tower blocks on Blackbird Leys. Every now and again the consortium received threats of sabotage from jealous rivals, or tip-offs of a potential raid from the DTI, at which times it wasn't uncommon for one of them to sit out on the rooftop armed with a baseball bat.

Few of the class of 1990 remained at Lux FM, which was poised for corporate consolidation and rebranding. Mal Knight and Jess Hewitt had both moved on to positions elsewhere in the independent radio network. Of all the former news staff, Tom Atton's career had gone on to be the most successful – at least according to mainstream society's interpretation of the term. He had been poached by Capital Radio as a result of his Gulf War reporting on Lux, moving on to a two-year stint at Independent Radio News, then, through some strategic networking and nepotistic string-pulling, had landed a key role at the BBC, (and in its specially-reserved fraternities.)

He was now a household name through his role as anchor-man on BBC TV's *Newsnight*, specialising in a ferociously hostile method of interviewing guests, (except when they were of the same political persuasion as himself, or when he had been warned off of giving a particular guest a hard time by his bosses.) Verity had remarked to Keith that she had always considered Atton to be 'something rhyming with anchor.' Regrettably for him, Atton's arrival at the Corporation had coincided with the lowest viewing figures in its 70-plus-year history.

Max Zeall had continued in his dogged determination to teach grass-roots spiritual law. Though cynical at first as to the results his efforts were truly bringing, in recent times, he had seen signs that had begun to give him optimism. His ongoing talks at Blackbird Leys

Community Centre had earned him recognition from outside of Oxford, and he was now getting booked by freedom activist groups to give presentations in London, Birmingham and Bristol.

Trends reported in the mainstream news filled him with hope – notably the crisis in the police and the military whose numbers were leaving in their droves, necessitating huge advertising campaigns to find new recruits, but to little avail. Public support for the upkeep of the Royal Family was at its lowest ever also, and voter turnout for the recent local elections was similarly at an all-time low. Zeall took all these as indicators of a public slowly becoming aware of the corrupt and deceptive nature of Organised Society and exercising their Free Will choice to extricate themselves from it in whatever small ways they could.

The appearance in recent years of books like William Cooper's *Behold A Pale Horse*, John Coleman's *Conspirators' Hierarchy: The Committee of 300*, and the titles released by BBC presenter-turned conspiracy researcher David Icke, had assisted in turning on adventurous readers to the harsh truth of how society was really structured, and to a control system dependent for its survival on perpetual human slavery.

Of most excitement to Zeall, as a keen tech-head, was the fledgling Worldwide Web. He had been quick to gain himself a dial-up modem connection as soon the option had been available, along with an e-mail address, earning himself the nickname of Max Dot Zeall among some of his acolytes. He had told friends that he saw the internet as presenting the best opportunity to dispense truthful information that humanity had ever had, and that, in his words, "this technology might just have the capabilities to free humankind, in the fullness of time." Most politely humoured him, but doubted the validity of his claims.

Something else which had assisted in Zeall's endeavours had been the input of a research assistant in the form of Keith Malcolm. Keith's tasks now included mastering Zeall's audio and video recordings, burning them to CD-ROM and mailing them out to subscribers, as well as researching content and creating slide images for his talks. It brought Keith a great sense of fulfilment to be on the right side of the information wars of the times. E-mail connections now also meant he could collaborate with Zeall remotely.

All evidence of Verity's being tailed back in 1991 had dissipated within a couple of weeks of Phil's disappearance. The rental contract becoming due on their house had served to be the catalyst for the couple following through on an idea that had been in the back of their minds since Verity had left Lux. Leaving Oxford had seemed a great hardship at first, mainly through no longer being close to their respective families, but they took a chance on their instincts to embark on a new journey into the unknown, relocating to Newquay in Cornwall, a favourite haunt of Verity's from her childhood summer holidays.

From their new home, Verity had set herself up as an independent investigative journalist, subsidising herself with bar work at first, but going on to sell stories to newspapers and magazines as her reputation and effectiveness grew. The internet connection in their home had helped immensely in this regard, though she and Keith had to work in separate shifts to both be able to avail themselves of it. She also had a book in the offing.

Now, as Spring '96 dawned, their lives were about to change again. Verity was eight months pregnant, the house already full of baby equipment in anticipation of their new arrival. Having learned they were to have a girl, the pair had already decided on the name; they were to call her

Hope. This particular weekend Verity was excited about the imminent social visit of May Pearce; the two had become and remained the closest of friends for the past few years.

\* \* \*

Almost 5,000 miles to the East, and five and a half hours ahead by time zone, a Full Moon dance party was in its opening stages on a beach of the type that graced travel agent brochures. This was the Indian state of Goa.

A sound system of the type that had typified the open-air raves in the UK of a few years before, was running off a mobile generator sheltered within a clump of palm trees. Beams from strobe lights zigzagged through the night sky. The bass bins pulsated as they pumped out the distinctive sounds of Goa Trance – heavy on the sweeping strings and synth harmonies, and with strategically-timed break-downs designed to fully enhance the euphoria generated by the serotonin-inducing pills being experienced by the majority of those in attendance – before the frantic, 145-beats-per-minute rhythms pounded back in.

The sun-bronzed DJ, wearing a string vest and Hawaiian shorts, his bees-waxed locks tied up under a red bandana, gesticulated wildly, controlling the crowd from his podium like some sonic sorcerer. Those in the throng who had been facing in his direction began mimicking his movements, arms flailing as if channelling some unseen spirit from the ether. Metaphysical, religious, spiritual, primal, super-natural, and UFO/ alien themes coloured the symbolism adorned on the many banners and drapes hung from trees and scattered liberally around the site.

The crowd stretched out as far as the eye could see along a landscape that would have constituted many peoples' idea of tropical paradise, the plentiful palm trees appearing in moonlit profile.

As they gyrated and writhed in the balmy night air, awareness of their physical location had dimmed in significance to most of the dancers, superseded as it was by the mystical, psychedelic experiences they were undergoing. Runaway teens and twenty-something adventure-seekers from every corner of the world interacted with grizzled old ravers, hippies, Bohemian New Agers, ex-cons, thieves, vagabonds, passport-forgers and junkies, all in their communal rejection of the norms of mainstream society, and their search for redemption from whatever personal demons they had come to Goa to forget.

Dancing unconvincingly and doing their best to blend in with the rest, were a small handful of middle-aged CIA and British Military Intelligence agents, in home-made tie-dye T-shirts and combat pants, quietly observing the proceedings from beneath their tinted sunglasses. The other dancers were giving them a wide berth.

Out among the flock being led, Pied-Piper-like, on a sonic million-year-voyage, was a near-23-year-old Molly Lowe. This was a long way from Milton Common, she reflected, as she allowed the electronic beats to flow up her spine like a kundalini energy rush – and yet so very, very close.

She had harboured a desire to absorb herself in the Full Moon experience ever since hearing Paul Oakenfold's landmark mix on Radio 1 two years previous, which had been credited with kick-starting an entire new genre within dance music known as Goa Trance. Molly had developed her business empire exponentially in the previous five years, so funding had not been a problem.

Now, as she lost herself in a sense of free-spirited emancipation and recalled past parties and past endeavours back in Oxford, she realised she had no intention of ever going home. This place. This felt like home.

Set back from the beach, on the far side of the clump of palm trees, were a group of seven shacks efficiently constructed from bamboo canes. The hut on the end, the furthest away from the beach party, had one side entirely exposed to the elements.

The loose strips of cane dangling down from the roof swayed in the warm breeze blowing in from the ocean. This particular shack served as a rudimentary beach bar. A few chairs and low tables constructed from canes lined the walls.

In the centre was a wooden counter that served as the bar. Three wooden stools were pulled up against it. One of them was occupied.

The Indian barman took a bottle from the shelf behind him and poured the clear liquid into a shot glass. The man in shabby clothes occupying the seat wore a lifetime of hardship upon his face. He was only 30, but the matted hair with flecks of grey, the long unkempt beard, and the deeply etched wrinkles made him look a decade older.

Tonight, though, aided by the shots of local brew that he knocked back as if they were water, he was without care or worry.

The barman spoke.

"Last one now, boss. We're closing."

"Sure thing," slurred the man with an intoxicated smile.

"You take care now, boss," said the barman.

"Oh, I will, my friend," replied the man.

"As it is willed, so shall it be."

CPSIA information can be obtained
at www.ICGtesting.com
Printed in the USA
LVHW080801060220
645949LV00011BA/854

9 781913 438098